PENGUIN CRIME FICTION

Editor: Julian Symons

FAREWELL, MY LOVELY

Raymond Chandler was born in Chicago of an American Quaker father and an Irish Quaker mother. At an early age he went to England, had his schooling at Dulwich College, and completed his education in France and Germany. After that he had many professions: teacher, book-reviewer, poet, paragraph writer, essayist, soldier in a Canadian infantry regiment, student pilot, accountant, oil executive, and 'pulp writer'. For many years he lived in the United States, his home being in the southern California area which forms the background of his books. He died in 1959.

RAYMOND CHANDLER

FAREWELL, MY LOVELY

PENGUIN BOOKS
in association with Hamish Hamilton

Penguin Books Ltd, Harmondsworth, Middlesex, England
Penguin Books Australia Ltd, Ringwood, Victoria, Australia
Penguin Books (N.Z.) Ltd, 182–190 Wairau Road, Auckland 10, New Zealand

—

First published in 1940
Published in Penguin Books 1949
Reprinted 1950, 1952, 1954, 1956, 1959, 1961, 1966, 1971, 1973, 1975 (twice)

—

Copyright © the Estate of Raymond Chandler, 1940

—

Made and printed in Great Britain
by C. Nicholls & Company Ltd
Set in Monotype Fournier

I

It was one of the mixed blocks over on Central Avenue, the blocks that are not yet all negro. I had just come out of a three-chair barber shop where an agency thought a relief barber named Dimitrios Aleidis might be working. It was a small matter. His wife said she was willing to spend a little money to have him come home.

I never found him, but Mrs Aleidis never paid me any money either.

It was a warm day, almost the end of March, and I stood outside the barber shop looking up at the jutting neon sign of a second floor dine and dice emporium called Florian's. A man was looking up at the sign too. He was looking up at the dusty windows with a sort of ecstatic fixity of expression, like a hunky immigrant catching his first sight of the Statue of Liberty. He was a big man but not more than six feet five inches tall and not wider than a beer truck. He was about ten feet away from me. His arms hung loose at his sides and a forgotten cigar smoked behind his enormous fingers.

Slim quiet negroes passed up and down the street and stared at him with darting side glances. He was worth looking at. He wore a shaggy borsalino hat, a rough grey sports coat with white golf balls on it for buttons, a brown shirt, a yellow tie, pleated grey flannel slacks and alligator shoes with white explosions on the toes. From his outer breast pocket cascaded a show handkerchief of the same brilliant yellow as his tie. There were a couple of coloured feathers tucked into the band of his hat, but he didn't really need them. Even on Central Avenue, not the quietest dressed street in the world, he looked about as inconspicuous as a tarantula on a slice of angel food.

His skin was pale and he needed a shave. He would always need a shave. He had curly black hair and heavy eyebrows that almost met over his thick nose. His ears were small and neat for a man of that size and his eyes had a shine close to tears that grey eyes often seem to have. He stood like a statue, and after a long time he smiled.

He moved slowly across the sidewalk to the double swinging doors which shut off the stairs to the second floor. He pushed them open, cast a cool expressionless glance up and down the street, and moved inside. If he had been a smaller man and more quietly dressed, I might have thought he was going to pull a stick-up. But not in those clothes, and not with that hat, and that frame.

The doors swung back outwards and almost settled to a stop. Before they had entirely stopped moving they opened again, violently, outwards. Something sailed across the sidewalk and landed in the gutter between two parked cars. It landed on its hands and knees and made a high keening noise like a cornered rat. It got up slowly, retrieved a hat and stepped back on to the sidewalk. It was a thin, narrow-shouldered brown youth in a lilac coloured suit and a carnation. It had slick black hair. It kept its mouth open and whined for a moment. People stared at it vaguely. Then it settled its hat jauntily, sidled over to the wall and walked silently splay-footed off along the block.

Silence. Traffic resumed. I walked along to the double doors and stood in front of them. They were motionless now. It wasn't any of my business. So I pushed them open and looked in.

A hand I could have sat in came out of the dimness and took hold of my shoulder and squashed it to a pulp. Then the hand moved me through the doors and casually lifted me up a step. The large face looked at me. A deep soft voice said to me, quietly:

'Smokes in here, huh? Tie that for me, pal.'

It was dark in there. It was quiet. From up above came vague sounds of humanity, but we were alone on the stairs. The big man stared at me solemnly and went on wrecking my shoulder with his hand.

'A dinge,' he said. 'I just thrown him out. You seen me throw him out?'

He let go of my shoulder. The bone didn't seem to be broken, but the arm was numb.

'It's that kind of a place,' I said, rubbing my shoulder. 'What did you expect?'

'Don't say that, pal,' the big man purred softly, like four tigers after dinner. 'Velma used to work here. Little Velma.'

He reached for my shoulder again. I tried to dodge him but he was as fast as a cat. He began to chew my muscles up some more with his iron fingers.

'Yeah,' he said. 'Little Velma. I ain't seen her in eight years. You say this here is a dinge joint?'

I croaked that it was.

He lifted me up two more steps. I wrenched myself loose and tried for a little elbow room. I wasn't wearing a gun. Looking for Dimitrios Aleidis hadn't seemed to require it. I doubted if it would do me any good. The big man would probably take it away from me and eat it.

'Go on up and see for yourself,' I said, trying to keep the agony out of my voice.

He let go of me again. He looked at me with a sort of sadness in his grey eyes. 'I'm feelin' good,' he said. 'I wouldn't want anybody to fuss with me. Let's you and me go on up and maybe nibble a couple.'

'They won't serve you. I told you it's a coloured joint.'

'I ain't seen Velma in eight years,' he said in his deep sad voice. 'Eight long years since I said good-bye. She ain't wrote to me in six. But she'll have a reason. She used to work here. Cute she was. Let's you and me go on up, huh?'

'All right,' I yelled. 'I'll go up with you. Just lay off carrying me. Let me walk. I'm fine. I'm all grown up. I go to the bathroom alone and everything. Just don't carry me.'

'Little Velma used to work here,' he said gently. He wasn't listening to me.

We went on up the stairs. He let me walk. My shoulder ached. The back of my neck was wet.

2

Two more swing doors closed off the head of the stairs from whatever was beyond. The big man pushed them open lightly with his thumbs and we went into the room. It was a long narrow room, not very clean, not very bright, not very cheerful. In the corner a group of negroes chanted and chattered in the cone of light over a crap table. There was a bar against the right hand wall. The rest of the room was mostly small round tables. There were a few customers, men and women, all negroes.

The chanting at the crap table stopped dead and the light over it jerked out. There was a sudden silence as heavy as a waterlogged boat. Eyes looked at us, chestnut coloured eyes, set in faces that ranged from grey to deep black. Heads turned slowly and the eyes in them glistened and stared in the dead alien silence of another race.

A large, thick-necked negro was leaning against the end of the bar with pink garters on his shirt sleeves and pink and white suspenders crossing his broad back. He had bouncer written all over him. He put his lifted foot down slowly and turned slowly and stared at us, spreading his feet gently and moving a broad tongue along his lips. He had a battered face that looked as if it had been hit by everything but the bucket of a dragline. It was scarred, flattened, thickened, chequered, and welted. It was a face that had nothing to fear. Everything had been done to it that anybody could think of.

The short crinkled hair had a touch of grey. One ear had lost its lobe.

The negro was heavy and wide. He had big heavy legs and they looked a little bowed, which is unusual in a negro. He moved his tongue some more and smiled and moved his body. He came towards us in a loose fighter's crouch. The big man waited for him silently.

The negro with the pink garters on his arms put a massive brown hand against the big man's chest. Large as it was the hand looked like a stud. The big man didn't move. The bouncer smiled gently.

'No white folks, brother. Jes' fo' the coloured people. I'se sorry.'

The big man moved his small sad grey eyes and looked around the room. His cheeks flushed a little. 'Shine box,' he said angrily, under his breath. He raised his voice. 'Where's Velma at?' he asked the bouncer.

The bouncer didn't quite laugh. He studied the big man's clothes, his brown shirt and yellow tie, his rough grey coat and the white golf balls on it. He moved his thick head around delicately and studied all this from various angles. He looked down at the alligator shoes. He chuckled lightly. He seemed amused. I felt a little sorry for him. He spoke softly again.

'Velma you says? No Velma heah, brother. No hooch, no gals, no nothing. Jes' the scram, white boy, jes' the scram.'

'Velma used to work here,' the big man said. He spoke almost dreamily, as if he was all by himself, out in the woods, picking johnny-jump-ups. I got my handkerchief out and wiped the back of my neck again.

The bouncer laughed suddenly. 'Shuah,' he said, throwing a quick look back over his shoulder at his public. 'Velma used to work here. But Velma don't work heah no mo'. She done reti'ed. Haw. Haw.'

'Kind of take your goddamned mitt off my shirt,' the big man said.

The bouncer frowned. He was not used to being talked to like that. He took his hand off the shirt and doubled it into a fist about the size and colour of a large eggplant. He had his job, his reputation for toughness, his public esteem to consider. He considered them for a second and made a mistake. He swung the fist very hard and short with a sudden outward jerk of the elbow and hit the big man on the side of the jaw. A soft sigh went around the room.

It was a good punch. The shoulder dropped and the body swung behind it. There was a lot of weight in that punch and the man who landed it had had plenty of practice. The big man didn't move his head more than an inch. He didn't try to block the punch. He took it, shook himself lightly, made a quiet sound in his throat and took hold of the bouncer by the throat.

The bouncer tried to knee him in the groin. The big man turned him in the air and slid his gaudy shoes apart on the scaly linoleum that covered the floor. He bent the bouncer backwards and shifted his right hand to the bouncer's belt. The belt broke like a piece of butcher's string. The big man put his enormous hand flat against the bouncer's spine and heaved. He threw him clear across the room, spinning and staggering and flailing with his arms. Three men jumped out of the way. The bouncer went over with a table and smacked into the baseboard with a crash that must have been heard in Denver. His legs twitched. Then he lay still.

'Some guys,' the big man said, 'has got wrong ideas about when to get tough.' He turned to me. 'Yeah,' he said. 'Let's you and me nibble one.'

We went over to the bar. The customers, by ones and twos and threes, became quiet shadows that drifted soundless across the floor, soundless through the doors at the head of the stairs. Soundless as shadows on grass. They didn't even let the doors swing.

We leaned against the bar. 'Whisky sour,' the big man said. 'Call yours.'

'Whisky sour,' I said.

We had whisky sours.

The big man licked his whisky sour impassively down the side of the thick squat glass. He stared solemnly at the barman, a thin, worried-looking negro in a white coat who moved as if his feet hurt him.

'*You* know where Velma is?'

'Velma, you says?' the barman whined. 'I ain't seen her 'round heah lately. Not right lately, nossuh.'

'How long you been here?'

'Le's see,' the barman put his towel down and wrinkled his forehead and started to count on his fingers. ''Bout ten months, I reckon. 'Bout a yeah. 'Bout——'

'Make your mind up,' the big man said.

The barman goggled and his Adam's apple flopped around like a headless chicken.

'How long's this coop been a dinge joint?' the big man demanded gruffly.

'Says which?'

The big man made a fist into which his whisky sour glass melted almost out of sight.

'Five years anyway,' I said. 'This fellow wouldn't know anything about a white girl named Velma. Nobody here would.'

The big man looked at me as if I had just hatched out. His whisky sour hadn't seemed to improve his temper.

'Who the hell asked you to stick your face in?' he asked me.

I smiled. I made it a big warm friendly smile. 'I'm the fellow that came in with you. Remember?'

He grinned back then, a flat white grin without meaning. 'Whisky sour,' he told the barman. 'Shake them fleas outa your pants. Service.'

The barman scuttled around, rolling the whites of his eyes.

I put my back against the bar and looked at the room. It was now empty, save for the barman, the big man and myself, and the bouncer crushed over against the wall. The bouncer was moving. He was moving slowly as if with great pain and effort. He was crawling softly along the baseboard like a fly with one wing. He was moving behind the tables, wearily, a man suddenly old, suddenly disillusioned. I watched him move. The barman put down two more whisky sours. I turned to the bar. The big man glanced casually over at the crawling bouncer and then paid no further attention to him.

'There ain't nothing left of the joint,' he complained. 'They was a little stage and band and cute little rooms where a guy could have fun. Velma did some warbling. A redhead she was. Cute as lace pants. We was to of been married when they hung the frame on me.'

I took my second whisky sour. I was beginning to have enough of the adventure. 'What frame?' I asked.

'Where you figure I been them eight years I said about?'

'Catching butterflies.'

He prodded his chest with a forefinger like a banana. 'In the caboose. Malloy is the name. They call me Moose Malloy, on account of I'm large. The Great Bend bank job. Forty grand. Solo job. Ain't that something?'

'You going to spend it now?'

He gave me a sharp look. There was a noise behind us. The bouncer was on his feet again, weaving a little. He had his hand on the knob of a dark door over behind the crap table. He got the door open, half fell through. The door clattered shut. A lock clicked.

'Where's that go?' Moose Malloy demanded.

The barman's eyes floated in his head, focussed with difficulty on the door through which the bouncer had stumbled.

'Tha – tha's Mistah Montgomery's office, suh. He's the boss. He's got his office back there.'

'He might know,' the big man said. He drank his drink at a

14

gulp. 'He better not crack wise neither. Two more of the same.'

He crossed the room slowly, lightfooted, without a care in the world. His enormous back hid the door. It was locked. He shook it and a piece of the panel flew off to one side. He went through and shut the door behind him.

There was silence. I looked at the barman. The barman looked at me. His eyes became thoughtful. He polished the counter and sighed and leaned down with his right arm.

I reached across the counter and took hold of the arm. It was thin, brittle. I held it and smiled at him.

'What you got down there, bo?'

He licked his lips. He leaned on my arm, and said nothing. Greyness invaded his shining face.

'This guy is tough,' I said. 'And he's liable to go mean. Drinks do that to him. He's looking for a girl he used to know. This place used to be a white establishment. Get the idea?'

The barman licked his lips.

'He's been away a long time,' I said. 'Eight years. He doesn't seem to realize how long that is, although I'd expect him to think it a lifetime. He thinks the people here should know where his girl is. Get the idea?'

The barman said slowly: 'I thought you was with him.'

'I couldn't help myself. He asked me a question down below and then dragged me up. I never saw him before. But I didn't feel like being thrown over any houses. What you got down there?'

'Got me a sawed-off,' the barman said.

'Tsk. That's illegal,' I whispered. 'Listen, you and I are together. Got anything else?'

'Got me a gat,' the barman said. 'In a cigar box. Leggo my arm.'

'That's fine,' I said. 'Now move along a bit. Easy now. Sideways. This isn't the time to pull the artillery.'

'Says you,' the barman sneered, putting his tired weight against my arm. 'Says——'

He stopped. His eyes rolled. His head jerked.

There was a dull flat sound at the back of the place, behind the closed door beyond the crap table. It might have been a slammed door. I didn't think it was. The barman didn't think so either.

The barman froze. His mouth drooled. I listened. No other sound. I started quickly for the end of the counter. I had listened too long.

The door at the back opened with a bang and Moose Malloy came through it with a smooth heavy lunge and stopped dead, his feet planted and a wide pale grin on his face.

A Colt Army .45 looked like a toy pistol in his hand.

'Don't nobody try to fancy pants,' he said cosily. 'Freeze the mitts on the bar.'

The barman and I put our hands on the bar.

Moose Malloy looked the room over with a raking glance. His grin was taut, nailed on. He shifted his feet and moved silently across the room. He looked like a man who could take a bank single-handed – even in those clothes.

He came to the bar. 'Rise up, nigger,' he said softly. The barman put his hands high in the air. The big man stepped to my back and prowled me over carefully with his left hand. His breath was hot on my neck. It went away.

'Mister Montgomery didn't know where Velma was neither,' he said. 'He tried to tell me – with this.' His hard hand patted the gun. I turned slowly and looked at him. 'Yeah,' he said. 'You'll know me. You ain't forgetting me, pal. Just tell them johns not to get careless is all.' He waggled the gun. 'Well, so long, punks. I gotta catch a street car.'

He started towards the head of the stairs.

'You didn't pay for the drinks,' I said.

He stopped and looked at me carefully.

'Maybe you got something there,' he said, 'but I wouldn't squeeze it too hard.'

He moved on, slipped through the double doors, and his steps sounded remotely going down the stairs.

The barman stooped. I jumped around behind the counter and jostled him out of the way. A sawed-off shot-gun lay under a towel on a shelf under the bar. Beside it was a cigar box. In the cigar box was a .38 automatic. I took both of them. The barman pressed back against the tier of glasses behind the bar.

I went back around the end of the bar and across the room to the gaping door behind the crap table. There was a hallway behind it, L-shaped, almost lightless. The bouncer lay sprawled on its floor unconscious, with a knife in his hand. I leaned down and pulled the knife loose and threw it down a back stairway. The bouncer breathed stertorously and his hand was limp.

I stepped over him and opened a door marked 'Office' in flaked black paint.

There was a small scarred desk close to a partly boarded-up window. The torso of a man was bolt upright in the chair. The chair had a high back which just reached to the nape of the man's neck. His head was folded back over the high back of the chair so that his nose pointed at the boarded-up window. Just folded, like a handkerchief or a hinge.

A drawer of the desk was open at the man's right. Inside it was a newspaper with a smear of oil in the middle. The gun would have come from there. It had probably seemed like a good idea at the time, but the position of Mr Montgomery's head proved that the idea had been wrong.

There was a telephone on the desk. I laid the sawed-off shotgun down and went over to lock the door before I called the police. I felt safer that way and Mr Montgomery didn't seem to mind.

When the prowl car boys stamped up the stairs, the bouncer and the barman had disappeared and I had the place to myself.

3

A man named Nulty got the case, a lean-jawed sourpuss with long yellow hands which he kept folded over his kneecaps most of the time he talked to me. He was a detective-lieutenant attached to the 77th Street Division and we talked in a bare room with two small desks against opposite walls and room to move between them, if two people didn't try it at once. Dirty brown linoleum covered the floor and the smell of old cigar butts hung in the air. Nulty's shirt was frayed and his coat sleeves had been turned in at the cuffs. He looked poor enough to be honest, but he didn't look like a man who could deal with Moose Malloy.

He lit half of a cigar and threw the match on the floor, where a lot of company was waiting for it. His voice said bitterly:

'Shines. Another shine killing. That's what I rate after eighteen years in this man's police department. No pix, no space, not even four lines in the want-ad section.'

I didn't say anything. He picked my card up and read it again and threw it down.

'Philip Marlowe, Private Investigator. One of those guys, huh? Jesus, you look tough enough. What was you doing all that time?'

'All what time?'

'All the time this Malloy was twisting the neck of this smoke.'

'Oh, that happened in another room,' I said. 'Malloy hadn't promised me he was going to break anybody's neck.'

'Ride me,' Nulty said bitterly. 'Okey, go ahead and ride me. Everybody else does. What's another one matter? Poor old Nulty. Let's go on up and throw a couple of nifties at him. Always good for a laugh, Nulty is.'

'I'm not trying to ride anybody,' I said. 'That's the way it happened – in another room.'

'Oh, sure,' Nulty said through a fan of rank cigar smoke. 'I was down there and saw it, didn't I? Don't you pack no rod?'

'Not on that kind of a job.'

'What kind of a job?'

'I was looking for a barber who had run away from his wife. She thought he could be persuaded to come home.'

'You mean a dinge?'

'No, a Greek.'

'Okey,' Nulty said and spit into his waste basket. 'Okey. You met the big guy how?'

'I told you already. I just happened to be there. He threw a negro out of the doors of Florian's and I unwisely poked my head in to see what was happening. So he took me upstairs.'

'You mean he stuck you up?'

'No, he didn't have the gun then. At least, he didn't show one. He took the gun away from Montgomery, probably. He just picked me up. I'm kind of cute sometimes.'

'I wouldn't know,' Nulty said. 'You seem to pick up awful easy.'

'All right,' I said. 'Why argue? I've seen the guy and you haven't. He could wear you or me for a watch charm. I didn't know he had killed anybody until after he left. I heard a shot, but I got the idea somebody had got scared and shot at Malloy and then Malloy took the gun away from whoever did it.'

'And why would you get an idea like that?' Nulty asked almost suavely. 'He used a gun to take that bank, didn't he?'

'Consider the kind of clothes he was wearing. He didn't go there to kill anybody; not dressed like that. He went there to look for this girl named Velma that had been his girl before he was pinched for the bank job. She worked there at Florian's or whatever place was there when it was still a white joint. He was pinched there. You'll get him all right.'

'Sure,' Nulty said. 'With that size and them clothes. Easy.'

'He might have another suit,' I said. 'And a car and a hide-out and money and friends. But you'll get him.'

Nulty spit in the waste basket again. 'I'll get him,' he said, 'about the time I get my third set of teeth. How many guys is put on it? One. Listen, you know why? No space. One time there was five smokes carved Harlem sunsets on each other down on East Eighty-four. One of them was cold already. There was blood on the furniture, blood on the walls, blood even on the ceiling. I go down and outside the house a guy that works on the *Chronicle*, a newshawk, is coming off the porch and getting into his car. He makes a face at us and says, "Aw, hell, shines," and gets in his heap and goes away. Don't even go in the house.'

'Maybe he's a parole breaker,' I said. 'You'd get some co-operation on that. But pick him up nice or he'll knock off a brace of prowlies for you. Then you'll get space.'

'And I wouldn't have the case no more neither,' Nulty sneered.

The phone rang on his desk. He listened to it and smiled sorrowfully. He hung up and scribbled on a pad and there was a faint gleam in his eyes, a light far back in a dusty corridor.

'Hell, they got him. That was Records. Got his prints, mug, and everything. Jesus, that's a little something anyway.' He read from his pad. 'Jesus, this is a man. Six five and one-half, two hundred sixty-four pounds, without his necktie. Jesus, that's a boy. Well, the hell with him. They got him on the air now. Probably at the end of the hot car list. Ain't nothing to do but just wait.' He threw his cigar into a spittoon.

'Try looking for the girl,' I said. 'Velma. Malloy will be looking for her. That's what started it all. Try Velma.'

'You try her,' Nulty said. 'I ain't been in a joy house in twenty years. '

I stood up. 'Okey,' I said, and started for the door.

'Hey, wait a minute,' Nulty said. 'I was only kidding. You ain't awful busy, are you?'

I rolled a cigarette around in my fingers and looked at him and waited by the door.

'I mean you got time to sort of take a gander around for this dame. That's a good idea you had there. You might pick something up. You can work under glass.'

'What's in it for me?'

He spread his yellow hands sadly. His smile was as cunning as a broken mousetrap. 'You been in jams with us boys before. Don't tell me no. I heard different. Next time it ain't doing you any harm to have a pal.'

'What good is it going to do me?'

'Listen,' Nulty urged. 'I'm just a quiet guy. But any guy in the department can do you a lot of good.'

'Is this for love – or are you paying anything in money?'

'No money,' Nulty said, and wrinkled his sad yellow nose. 'But I'm needing a little credit bad. Since the last shake-up, things is really tough. I wouldn't forget it, pal. Not ever.'

I looked at my watch. 'Okey, if I think of anything, it's yours. And when you get the mug, I'll identify it for you. After lunch.' We shook hands and I went down the mud-coloured hall and stairway to the front of the building and my car.

It was two hours since Moose Malloy had left Florian's with the Army Colt in his hand. I ate lunch at a drugstore, bought a pint of bourbon, and drove eastward to Central Avenue and north on Central again. The hunch I had was as vague as the heat waves that danced above the sidewalk.

Nothing made it my business except curiosity. But strictly speaking, I hadn't had any business in a month. Even a no-charge job was a change.

4

Florian's was closed up, of course. An obvious plain-clothes-man sat in front of it in a car, reading a paper with one eye. I didn't know why they bothered. Nobody there knew anything about Moose Malloy. The bouncer and the barman had not been found. Nobody on the block knew anything about them, for talking purposes.

I drove past slowly and parked around the corner and sat looking at a negro hotel which was diagonally across the block from Florian's and beyond the nearest intersection. It was called the Hotel Sans Souci. I got out and walked back across the intersection and went into it. Two rows of hard empty chairs stared at each other across a strip of tan fibre carpet. A desk was back in the dimness and behind the desk a bald-headed man had his eyes shut and his soft brown hands clasped peacefully on the desk in front of him. He dozed, or appeared to. He wore an Ascot tie that looked as if it had been tied about the year 1880. The green stone in his stickpin was not quite as large as an apple. His large loose chin was folded down gently on the tie, and his folded hands were peaceful and clean, with manicured nails, and grey half-moons in the purple of the nails.

A metal embossed sign at his elbow said: 'This Hotel is Under the Protection of The International Consolidated Agencies Ltd. Inc.'

When the peaceful brown man opened one eye at me thoughtfully I pointed at the sign.

'H.P.D. man checking up. Any trouble here?'

H.P.D. means Hotel Protective Department, which is the department of a large agency that looks after cheque bouncers and people who move out by the back stairs leaving unpaid bills and second-hand suitcases full of bricks.

'Trouble, brother,' the clerk said in a high sonorous voice, 'is something we is fresh out of.' He lowered his voice four or five notches and added: 'What was the name again?'

'Marlowe. Philip Marlowe——'

'A nice name, brother. Clean and cheerful. You're looking right well to-day.' He lowered his voice again. 'But you ain't no H.P.D. man. Ain't seen one in years.' He unfolded his hands and pointed languidly at the sign. 'I acquired that second-hand, brother, just for the effect.'

'Okey,' I said. I leaned on the counter and started to spin a half dollar on the bare, scarred wood of the counter.

'Heard what happened over at Florian's this morning?'

'Brother, I forgot.' Both his eyes were open now and he was watching the blur of light made by the spinning coin.

'The boss got bumped off,' I said. 'Man named Montgomery. Somebody broke his neck.'

'May the Lawd receive his soul, brother.' Down went the voice again. 'Cop?'

'Private – on a confidential lay. And I know a man who can keep things confidential when I see one.'

He studied me, then closed his eyes and thought. He reopened them cautiously and stared at the spinning coin. He couldn't resist looking at it.

'Who done it?' he asked softly. 'Who fixed Sam?'

'A tough guy out of the jailhouse got sore because it wasn't a white joint. It used to be, it seems. Maybe you remember?'

He said nothing. The coin fell over with a light ringing whirr and lay still.

'Call your play,' I said. 'I'll read you a chapter of the Bible or buy you a drink. Say which.'

'Brother, I kind of like to read my Bible in the seclusion of my family.' His eyes were bright, toadlike, steady.

'Maybe you've just had lunch,' I said.

'Lunch,' he said, 'is something a man of my shape and disposition aims to do without.' Down went the voice. 'Come 'round this here side of the desk.'

I went around and drew the flat pint of bonded bourbon out of my pocket and put it on the shelf. I went back to the front of the desk. He bent over and examined it. He looked satisfied.

'Brother, this don't buy you nothing at all,' he said. 'But I is pleased to take a light snifter in your company.'

He opened the bottle, put two small glasses on the desk and quietly poured each full to the brim. He lifted one, sniffed it carefully, and poured it down his throat with his little finger lifted.

He tasted it, thought about it, nodded and said: 'This come out of the correct bottle, brother. In what manner can I be of service to you? There ain't a crack in the sidewalk 'round here I don't know by its first name. Yessuh, this liquor has been keepin' the right company.' He refilled his glass.

I told him what had happened at Florian's and why. He stared at me solemnly and shook his bald head.

'A nice quiet place Sam run too,' he said. 'Ain't nobody been knifed there in a month.'

'When Florian's was a white joint some six or eight years ago or less, what was the name of it?'

'Electric signs come kind of high, brother.

I nodded. 'I thought it might have had the same name. Malloy would probably have said something if the name had been changed. But who ran it?'

'I'm a mite surprised at you, brother. The name of that pore sinner was Florian. Mike Florian——'

'And what happened to Mike Florian?'

The negro spread his gentle brown hands. His voice was sonorous and sad. 'Daid, brother. Gathered to the Lawd. Nineteen hundred and thirty-four, maybe thirty-five. I ain't precise on that. A wasted life, brother, and a case of pickled kidneys, I heard say. The ungodly man drops like a polled steer, brother, but mercy waits for him up yonder.' His voice went down to the business level. 'Damn if I know why.'

'Who did he leave behind him? Pour another drink.'

He corked the bottle firmly and pushed it across the counter. 'Two is all, brother – before sundown. I thank you. Your method of approach is soothin' to a man's dignity. ... Left a widow. Name of Jessie.'

'What happened to her?'

'The pursuit of knowledge, brother, is the askin' of many questions. I ain't heard. Try the phone book.'

There was a booth in the dark corner of the lobby. I went over and shut the door far enough to put the light on. I looked up the name in the chained and battered book. No Florian in it at all. I went back to the desk.

'No soap,' I said.

The negro bent regretfully and heaved a city directory up on top of the desk and pushed it towards me. He closed his eyes. He was getting bored. There was a Jessie Florian, Widow, in the book. She lived at 1644 West 54th Place. I wondered what I had been using for brains all my life.

I wrote the address down on a piece of paper and pushed the directory back across the desk. The negro put it back where he had found it, shook hands with me, then folded his hands on the desk exactly where they had been when I came in. His eyes drooped slowly and he appeared to fall asleep.

The incident for him was over. Half-way to the door I shot a glance back at him. His eyes were closed and he breathed softly and regularly, blowing a little with his lips at the end of each breath. His bald head shone.

I went out of the Hotel Sans Souci and crossed the street to my car. It looked too easy. It looked much too easy.

5

1644 West 54th Place was a dried-out brown house with a dried-out brown lawn in front of it. There was a large bare patch around a tough-looking palm tree. On the porch stood one lonely wooden rocker, and the afternoon breeze made the unpruned shoots of last year's poinsettias tap-tap against the cracked stucco wall. A line of stiff yellowish half-washed clothes jittered on a rusty wire in the side yard.

I drove on a quarter block, parked my car across the street and walked back.

The bell didn't work so I rapped on the wooden margin of the screen door. Slow steps shuffled and the door opened and I was looking into dimness at a blowsy woman who was blowing her nose as she opened the door. Her face was grey and puffy. She had weedy hair of that vague colour which is neither brown nor blond, that hasn't enough life in it to be ginger, and isn't clean enough to be grey. Her body was thick in a shapeless outing flannel bathrobe many moons past colour and design. It was just something around her body. Her toes were large and obvious in a pair of man's slippers of scuffed brown leather.

I said: 'Mrs Florian? Mrs Jessie Florian?'

'Uh-huh,' the voice dragged itself out of her throat like a sick man getting out of bed.

'You are the Mrs Florian whose husband once ran a place of entertainment on Central Avenue? Mike Florian?'

She thumbed a wick of hair past her large ear. Her eyes glittered with surprise. Her heavy clogged voice said:

'Wha – what? My goodness sakes alive. Mike's been gone these five years. Who did you say you was?'

The screen door was still shut and hooked.

'I'm a detective,' I said. 'I'd like a little information.'

She stared at me a long dreary minute. Then with effort she unhooked the door and turned away from it.

'Come on in then. I ain't had time to get cleaned up yet,' she whined. 'Cops, huh?'

I stepped through the door and hooked the screen again. A large handsome cabinet radio droned to the left of the door in the corner of the room. It was the only decent piece of furniture the place had. It looked brand new. Everything else was junk – dirty overstuffed pieces, a wooden rocker that matched the one on the porch, a square arch into a dining-room with a stained table, finger marks all over the swing door to the kitchen beyond. A couple of frayed lamps with once gaudy shades that were now as gay as superannuated streetwalkers.

The woman sat down in the rocker and flopped her slippers and looked at me. I looked at the radio and sat down on the end of a davenport. She saw me looking at it. A bogus heartiness, as weak as a Chinaman's tea, moved into her face and voice. 'All the comp'ny I got,' she said. Then she tittered. 'Mike ain't done nothing new, has he? I don't get cops calling on me much.'

Her titter contained a loose alcoholic overtone. I leaned back against something hard, felt for it and brought up an empty quart gin bottle. The woman tittered again.

'A joke that was,' she said. 'But I hope to Christ they's enough cheap blondes where he is. He never got enough of them here.'

'I was thinking more about a redhead,' I said.

'I guess he could use a few of them too.' Her eyes, it seemed to me, were not so vague now. 'I don't call to mind. Any special redhead?'

'Yes. A girl named Velma. I don't know what last name she used except that it wouldn't be her real one. I'm trying to trace her for her folks. Your place on Central is a coloured place now, although they haven't changed the name, and of course the people there never heard of her. So I thought of you.'

'Her folks taken their time getting around to it – looking for her,' the woman said thoughtfully.

'There's a little money involved. Not much. I guess they have to get her in order to touch it. Money sharpens the memory.'

'So does liquor,' the woman said. 'Kind of hot to-day, ain't it? You said you was a copper though.' Cunning eyes, steady attentive face. The feet in the man's slippers didn't move.

I held up the dead soldier and shook it. Then I threw it to one side and reached back on my hip for the pint of bond bourbon the negro hotel clerk and I had barely tapped. I held it out on my knee. The woman's eyes became fixed in an incredulous stare. Then suspicion climbed all over her face, like a kitten, but not so playfully.

'You ain't no copper,' she said softly. 'No copper ever bought a drink of that stuff. What's the gag, mister?'

She blew her nose again, on one of the dirtiest handkerchiefs I ever saw. Her eyes stayed on the bottle. Suspicion fought with thirst, and thirst was winning. It always does.

'This Velma was an entertainer, a singer. You wouldn't know her? I don't suppose you went there much.'

Seaweed-coloured eyes stayed on the bottle. A coated tongue coiled on her lips.

'Man, that's liquor,' she sighed. 'I don't give a damn who you are. Just hold it careful, mister. This ain't no time to drop anything.'

She got up and waddled out of the room and came back with two thick smeared glasses.

'No fixin's. Just what you brought is all,' she said.

I poured her a slug that would have made me float over a wall. She reached for it hungrily and put it down her throat like an aspirin tablet and looked at the bottle. I poured her another and a smaller one for me. She took it over to her rocker. Her eyes had turned two shades browner already.

'Man, this stuff dies painless with me,' she said and sat down. 'It never knows what hit it. What was we talkin' about?'

'A redhaired girl named Velma who used to work in your place on Central Avenue.'

'Yeah.' She used her second drink. I went over and stood the bottle on an end beside her. She reached for it. 'Yeah. Who you say you was?'

I took out a card and gave it to her. She read it with her tongue and lips, dropped it on a table beside her and set her empty glass on it.

'Oh, a private guy. You ain't said that, mister.' She waggled a finger at me with gay reproach. 'But your liquor says you're an all right guy at that. Here's to crime.' She poured a third drink for herself and drank it down.

I sat down and rolled a cigarette around in my fingers and waited. She either knew something or she didn't. If she knew something, she either would tell me or she wouldn't. It was that simple.

'Cute little redhead,' she said slowly and thickly. 'Yeah, I remember her. Song and dance. Nice legs and generous with 'em. She went off somewheres. How would I know what them tramps do?'

'Well, I didn't really think you would know,' I said. 'But it was natural to come and ask you, Mrs Florian. Help yourself to the whisky – I could run out for more when we need it.'

'You ain't drinkin',' she said suddenly.

I put my hand around my glass and swallowed what was in it slowly to make it seem more than it was.

'Where's her folks at?' she asked suddenly.

'What does that matter?'

'Okey,' she sneered. 'All cops is the same. Okey, handsome. A guy that buys me a drink is a pal.' She reached for the bottle and set up Number 4. 'I shouldn't ought to barber with you. But when I like a guy, the ceiling's the limit.' She simpered. She was as cute as a washtub. 'Hold on to your chair and don't step on no snakes,' she said. 'I got me an idea.'

She got up out of the rocker, sneezed, almost lost the bathrobe, slapped it back against her stomach and stared at me coldly.

'No peekin',' she said, and went out of the room again, hitting the door frame with her shoulder.

I heard her fumbling steps going into the back part of the house.

The poinsettia shoots tap-tapped dully against the front wall. The clothes line creaked vaguely at the side of the house. The ice cream peddler went by ringing his bell. The big new handsome radio in the corner whispered of dancing and love with a deep soft throbbing note like the catch in a torch singer's voice.

Then from the back of the house there were various types of crashing sounds. A chair seemed to fall over backwards, a bureau drawer was pulled out too far and crashed to the floor, there was fumbling and thudding and muttered thick language. Then the slow click of a lock and the squeak of a trunk top going up. More fumbling and banging. A tray landed on the floor. I got up from the davenport and sneaked into the dining-room and from that into a short hall. I looked around the edge of an open door.

She was in there swaying in front of the trunk, making grabs at what was in it, and then throwing her hair back over her forehead with anger. She was drunker than she thought. She leaned down and steadied herself on the trunk and coughed and sighed. Then she went down on her thick knees and plunged both hands into the trunk and groped.

They came up holding something unsteadily. A thick package tied with faded pink tape. Slowly, clumsily, she undid the tape. She slipped an envelope out of the package and

30

leaned down again to thrust the envelope out of sight into the right-hand side of the trunk. She retied the tape with fumbling fingers.

I sneaked back the way I had come and sat down on the davenport. Breathing stertorous noises, the woman came back into the living-room and stood swaying in the doorway with the tape-tied package.

She grinned at me triumphantly, tossed the package and it fell somewhere near my feet. She waddled back to the rocker and sat down and reached for the whisky.

I picked the package off the floor and untied the faded pink tape.

'Look 'em over,' the woman grunted. 'Photos. Newspaper stills. Not that them tramps ever got in no newspapers except by way of the police blotter. People from the joint they are. They're all the bastard left me – them and his old clothes.'

I leafed through the bunch of shiny photographs of men and women in professional poses. The men had sharp foxy faces and racetrack clothes or eccentric clown-like make-up. Hoofers and comics from the filling station circuit. Not many of them would ever get west of Main Street. You would find them in tank town vaudeville acts, cleaned up, or down in the cheap burlesque houses, as dirty as the law allowed and once in a while just enough dirtier for a raid and a noisy police court trial, and then back in their shows again, grinning, sadistically filthy and as rank as the smell of stale sweat. The women had good legs and displayed their inside curves more than Will Hays would have liked. But their faces were as threadbare as a book-keeper's office cat. Blondes, brunettes, large cow-like eyes with a peasant dullness in them. Small sharp eyes with urchin greed in them. One or two of the faces obviously vicious. One or two of them might have had red hair. You couldn't tell from the photographs. I looked them over casually, without interest and tied the tape again.

'I wouldn't know any of these,' I said. 'Why am I looking at them?'

She leered over the bottle her right hand was grappling with unsteadily. 'Ain't you looking for Velma?'

'Is she one of these?'

Thick cunning played on her face, had no fun there and went somewhere else. 'Ain't you got a photo of her – from her folks?'

'No.'

That troubled her. Every girl has a photo somewhere, if it's only in short dresses with a bow in her hair. I should have had it.

'I ain't beginnin' to like you again,' the woman said almost quietly.

I stood up with my glass and went over and put it down beside hers on the end table.

'Pour me a drink before you kill the bottle.'

She reached for the glass and I turned and walked swiftly through the square arch into the dining-room, into the hall, into the cluttered bedroom with the open trunk and the spilled tray. A voice shouted behind me. I plunged ahead down into the right side of the trunk, felt an envelope and brought it up swiftly.

She was out of her chair when I got back to the living-room, but she had only taken two or three steps. Her eyes had a peculiar glassiness. A murderous glassiness.

'Sit down,' I snarled at her deliberately. 'You're not dealing with a simple-minded lug like Moose Malloy this time.'

It was a shot more or less in the dark, and it didn't hit anything. She blinked twice and tried to lift her nose with her upper lip. Some dirty teeth showed in a rabbit leer.

'Moose? The Moose? What about him?' she gulped.

'He's loose,' I said. 'Out of jail. He's wandering, with a forty-five gun in his hand. He killed a nigger over on Central this morning because he wouldn't tell him where Velma was.

Now he's looking for the fink that turned him up eight years ago.'

A white look smeared the woman's face. She pushed the bottle against her lips and gurgled at it. Some of the whisky ran down her chin.

'And the cops are looking for *him*,' she said and laughed. 'Cops. Yah!'

A lovely old woman. I liked being with her. I liked getting her drunk for my own sordid purposes. I was a swell guy. I enjoyed being me. You find almost anything under your hand in my business, but I was beginning to be a little sick at my stomach.

I opened the envelope my hand was clutching and drew out a glazed still. It was like the others but it was different, much nicer. The girl wore a Pierrot costume from the waist up. Under the white conical hat with a black pompon on the top, her fluffed-out hair had a dark tinge that might have been red. The face was in profile but the visible eye seemed to have gaiety in it. I wouldn't say the face was lovely and un-spoiled, I'm not that good at faces. But it was pretty. People had been nice to that face, or nice enough for their circle. Yet it was a very ordinary face and its prettiness was strictly assembly line. You would see a dozen faces like it on a city block in the noon hour.

Below the waist the photo was mostly legs and very nice legs at that. It was signed across the lower right-hand corner: 'Always yours – Velma Valento.'

I held it up in front of the Florian woman, out of her reach. She lunged but came short.

'Why hide it?' I asked.

She made no sound except thick breathing. I slipped the photo back into the envelope and the envelope into my pocket.

'Why hide it?' I asked again. 'What makes it different from the others? Where is she?'

'She's dead,' the woman said. 'She was a good kid, but she's dead, copper. Beat it.'

The tawny mangled brows worked up and down. Her hand opened and the whisky bottle slid to the carpet and began to gurgle. I bent to pick it up. She tried to kick me in the face. I stepped away from her.

'And that still doesn't say why you hid it,' I told her. 'When did she die? How?'

'I am a poor sick old woman,' she grunted. 'Get away from me, you son of a bitch.'

I stood there looking at her, not saying anything, not thinking of anything particular to say. I stepped over to her side after a moment and put the flat bottle, now almost empty, on the table at her side.

She was staring down at the carpet. The radio droned pleasantly in the corner. A car went by outside. A fly buzzed in a window. After a long time she moved one lip over the other and spoke to the floor, a meaningless jumble of words from which nothing emerged. Then she laughed and threw her head back and drooled. Then her right hand reached for the bottle and it rattled against her teeth as she drained it. When it was empty she held it up and shook it and threw it at me. It went off in the corner somewhere, skidding along the carpet and bringing up with a thud against the baseboard.

She leered at me once more, then her eyes closed and she began to snore.

It might have been an act, but I didn't care. Suddenly I had enough of the scene, too much of it, far too much of it.

I picked my hat off the davenport and went over to the door and opened it and went out past the screen. The radio still droned in the corner and the woman still snored gently in her chair. I threw a quick look back at her before I closed the door, then shut it, opened it again silently and looked again.

Her eyes were still shut but something gleamed below the lids. I went down the steps, along the cracked walk to the street.

In the next house a window curtain was drawn aside and a narrow intent face was close to the glass, peering, an old woman's face with white hair and a sharp nose.

Old Nosey checking up on the neighbours. There's always at least one like her to the block. I waved a hand at her. The curtain fell.

I went back to my car and got into it and drove back to the 77th Street Division, and climbed upstairs to Nulty's smelly little cubbyhole of an office on the second floor.

6

Nulty didn't seem to have moved. He sat in his chair in the same attitude of sour patience. But there were two more cigar stubs in his ash-tray and the floor was a little thicker in burnt matches.

I sat down at the vacant desk and Nulty turned over a photo that was lying face down on his desk and handed it to me. It was a police mug, front and profile, with a fingerprint classification underneath. It was Malloy all right, taken in a strong light, and looking as if he had no more eyebrows than a French roll.

'That's the boy.' I passed it back.

'We got a wire from Oregon State pen on him,' Nulty said. 'All time served except his copper. Things look better. We got him cornered. A prowl car was talking to a conductor the end of the Seventh Street line. The conductor mentioned a guy that size, looking like that. He got off Third and Alexandria. What he'll do is break into some big house where the folks are away. Lots of 'em there, old-fashioned places too far down-town now and hard to rent. He'll break in one and we got him bottled. What you been doing?'

'Was he wearing a fancy hat and white golf balls on his jacket?'

Nulty frowned and twisted his hands on his kneecaps. 'No, a blue suit. Maybe brown.'

'Sure it wasn't a sarong?'

'Huh? Oh yeah, funny. Remind me to laugh on my day off.'

I said: 'That wasn't the Moose. He wouldn't ride a street car. He had money. Look at the clothes he was wearing. He couldn't wear stock sizes. They must have been made to order.'

'Okey, ride me,' Nulty scowled. 'What you been doing?'

'What you ought to have done. This place called Florian's was under the same name when it was a white night trap. I talked to a negro hotel-man who knows the neighbourhood. The sign was expensive so the shines just went on using it when they took over. The man's name was Mike Florian. He's dead some years, but his widow is still around. She lives at 1644 West 54th Place. Her name is Jessie Florian. She's not in the phone book, but she is in the city directory.'

'Well, what do I do – date her up?' Nulty asked.

'I did it for you. I took in a pint of bourbon with me. She's a charming middle-aged lady with a face like a bucket of mud and if she has washed her hair since Coolidge's second term, I'll eat my spare tyre, rim and all.'

'Skip the wisecracks,' Nulty said.

'I asked Mrs Florian about Velma. You remember, Mr Nulty, the redhead named Velma that Moose Malloy was looking for? I'm not tiring you, am I, Mr Nulty?'

'What you sore about?'

'You wouldn't understand. Mrs Florian said she didn't remember Velma. Her home is very shabby except for a new radio, worth seventy or eighty dollars.'

'You ain't told me why that's something I should start screaming about.'

'Mrs Florian – Jessie to me – said her husband left her nothing but his old clothes and a bunch of stills of the gang who worked at his joint from time to time. I plied her with liquor and she is a girl who will take a drink if she had to knock you down to get the bottle. After the third or fourth she went into her modest bedroom and threw things around and dug the bunch of stills out of the bottom of an old trunk. But I was watching her without her knowing it and she slipped one out of the packet and hid it. So after a while I snuck in there and grabbed it.'

I reached into my pocket and laid the Pierrot girl on his desk. He lifted it and stared at it and his lips quirked at the corners.

'Cute,' he said. 'Cute enough. I could of used a piece of that once. Haw, haw. Velma Valento, huh? What happened to this doll?'

'Mrs Florian says she died – but that hardly explains why she hid the photo.'

'It don't do at that. Why did she hide it?'

'She wouldn't tell me. In the end, after I told her about the Moose being out, she seemed to take a dislike to me. That seems impossible, doesn't it?'

'Go on,' Nulty said.

'That's all. I've told you the facts and given you the exhibit. If you can't get somewhere on this set-up, nothing I could say would help.'

'Where would I get? It's still a shine killing. Wait'll we get the Moose. Hell, it's eight years since he saw the girl unless she visited him in the pen.'

'All right,' I said. 'But don't forget he's looking for her and he's a man who would bear down. By the way, he was in for a bank job. That means a reward. Who got it?'

'I don't know,' Nulty said. 'Maybe I could find out. Why?'

'Somebody turned him up. Maybe he knows who. That would be another job he would give time to.' I stood up. 'Well, good-bye and good luck.'

'You walking out on me?'

I went over to the door. 'I have to go home and take a bath and gargle my throat and get my nails manicured.'

'You ain't sick, are you?'

'Just dirty,' I said. 'Very, very dirty.'

'Well, what's your hurry? Sit down a minute.' He leaned back and hooked his thumbs in his vest, which made him look a little more like a cop, but didn't make him look any more magnetic.

'No hurry,' I said. 'No hurry at all. There's nothing more I can do. Apparently this Velma is dead, if Mrs Florian is telling the truth – and I don't at the moment know of any reason why she should lie about it. That was all I was interested in.'

'Yeah,' Nulty said suspiciously – from force of habit.

'And you have Moose Malloy all sewed up anyway, and that's that. So I'll just run on home now and go about the business of trying to earn a living.'

'We might miss out on the Moose,' Nulty said. 'Guys get away once in a while. Even big guys.' His eyes were suspicious also, in so far as they contained any expression at all. 'How much she slip you?'

'What?'

'How much this old lady slip you to lay off?'

'Lay off what?'

'Whatever it is you're layin' off from now on.' He moved his thumbs from his armholes and placed them together in front of his vest and pushed them against each other. He smiled.

'Oh, for Christ's sake,' I said, and went out of the office, leaving his mouth open.

When I was about a yard from the door, I went back and opened it again quietly and looked in. He was sitting in the same position, pushing his thumbs at each other. But he wasn't smiling any more. He looked worried. His mouth was still open.

He didn't move or look up. I didn't know whether he heard me or not. I shut the door again and went away.

7

They had Rembrandt on the calendar that year, a rather smeary self-portrait due to imperfectly registered colour plates. It showed him holding a smeared palette with a dirty thumb and wearing a tam-o'-shanter which wasn't any too clean either. His other hand held a brush poised in the air, as if he might be going to do a little work after a while, if somebody made a down payment. His face was ageing, saggy, full of the disgust of life and the thickening effects of liquor. But it had a hard cheerfulness that I liked, and the eyes were as bright as drops of dew.

I was looking at him across my office desk at about four-thirty when the phone rang and I heard a cool, supercilious voice that sounded as if it thought it was pretty good. It said drawlingly, after I had answered:

'You are Philip Marlowe, a private detective?'

'Check.'

'Oh – you mean, yes. You have been recommended to me as a man who can be trusted to keep his mouth shut. I should like you to come to my house at seven o'clock this evening. We can discuss a matter. My name is Lindsay Marriott and I live at 4212 Cabrillo Street, Montemar Vista. Do you know where that is?'

'I know where Montemar Vista is, Mr Marriott.'

'Yes. Well, Cabrillo Street is rather hard to find. The streets down here are all laid out in a pattern of interesting but intricate curves. I should suggest that you walk up the steps from the sidewalk café. If you do that, Cabrillo is the third street you come to and my house is the only one on the block. At seven then?'

'What is the nature of the employment, Mr Marriott?'

'I should prefer not to discuss that over the phone.'

'Can't you give me some idea? Montemar Vista is quite a distance.'

'I shall be glad to pay your expenses, if we don't agree. Are you particular about the nature of the employment?'

'Not as long as it's legitimate.'

The voice grew icicles. 'I should not have called you, if it were not.'

A Harvard boy. Nice use of the subjunctive mood. The end of my foot itched, but my bank account was still trying to crawl under a duck. I put honey into my voice and said: 'Many thanks for calling me, Mr Marriott. I'll be there.'

He hung up and that was that. I thought Mr Rembrandt had a faint sneer on his face. I got the office bottle out of the deep drawer of the desk and took a short drink. That took the sneer out of Mr Rembrandt in a hurry.

A wedge of sunlight slipped over the edge of the desk and fell noiselessly to the carpet. Traffic lights bong-bonged outside on the boulevard, interurban cars pounded by, a typewriter clacked monotonously in the lawyer's office beyond the party wall. I had just filled and lit a pipe when the telephone rang again.

It was Nulty this time. His voice sounded full of baked potato. 'Well, I guess I ain't quite bright at that,' he said, when he knew who he was talking to. 'I miss one. Malloy went to see that Florian dame.'

I held the phone tight enough to crack it. My upper lip suddenly felt a little cold. 'Go on. I thought you had him cornered.'

'Was some other guy. Malloy ain't around there at all. We

got a call from some old window-peaker on West Fifty-four. Two guys was to see the Florian dame. Number one parked the other side of the street and acted kind of cagey. Looked the dump over good before he went in. Was in about an hour. Six feet, dark hair, medium heavy built. Come out quiet.'

'He had liquor on his breath too,' I said.

'Oh, sure. That was you, wasn't it? Well, Number Two was the Moose. Guy in loud clothes as big as a house. He come in a car too but the old lady don't get the licence, can't read the number that far off. This was about a hour after you was there, she says. He goes in fast and is in about five minutes only. Just before he gets back in his car he takes a big gat out and spins the chamber. I guess that's what the old lady saw he done. That's why she calls up. She don't hear no shots though, inside the house.'

'That must have been a big disappointment,' I said.

'Yeah. A nifty. Remind me to laugh on my day off. The old lady misses one too. The prowl boys go down there and don't get no answer on the door, so they walk in, the front door not being locked. Nobody's dead on the floor. Nobody's home. The Florian dame has skipped out. So they stop by next door and tell the old lady and she's sore as a boil on account of she didn't see the Florian dame go out. So they report back and go on about the job. So about an hour, maybe hour and a half after that, the old lady phones in again and says Mrs Florian is home again. So they give the call to me and I ask her what makes that important and she hangs up in my face.'

Nulty paused to collect a little breath and wait for my comments. I didn't have any. After a moment he went on grumbling.

'What you make of it?'

'Nothing much. The Moose would be likely to go by there, of course. He must have known Mrs Florian pretty well. Naturally he wouldn't stick around very long. He would be afraid the law might be wise to Mrs Florian.'

'What I figure,' Nulty said calmly, 'Maybe I should go over and see her – kind of find out where she went to.'

'That's a good idea,' I said. 'If you can get somebody to lift you out of your chair.'

'Huh? Oh, another nifty. It don't make a lot of difference any more now though. I guess I won't bother.'

'All right,' I said. 'Let's have it whatever it is.'

He chuckled. 'We got Malloy all lined up. We really got him this time. We make him at Girard, headed north in a rented hack. He gassed up there and the service station kid recognized him from the description we broadcast a while back. He said everything jibed except Malloy had changed to a dark suit. We got county and state law on it. If he goes on north we get him at the Ventura line, and if he slides over to the Ridge Route, he has to stop at Castaic for his check ticket. If he don't stop, they phone ahead and block the road. We don't want no cop shot up, if we can help it. That sound good?'

'It sounds all right,' I said. 'If it really is Malloy, and if he does exactly what you expect him to do.'

Nulty cleared his throat carefully. 'Yeah. What you doing on it – just in case?'

'Nothing. Why should I be doing anything on it?'

'You got along pretty good with that Florian dame. Maybe she would have some more ideas.'

'All you need to find out is a full bottle,' I said.

'You handled her real nice. Maybe you ought to kind of spend a little more time on her.'

'I thought this was a police job.'

'Oh, sure. Was your idea about the girl though.'

'That seems to be out – unless the Florian is lying about it.'

'Dames lie about anything – just for practice,' Nulty said grimly. 'You ain't real busy, huh?'

'I've got a job to do. It came in since I saw you. A job where I get paid. I'm sorry.'

'Walking out, huh?'

'I wouldn't put it that way. I just have to work to earn a living.'

'Okey, pal. If that's the way you feel about it, okey.'

'I don't feel any way about it,' I almost yelled. 'I just don't have time to stooge for you or any other cop.'

'Okey, get sore,' Nulty said, and hung up.

I held the dead phone and snarled into it: 'Seventeen hundred and fifty cops in this town and they want me to do their leg work for them.'

I dropped the phone into its cradle and took another drink from the office bottle.

After a while I went down to the lobby of the building to buy an evening paper. Nulty was right in one thing at least. The Montgomery killing hadn't even made the want-ad section so far.

I left the office again in time for an early dinner.

8

I got down to Montemar Vista as the light began to fade, but there was still a fine sparkle on the water and the surf was breaking far out in long smooth curves. A group of pelicans was flying bomber formation just under the creaming lip of the waves. A lonely yacht was taking in toward the yacht harbour at Bay City. Beyond it the huge emptiness of the Pacific was purple-grey.

Montemar Vista was a few dozen houses of various sizes and shapes hanging by their teeth and eyebrows to a spur of mountain and looking as if a good sneeze would drop them down among the box lunches on the beach.

Above the beach the highway ran under a wide concrete arch which was in fact a pedestrian bridge. From the inner end of this a flight of concrete steps with a thick galvanized handrail on one side ran straight as a ruler up the side of the mountain. Beyond the arch the sidewalk café my client had spoken of was bright and cheerful inside, but the iron-legged tile-topped tables outside under the striped awning were empty save for a single dark woman in slacks who smoked and stared moodily out to sea, with a bottle of beer in front of her. A fox terrier was using one of the iron chairs for a lamp-post. She chided the dog absently as I drove past and gave the sidewalk café my business to the extent of using its parking space.

I walked back through the arch and started up the steps. It was a nice walk if you liked grunting. There were two hundred and eighty steps up to Cabrillo Street. They were drifted over with windblown sand and the handrail was as cold and wet as a toad's belly.

When I reached the top the sparkle had gone from the water and a seagull with a broken trailing leg was twisting against the offsea breeze. I sat down on the damp cold top step and shook the sand out of my shoes and waited for my pulse to come down into the low hundreds. When I was breathing more or less normally again I shook my shirt loose from my back and went along to the lighted house which was the only one within yelling distance of the steps.

It was a nice little house with a salt-tarnished spiral of staircase going up to the front door and an imitation coach-lamp for a porch light. The garage was underneath and to one side. Its door was lifted up and rolled back and the light of the porch-lamp shone obliquely on a huge black battleship of a car with chromium trimmings, a coyote tail tied to the Winged Victory on the radiator cap and engraved initials where the emblem should be. The car had a right-hand drive and looked as if it had cost more than the house.

I went up the spiral steps, looked for a bell, and used a knocker in the shape of a tiger's head. Its clatter was swallowed in the early evening fog. I heard no steps in the house.

My damp shirt felt like an icepack on my back. The door opened silently, and I was looking at a tall blond man in a white flannel suit with a violet satin scarf around his neck.

There was a cornflower in the lapel of his white coat and his pale blue eyes looked faded out by comparison. The violet scarf was loose enough to show that he wore no tie and that he had a thick, soft brown neck, like the neck of a strong woman. His features were a little on the heavy side, but handsome; he had an inch more of height than I had, which made him six feet one. His blond hair was arranged, by art or nature, in three precise blond ledges which reminded me of steps, so that I didn't like them. I wouldn't have liked them anyway. Apart from all this he had the general appearance of a lad who would wear a white flannel suit with a violet scarf round his neck and a cornflower in his lapel.

He cleared his throat lightly and looked past my shoulder at the darkening sea. His cool supercilious voice said: 'Yes?'

'Seven o'clock,' I said. 'On the dot.'

'Oh yes. Let me see, your name is——' he paused and frowned in the effort of memory. The effect was as phony as the pedigree of a used car. I let him work at it for a minute, then I said:

'Philip Marlowe. The same as it was this afternoon.'

He gave me a quick darting frown, as if perhaps something ought to be done about that. Then he stepped back and said coldly:

'Ah yes. Quite so. Come in, Marlowe. My house boy is away this evening.'

He opened the door wide with a fingertip, as though opening the door himself dirtied him a little.

I went in past him and smelled perfume. He closed the door. The entrance put us on a low balcony with a metal railing that ran around three sides of a big studio living-room. The fourth side contained a big fireplace and two doors. A fire was crackling in the fireplace. The balcony was lined with bookshelves and there were pieces of glazed metallic-looking bits of sculpture on pedestals.

We went down three steps to the main part of the living-room. The carpet almost tickled my ankles. There was a concert grand piano, closed down. On one corner of it stood a tall silver vase on a strip of peach-coloured velvet, and a single yellow rose in the vase. There was plenty of nice soft furniture, a great many floor cushions, some with golden tassels and some just naked. It was a nice room, if you didn't get rough. There was a wide damask covered divan in a shadowy corner, like a casting couch. It was the kind of room where people sit with their feet in their laps and sip absinthe through lumps of sugar and talk with high affected voices and sometimes just squeak. It was a room where anything could happen except work.

Mr Lindsay Marriott arranged himself in the curve of the grand piano, leaned over to sniff at the yellow rose, then opened a French enamel cigarette case and lit a long brown cigarette with a gold tip. I sat down on a pink chair and hoped I wouldn't leave a mark on it. I lit a Camel, blew smoke through my nose and looked at a piece of black shiny metal on a stand. It showed a full, smooth curve with a shallow fold in it and two protuberances on the curve. I stared at it. Marriott saw me staring at it.

'An interesting bit,' he said negligently, 'I picked it up just the other day. Asta Dial's *Spirit of Dawn.*'

'I thought it was Klopstein's *Two Warts on a Fanny,*' I said.

Mr Lindsay Marriott's face looked as if he had swallowed a bee. He smoothed it out with an effort.

'You have a somewhat peculiar sense of humour,' he said.

'Not peculiar,' I said. 'Just uninhibited.'

'Yes,' he said very coldly. 'Yes – of course. I've no doubt. ... Well, what I wished to see you about is, as a matter of fact, a very slight matter indeed. Hardly worth bringing you down here for. I am meeting a couple of men to-night and paying them some money. I thought I might as well have someone with me. You carry a gun?'

'At times. Yes,' I said. I looked at the dimple in his broad, fleshy chin. You could have lost a marble in it.

'I shan't want you to carry that. Nothing of that sort at all. This is a purely business transaction.'

'I hardly ever shoot anybody,' I said. 'A matter of blackmail?'

He frowned. 'Certainly not. I'm not in the habit of giving people grounds for blackmail.'

'It happens to the nicest people. I might say particularly to the nicest people.'

He waved his cigarette. His aquamarine eyes had a faintly thoughtful expression, but his lips smiled. The kind of smile that goes with a silk noose.

He blew some more smoke and tilted his head back. This accentuated the soft firm lines of his throat. His eyes came down slowly and studied me.

'I'm meeting these men – most probably – in a rather lonely place. I don't know where yet. I expect a call giving me the particulars. I have to be ready to leave at once. It won't be very far away from here. That's the understanding.'

'You've been making this deal some time?'

'Three or four days, as a matter of fact.'

'You left your bodyguard problem until pretty late.'

He thought that over. He snicked some dark ash from his cigarette. 'That's true. I had some difficulty making my mind up. It would be better for me to go alone, although nothing has been said definitely about my having someone with me. On the other hand I'm not much of a hero.'

'They know you by sight, of course?'

'I – I'm not sure. I shall be carrying a large amount of money and it is not my money. I'm acting for a friend. I shouldn't feel justified in letting it out of my possession, of course.'

I snubbed out my cigarette and leaned back in the pink chair and twiddled my thumbs. 'How much money – and what for?'

'Well, really——' it was a fairly nice smile now, but I still didn't like it. 'I can't go into that.'

'You just want me to go along and hold your hat?'

His hand jerked again and some ash fell off on his white cuff. He shook it off and stared down at the place where it had been.

'I'm afraid I don't like your manner,' he said, using the edge of his voice.

'I've had complaints about it,' I said. 'But nothing seems to do any good. Let's look at this job a little. You want a bodyguard, but he can't wear a gun. You want a helper, but he isn't supposed to know what he's supposed to do. You want me to risk my neck without knowing why or what for or what the risk is. What are you offering for all this?'

'I hadn't really got around to thinking about it.' His cheekbones were dusky red.

'Do you suppose you could get around to thinking about it?'

He leaned forward gracefully and smiled between his teeth. 'How would you like a swift punch on the nose?'

I grinned and stood up and put my hat on. I started across the carpet towards the front door, but not very fast.

His voice snapped at my back. 'I'm offering you a hundred dollars for a few hours of your time. If that isn't enough, say so. There's no risk. Some jewels were taken from a friend of mine in a hold-up – and I'm buying them back. Sit down and don't be so touchy.'

I went back to the pink chair and sat down again.

'All right,' I said. 'Let's hear about it.'

We stared at each other for all of ten seconds. 'Have you

ever heard of Fei Tsui jade?' he asked slowly, and lit another of his dark cigarettes.

'No.'

'It's the only really valuable kind. Other kinds are valuable to some extent for the material, but chiefly for the workmanship on them. Fei Tsui is valuable in itself. All known deposits were exhausted hundreds of years ago. A friend of mine owns a necklace of sixty beads of about six carats each, intricately carved. Worth eighty or ninety thousand dollars. The Chinese Government has a very slightly larger one valued at a hundred and twenty-five thousand. My friend's necklace was taken in a hold-up a few nights ago. I was present, but quite helpless. I had driven my friend to an evening party and later to the Trocadero and we were on our way back to her home from there. A car brushed the left front fender and stopped, as I thought, to apologize. Instead of that it was a very quick and very neat hold-up. Either three or four men, I really saw only two, but I'm sure another stayed in the car behind the wheel, and I thought I saw a glimpse of still a fourth at the rear window. My friend was wearing the jade necklace. They took that and two rings and a bracelet. The one who seemed to be the leader looked the things over without any apparent hurry under a small flashlight. Then he handed one of the rings back and said that would give us an idea what kind of people we were dealing with and to wait for a phone call before reporting to the police or the insurance company. So we obeyed their instructions. There's plenty of that sort of thing going on, of course. You keep the affair to yourself and pay ransom, or you never see your jewels again. If they're fully insured, perhaps you don't mind, but if they happen to be rare pieces, you would rather pay ransom.'

I nodded. 'And this jade necklace is something that can't be picked up every day.'

He slid a finger along the polished surface of the piano

with a dreamy expression, as if touching smooth things pleased him.

'Very much so. It's irreplaceable. She shouldn't have worn it out – ever. But she's a reckless sort of woman. The other things were good but ordinary.

'Uh-huh. How much are you paying?'

'Eight thousand dollars. It's dirt cheap. But if my friend couldn't get another like it, these thugs couldn't very easily dispose of it either. It's probably known to everyone in the trade, all over the country.'

'This friend of yours – does she have a name?'

'I'd prefer not to mention it at the moment.'

'What are the arrangements?'

He looked at me along his pale eyes. I thought he seemed a bit scared, but I didn't know him very well. Maybe it was a hangover. The hand that held the dark cigarette couldn't keep still.

'We have been negotiating by telephone for several days – through me. Everything is settled except the time and place of meeting. It is to be some time to-night. I shall presently be getting a call to tell me of that. It will not be very far away, they say, and I must be prepared to leave at once. I suppose that is so that no plant could be arranged. With the police, I mean.'

'Uh-huh. Is the money marked? I suppose it *is* money?'

'Currency, of course. Twenty dollar bills. No, why should it be marked?'

'It can be done so that it takes black light to detect it. No reason – except that the cops like to break up these gangs – if they can get any co-operation. Some of the money might turn up on some lad with a record.'

He wrinkled his brow thoughtfully. 'I'm afraid I don't know what black light is.'

'Ultra-violet. It makes certain metallic inks glisten in the dark. I could get it done for you.'

'I'm afraid there isn't time for that now,' he said shortly.

'That's one of the things that worries me.'

'Why?'

'Why you only called me this afternoon. Why you picked on me. Who told you about me?'

He laughed. His laugh was rather boyish, but not a very young boy. 'Well, as a matter of fact I'll have to confess I merely picked your name at random out of the phone book. You see I hadn't intended to have anyone go with me. Then this afternoon I got to thinking why not.'

I lit another of my squashed cigarettes and watched his throat muscles. 'What's the plan?'

He spread his hands. 'Simply to go where I am told, hand over the package of money, and receive back the jade necklace.'

'Uh-huh.'

'You seem fond of that expression.'

'What expression?'

'Uh-huh.'

'Where will I be – in the back of the car?'

'I suppose so. It's a big car. You could easily hide in the back of it.'

'Listen,' I said slowly. 'You plan to go out with me hidden in your car to a destination you are to get over the phone some time to-night. You will have eight grand in currency on you and with that you are supposed to buy back a jade necklace worth ten or twelve times that much. What you will probably get will be a package you won't be allowed to open – providing you get anything at all. It's just as likely they will simply take your money, count it over in some other place, and mail you the necklace, if they feel big-hearted. There's nothing to prevent them double-crossing you. Certainly nothing I could do would stop them. These are heist guys. They're tough. They might even knock you on the head – not hard – just enough to delay you while they go on their way.'

'Well, as a matter of fact, I'm a little afraid of something like that,' he said quietly, and his eyes twitched. 'I suppose that's really why I wanted somebody with me.'

'Did they put a flash on you when they pulled the stick-up?'

He shook his head, no.

'No matter. They've had a dozen chances to look you over since. They probably knew all about you before that anyway. These jobs are cased. They're cased the way a dentist cases your tooth for a gold inlay. You go out with this dame much?'

'Well – not infrequently,' he said stiffly.

'Married?'

'Look here,' he snapped. 'Suppose we leave the lady out of this entirely.'

'Okey,' I said. 'But the more I know the fewer cups I break. I ought to walk away from this job, Marriott. I really ought. If the boys want to play ball, you don't need me. If they don't want to play ball, I can't do anything about it.'

'All I want is your company,' he said quickly.

I shrugged and spread my hands. 'Okey – but I drive the car and carry the money – and you do the hiding in the back. We're about the same height. If there's any question, we'll just tell them the truth. Nothing to lose by it.'

'No.' He bit his lip.

'I'm getting a hundred dollars for doing nothing. If anybody gets conked, it ought to be me.'

He frowned and shook his head, but after quite a long time his face cleared slowly and he smiled.

'Very well,' he said slowly. 'I don't suppose it matters much. We'll be together. Would you care for a spot of brandy?'

'Uh-huh. And you might bring me my hundred bucks. I like to feel money.'

He moved away like a dancer, his body almost motionless from the waist up.

The phone rang as he was on his way out. It was in a little alcove off the living-room proper, cut into the balcony. It wasn't the call we were thinking about though. He sounded too affectionate.

He danced back after a while with a bottle of Five-Star Martell and five nice crisp twenty-dollar bills. That made it a nice evening – so far.

9

The house was very still. Far off there was a sound which might have been beating surf or cars zooming along a highway, or wind in pine trees. It was the sea, of course, breaking far down below. I sat there and listened to it and thought long, careful thoughts.

The phone rang four times within the next hour and a half. The big one came at eight minutes past ten. Marriott talked briefly, in a very low voice, cradled the instrument without a sound and stood up with a sort of hushed movement. His face looked drawn. He had changed to dark clothes now. He walked silently back into the room and poured himself a stiff drink in a brandy glass. He held it against the light a moment with a queer unhappy smile, swirled it once quickly and tilted his head back to pour it down his throat.

'Well – we're all set, Marlowe. Ready?'

'That's all I've been all evening. Where do we go?'

'A place called Purissima Canyon.'

'I never heard of it.'

'I'll get a map.' He got one and spread it out quickly and the light blinked in his brassy hair as he bent over it. Then he pointed with his finger. The place was one of the many canyons off the foothill boulevard that turns into town from the coast highway north of Bay City. I had a vague idea where it was, but no more. It seemed to be at the end of a street called Camino de la Costa.

'It will be not more than twelve minutes from here,' Marriott said quickly. 'We'd better get moving. We only have twenty minutes to play with.'

He handed me a light-coloured overcoat which made me a fine target. It fitted pretty well. I wore my own hat. I had a gun under my arm, but I hadn't told him about that.

While I put the coat on, he went on talking in a light nervous voice and dancing on his hands the thick manila envelope with the eight grand in it.

'Purissima Canyon has a sort of level shelf at the inner end of it, they say. This is walled off from the road by a white fence of four-by-fours, but you can just squeeze by. A dirt road winds down into a little hollow and we are to wait there without lights. There are no houses around.'

'We?'

'Well, I mean "I" – theoretically.'

'Oh.'

He handed me the manila envelope and I opened it up and looked at what was inside. It was money all right, a huge wad of currency. I didn't count it. I snapped the rubber around again and stuffed the packet down inside my overcoat. It almost caved in a rib.

We went to the door and Marriott switched off all the lights. He opened the front door cautiously and peered out at the foggy air. We went out and down the salt-tarnished spiral stairway to the street level and the garage.

It was a little foggy, the way it always is down there at night. I had to start up the windshield wiper for a while.

The big foreign car drove itself, but I held the wheel for the sake of appearances.

For two minutes we figure-eighted back and forth across the face of the mountain and then popped out right beside the sidewalk café. I could understand now why Marriott had told me to walk up the steps. I could have driven about in those curving, twisting streets for hours without making any more yardage than an angle-worm in a bait can.

On the highway the lights of the streaming cars made an almost solid beam in both directions. The big corn-poppers were rolling north growling as they went and festooned all over with green and yellow overhang lights. Three minutes of that and we turned inland, by a big service station, and wound along the flank of the foothills. It got quiet. There was loneliness and the smell of kelp and the smell of wild sage from the hills. A yellow window hung here and there, all by itself, like the last orange. Cars passed, spraying the pavement with cold white light, then growled off into the darkness again. Wisps of fog chased the stars down the sky.

Marriott leaned forward from the dark rear seat and said:

'Those lights off to the right are the Belvedere Beach Club. The next canyon is Las Pulgas and the next after that Purissima. We turn right at the top of the second rise.' His voice was hushed and taut.

I grunted and kept on driving. 'Keep your head down,' I said over my shoulder. 'We may be watched all the way. This car sticks out like spats at an Iowa picnic. Could be the boys don't like your being twins.'

We went down into a hollow at the inward end of a canyon and then up on the high ground and after a little while down again and up again. Then Marriott's tight voice said in my ear:

'Next street on the right. The house with the square turret. Turn beside that.'

'You didn't help them pick this place out, did you?'

'Hardly,' he said, and laughed grimly. 'I just happen to know these canyons pretty well.'

I swung the car to the right past a big corner house with a square white turret topped with round tiles. The headlights sprayed for an instant on a street sign that read: Camino de la

Costa. We slid down a broad avenue lined with unfinished electroliers and weed-grown sidewalks. Some realtor's dream had turned into a hangover there. Crickets chirped and bull-frogs whooped in the darkness behind the overgrown side-walks. Marriott's car was that silent.

There was a house to a block, then a house to two blocks, then no houses at all. A vague window or two was still lighted, but the people around there seemed to go to bed with the chickens. Then the paved avenue ended abruptly in a dirt road packed as hard as concrete in dry weather. The dirt road narrowed and dropped slowly downhill between walls of brush. The lights of the Belvedere Beach Club hung in the air to the right and far ahead there was a gleam of moving water. The acrid smell of the sage filled the night. Then a white-painted barrier loomed across the dirt road and Marriott spoke at my shoulder again.

'I don't think you can get past it,' he said. 'The space doesn't look wide enough.'

I cut the noiseless motor, dimmed the lights and sat there, listening. Nothing. I switched the lights off altogether and got out of the car. The crickets stopped chirping. For a little while the silence was so complete that I could hear the sound of tyres on the highway at the bottom of the cliffs, a mile away. Then one by one the crickets started up again until the night was full of them.

'Sit tight. I'm going down there and have a look see,' I whispered into the back of the car.

I touched the gun butt inside my coat and walked forward. There was more room between the brush and the end of the white barrier than there had seemed to be from the car. Some-one had hacked the brush away and there were car marks in the dirt. Probably kids going down there to neck on warm nights. I went on past the barrier. The road dropped and curved. Below was darkness and a vague far off sea-sound. And the lights of cars on the highway. I went on. The road ended in a shallow bowl entirely surrounded by brush. It was empty. There seemed to be no way into it but the way I had come. I stood there in the silence and listened.

Minute passed slowly after minute, but I kept on waiting for some new sound. None came. I seemed to have that hollow entirely to myself.

I looked across to the lighted beach club. From its upper windows a man with a good night glass could probably cover this spot fairly well. He could see a car come and go, see who got out of it, whether there was a group of men or just one. Sitting in a dark room with a good night glass you can see a lot more detail than you would think possible.

I turned to go back up the hill. From the base of a bush a cricket chirped loud enough to make me jump. I went on up around the curve and past the white barricade. Still nothing. The black car stood dimly shining against a greyness which was neither darkness nor light. I went over to it and put a foot on the running board beside the driver's seat.

'Looks like a tryout,' I said under my breath, but loud enough for Marriott to hear me from the back of the car. 'Just to see if you obey orders.'

There was a vague movement behind but he didn't answer. I went on trying to see something besides bushes.

Whoever it was had a nice easy shot at the back of my head. Afterwards I thought I might have heard the swish of a sap. Maybe you always think that – afterwards.

10

'Four minutes,' the voice said. 'Five, possibly six. They must have moved quick and quiet. He didn't even let out a yell.'

I opened my eyes and looked fuzzily at a cold star. I was lying on my back. I felt sick.

The voice said: 'It could have been a little longer. Maybe even eight minutes altogether. They must have been in the brush, right where the car stopped. The guy scared easily. They must have thrown a small light in his face and he passed out – just from panic. The pansy.'

There was silence. I got up on one knee. Pains shot from the back of my head clear to my ankles.

'Then one of them got into the car,' the voice said, 'and waited for you to come back. The others hid again. They must have figured he would be afraid to come alone. Or something in his voice made them suspicious, when they talked to him on the phone.'

I balanced myself woozily on the flat of my hands, listening.

'Yeah, that was about how it was,' the voice said.

It was my voice. I was talking to myself, coming out of it. I was trying to figure the thing out subconsciously.

'Shut up, you damwit,' I said, and stopped talking to myself.

Far off the purl of motors, nearer the chirp of crickets, the peculiar long drawn ee-ee-ee of tree frogs. I didn't think I was going to like those sounds any more.

I lifted a hand off the ground and tried to shake the sticky sage ooze off it, then rubbed it on the side of my coat. Nice work, for a hundred dollars. The hand jumped at the inside pocket of the overcoat. No manila envelope, naturally. The hand jumped inside my own suit coat. My wallet was still there. I wondered if my hundred was still in it. Probably not. Something felt heavy against my left ribs. The gun in the shoulder holster.

That was a nice touch. They left me my gun. A nice touch of something or other – like closing a man's eyes after you knife him.

I felt the back of my head. My hat was still on. I took it off, not without discomfort, and felt the head underneath. Good old head, I'd had it a long time. It was a little soft now, a little pulpy, and more than a little tender. But a pretty light sapping at that. The hat had helped. I could still use the head. I could use it another year anyway.

I put my right hand back on the ground and took the left off and swivelled it around until I could see my watch. The illuminated dial showed 10.56, as nearly as I could focus on it.

The call had come at 10.08. Marriott had talked maybe two minutes. Another four had got us out of the house. Time passes very slowly when you are actually doing something. I mean, you can go through a lot of movements in very few minutes. Is that what I mean? What the hell do I care what I mean? Okey, better men than me have meant less. Okey, what I mean is, that would be 10.15, say. The place was about twelve minutes away. 10.27. I get out, walk down in the hollow, spend at the most eight minutes fooling around and come on back up to get my head treated. 10.35. Give me a minute to fall down and hit the ground with my face. The reason I hit it with my face, I got my chin scraped. It hurts. It feels scraped. That way I know it's scraped. No, I can't see it. I don't have to see it. It's my chin and I know whether it's scraped or not. Maybe you want to make something of it. Okey, shut up and let me think. What with? ...

The watch showed 10.56 p.m. That meant I had been out for twenty minutes.

Twenty minutes' sleep. Just a nice doze. In that time I had muffed a mob and lost eight thousand dollars. Well, why not? In twenty minutes you can sink a battleship, down three or four planes, hold a double execution. You can die, get married, get fired and find a new job, have a tooth pulled, have your tonsils out. In twenty minutes you can even get up in the morning. You can get a glass of water at a night club — maybe.

Twenty minutes' sleep. That's a long time. Especially on a cold night, out in the open. I began to shiver.

I was still on my knees. The smell of the sage was beginning to bother me. The sticky ooze from which wild bees get their honey. Honey was sweet, much too sweet. My stomach took a whirl. I clamped my teeth tight and just managed to keep it down my throat. Cold sweat stood out in lumps on my forehead, but I shivered just the same. I got up on one foot, then on both feet, straightened up, wobbling a little. I felt like an amputated leg.

I turned slowly. The car was gone. The dirt road stretched empty, back up the shallow hill towards the paved street, the end of Camino de la Costa. To the left the barrier of white-painted four-by-fours stood out against the darkness. Beyond the low wall of brush the pale glow in the sky would be the lights of Bay City. And over farther to the right and near by were the lights of the Belvedere Club.

I went over where the car had stood and got a fountain pen flash unclipped from my pocket and poked the little light down at the ground. The soil was red loam, very hard in dry weather, but the weather was not bone dry. There was a little fog in the air, and enough of the moisture had settled on the surface of the ground to show where the car had stood. I could see, very faint, the tread marks of the heavy ten-ply Vogue tyres. I put the light on them and bent over and the pain made my head dizzy. I started to follow the tracks. They went straight ahead for a dozen feet, then swung over to the left. They didn't turn. They went towards the gap at the left-hand end of the white barricade. Then I lost them.

I went over to the barricade and shone the little light on the brush. Fresh-broken twigs. I went through the gap, on down the curving road. The ground was still softer here. More marks of the heavy tyres. I went on down, rounded the curve and was at the edge of the hollow closed in by brush.

It was there all right, the chromium and glossy paint shining a little even in the dark, and the red reflector glass of the tail-lights shining back at the pencil flash. It was there, silent, lightless, all the doors shut. I went towards it slowly, gritting my teeth at every step. I opened one of the rear doors and put the beam of the flash inside. Empty. The front was empty too. The ignition was off. The key hung in the lock on a thin chain. No torn upholstery, no scarred glass, no blood, no bodies. Everything neat and orderly. I shut the doors and circled the car slowly, looking for a sign and not finding any.

A sound froze me.

A motor throbbed above the rim of the brush. I didn't jump more than a foot. The flash in my hand went out. A gun slid into my hand all by itself. Then headlight beams tilted up towards the sky, then tilted down again. The motor sounded like a small car. It had that contented sound that comes with moisture in the air.

The lights tilted down still more and got brighter. A car was coming down the curve of the dirt road. It came two-thirds of the way and then stopped. A spotlight clicked on and swung out to the side, held there for a long moment, went out again. The car came on down the hill. I slipped the gun out of my pocket and crouched behind the motor of Marriott's car.

A small coupé of no particular shape or colour slid into the hollow and turned so that its headlights raked the sedan from one end to the other. I got my head down in a hurry. The lights swept above me like a sword. The coupé stopped. The motor died. The headlights died. Silence. Then a door opened and a light foot touched the ground. More silence. Even the crickets were silent. Then a beam of light cut the darkness low down, parallel to the ground and only a few inches above it. The beam swept, and there was no way I could get my ankles out of it quickly enough. The beam stopped on my feet. Silence. The beam came up and raked the top of the hood again.

Then a laugh. It was a girl's laugh. Strained, taut as a

mandolin wire. A strange sound in that place. The white beam shot under the car again and settled on my feet.

The voice said, not quite shrilly: 'All right, you. Come out of there with your hands up and very damned empty. You're covered.'

I didn't move.

The light wavered a little, as though the hand that held it wavered. It swept slowly along the hood once more. The voice stabbed at me again.

'Listen, stranger. I'm holding a ten shot automatic. I can shoot straight. Both your feet are vulnerable. What do you bid?'

'Put it up – or I'll blow it out of your hand!' I snarled. My voice sounded like somebody tearing slats off a chicken coop.

'Oh – a hard-boiled gentleman.' There was a quaver in the voice, a nice little quaver. Then it hardened again. 'Coming out? I'll count three. Look at the odds I'm giving you – twelve fat cylinders, maybe sixteen. But your feet will hurt. And ankle bones take years and years to get well and some-times they never do really——'

I straightened up slowly and looked into the beam of the flashlight.

'I talk too much when I'm scared too,' I said.

'Don't – don't move another inch! Who are you?'

I moved around the front of the car towards her. When I was six feet from the slim dark figure behind the flash I stopped. The flash glared at me steadily.

'You stay right there,' the girl snapped angrily, after I had stopped. 'Who are you?'

'Let's see your gun.'

She held it forward into the light. It was pointed at my stomach. It was a little gun, it looked like a small Colt vest pocket automatic.

'Oh, that,' I said. 'That toy. It doesn't either hold ten shots. It holds six. It's just a little bitty gun, a butterfly gun. They shoot butterflies with them. Shame on you for telling a deliberate lie like that.'

'Are you crazy?'

'Me? I've been sapped by a hold-up man. I might be a little goofy.'

'Is that – is that your car?'

'No.'

'Who are you?'

'What were you looking at back there with your spot-light?'

'I get it. You ask the answers. He-man stuff. I was looking at a man.'

'Does he have blond hair in waves?'

'Not now,' she said quietly. 'He might have had – once.'

That jarred me. Somehow I hadn't expected it. 'I didn't see him,' I said lamely. 'I was following the tyre marks with a flashlight down the hill. Is he badly hurt?' I went another step towards her. The little gun jumped at me and the flash held steady.

'Take it easy,' she said quietly. 'Very easy. Your friend is dead.'

I didn't say anything for a moment. Then I said: 'All right, let's go look at him.'

'Let's stand right here and not move and you tell me who you are and what happened.' The voice was crisp. It was not afraid. It meant what it said.

'Marlowe. Philip Marlowe. An investigator. Private.'

'That's who you are – if it's true. Prove it.'

'I'm going to take my wallet out.'

'I don't think so. Just leave your hands where they happen to be. We'll skip the proof for the time being. What's your story?'

'This man may not be dead.'

'He's dead all right. With his brains on his face. The story, mister. Make it fast.'

'As I said – he may not be dead. We'll go look at him.' I moved one foot forward.

'Move and I'll drill you!' she snapped.

I moved the other foot forward. The flash jumped about a little. I think she took a step back.

'You take some awful chances, mister,' she said quietly. 'All right, go on ahead and I'll follow. You look like a sick man. If it hadn't been for that——'

'You'd have shot me. I've been sapped. It always makes me a little dark under the eyes.'

'A nice sense of humour – like a morgue attendant,' she almost wailed.

I turned away from the light and immediately it shone on the ground in front of me. I walked past the little coupé, an ordinary little car, clean and shiny under the misty starlight. I went on, up the dirt road, around the curve. The steps were close behind me and the flashlight guided me. There was no sound anywhere now except our steps and the girl's breathing. I didn't hear mine.

11

Half-way up the slope I looked off to the right and saw his foot. She swung the light. Then I saw all of him. I ought to have seen him as I came down, but I had been bent over, peering at the ground with a fountain pen flash, trying to read tyre marks by a light the size of a quarter.

'Give me the flash,' I said and reached back.

She put it into my hand, without a word. I went down on a knee. The ground felt cold and damp through the cloth.

He lay smeared to the ground, on his back, at the base of a bush, in that bag-of-clothes position that always means the same thing. His face was a face I had never seen before. His hair was dark with blood, the beautiful blond ledges were tangled with blood, and some thick greyish ooze, like primeval slime.

The girl behind me breathed hard, but she didn't speak. I held the light on his face. He had been beaten to a pulp. One of his hands was flung out in a frozen gesture, the fingers curled. His overcoat was half twisted under him, as though he had rolled as he fell. His legs were crossed. There was a trickle as black as dirty oil at the corner of his mouth.

'Hold the flash on him,' I said, passing it back to her. 'If it doesn't make you sick.'

She took it and held it without a word, as steady as an old homicide veteran. I got my fountain pen flash out again and started to go through his pockets, trying not to move him.

'You shouldn't do that,' she said tensely. 'You shouldn't touch him until the police come.'

'That's right,' I said. 'And the prowl car boys are not supposed to touch him until the K-car men come and they're not supposed to touch him until the coroner's examiner sees him and the photographers have photographed him and the fingerprint man has taken his prints. And do you know how long all that is liable to take out here? A couple of hours.'

'All right,' she said. 'I suppose you're always right. I guess you must be that kind of person. Somebody must have hated him to smash his head in like that.'

'I don't suppose it was personal,' I growled. 'Some people just like to smash heads.'

'Seeing that I don't know what it's all about, I couldn't guess,' she said tartly.

I went through his clothes. He had loose silver and bills in one trouser pocket, a tooled leather keycase in the other, also a small knife. His left hip pocket yielded a small billfold with more currency, insurance cards, a driver's licence, a couple of receipts. In his coat loose match folders, a gold pencil clipped to a pocket, two thin cambric handkerchiefs as fine and white as dry powdered snow. Then the enamel cigarette case from which I had seen him take his brown gold-tipped cigarettes. They were South American, from Montevideo. And in the other inside pocket a second cigarette case I hadn't seen before. It was made of embroidered silk, a dragon on each side, a frame of imitation tortoiseshell so thin it was hardly there at all. I tickled the catch open and looked in at three oversized Russian cigarettes under the band of elastic. I pinched one. They felt old and dry and loose. They had hollow mouth-pieces.

'He smoked the others,' I said over my shoulder. 'These must have been for a lady friend. He would be a lad who would have a lot of lady friends.'

The girl was bent over, breathing on my neck now. 'Didn't you know him?'

'I only met him to-night. He hired me for a bodyguard.'

'Some bodyguard.'

I didn't say anything to that.

'I'm sorry,' she almost whispered. 'Of course I don't know the circumstances. Do you suppose those could be jujus? Can I look?'

I passed the embroidered case back to her.

'I knew a guy once who smoked jujus,' she said. 'Three highballs and three sticks of tea and it took a pipe wrench to get him off the chandelier.'

'Hold the light steady.'

There was a rustling pause. Then she spoke again.

'I'm sorry.' She handed the case down again and I slipped it back in his pocket. That seemed to be all. All it proved was that he hadn't been cleaned out.

I stood up and took my wallet out. The five twenties were still in it.

'High class boys,' I said. 'They only took the large money.'

The flash was drooping to the ground. I put my wallet away again, clipped my own small flash to my pocket and reached suddenly for the little gun she was still holding in the same hand with the flashlight. She dropped the flashlight, but I got the gun. She stepped back quickly and I reached down for the light. I put it on her face for a moment, then snapped it off.

'You didn't have to be rough,' she said, putting her hands down into the pockets of a long rough coat with flaring shoulders. 'I didn't think you killed him.'

I liked the cool quiet of her voice. I liked her nerve. We stood in the darkness, face to face, not saying anything for a moment. I could see the brush and light in the sky.

I put the light on her face and she blinked. It was a small neat vibrant face with large eyes. A face with bone under the skin, fine drawn like a Cremona violin. A very nice face.

'Your hair's red,' I said. 'You look Irish.'

'And my name's Riordan. So what? Put that light out. It's not red, it's auburn.'

I put it out. 'What's your first name?'

'Anne. And don't call me Annie.'

'What are you doing around here?'

'Sometimes at night I go riding. Just restless. I live alone. I'm an orphan. I know all this neighbourhood like a book. I just happened to be riding along and noticed a light flickering down in the hollow. It seemed a little cold for young love. And they don't use lights, do they?'

'I never did. You take some awful chances, Miss Riordan.'

'I think I said the same about you. I had a gun. I wasn't afraid. There's no law against going down there.'

'Uh-huh. Only the law of self-preservation. Here. It's not my night to be clever. I suppose you have a permit for the gun.' I held it out to her, butt first.

She took it and tucked it down into her pocket. 'Strange how curious people can be, isn't it? I write a little. Feature articles.'

'Any money in it?'

'Very damned little. What were you looking for – in his pockets?'

'Nothing in particular. I'm a great guy to snoop around. We had eight thousand dollars to buy back some stolen jewellery for a lady. We got hijacked. Why they killed him I don't know. He didn't strike me as a fellow who would put up much of a fight. And I didn't hear a fight. I was down in the hollow when he was jumped. He was in the car, up above. We were supposed to drive down into the hollow but there didn't seem to be room for the car without scratching it up. So I went down there on foot and while I was down there they must have stuck him up. Then one of them got into the car and dry-gulched me. I thought he was still in the car, of course.'

'That doesn't make you so terribly dumb,' she said.

'There was something wrong with the job from the start. I could feel it. But I needed the money. Now I have to go to the cops and eat dirt. Will you drive me to Montemar Vista? I left my car there. He lived there.'

'Sure. But shouldn't somebody stay with him? You could take my car – or I could go call the cops.'

I looked at the dial of my watch. The faintly glowing hands said that it was getting towards midnight.

'No.'

'Why not?'

'I don't know why not. I just feel it that way. I'll play it alone.'

She said nothing. We went back down the hill and got into her little car and she started it and jockeyed it around without lights and drove it back up the hill and eased it past the barrier. A block away she sprang the lights on.

My head ached. We didn't speak until we came level with the first house on the paved part of the street. Then she said:

'You need a drink. Why not go back to my house and have one? You can phone the law from there. They have to come from West Los Angeles anyway. There's nothing up here but a fire station.'

'Just keep on going down to the coast. I'll play it solo.'

'But why? I'm not afraid of them. My story might help you.'

'I don't want any help. I've got to think. I want to be by myself for a while.'

'I – okey,' she said.

She made a vague sound in her throat and turned on to the boulevard. We came to the service station at the coast highway and turned north to Montemar Vista and the sidewalk café there. It was lit up like a luxury liner. The girl pulled over on to the shoulder and I got out and stood holding the door.

I fumbled a card out of my wallet and passed it in to her. 'Some day you may need a strong back,' I said. 'Let me know. But don't call me if it's brain work.'

She tapped the card on the wheel and said slowly: 'You'll find me in the Bay City phone book, 819 Twenty-fifth Street. Come around and pin a putty medal on me for minding my own business. I think you're still woozy from that crack on the head.'

She swung her car swiftly around on the highway and I watched its twin tail-lights fade into the dark.

I walked past the arch and the sidewalk café into the parking space and got into my car. A bar was right in front of me and I was shaking again. But it seemed smarter to walk into the West Los Angeles police station the way I did twenty minutes later, as cold as a frog and as green as the back of a new dollar bill.

12

It was an hour and a half later. The body had been taken away, the ground gone over, and I had told my story three or four times. We sat, four of us, in the day captain's room at the West Los Angeles station. The building was quiet except for a drunk in a cell who kept giving the Australian bush call while he waited to go downtown for sunrise court.

A hard white light inside a glass reflector shone down on the flat-topped table on which were spread the things that had come from Lindsay Marriott's pockets, things now that seemed as dead and homeless as their owner. The man across the table from me was named Randall and he was from Central Homicide in Los Angeles. He was a thin quiet man of fifty with smooth creamy-grey hair, cold eyes, a distant manner. He wore a dark red tie with black spots on it and the spots kept dancing in front of my eyes. Behind him, beyond the cone of light two beefy men lounged like bodyguards, each of them watching one of my ears.

I fumbled a cigarette around in my fingers and lit it and didn't like the taste of it. I sat watching it burn between my fingers. I felt about eighty years old and slipping fast.

Randall said coldly: 'The oftener you tell this story the sillier it sounds. This man Marriott had been negotiating for days, no doubt, about this pay-off and then just a few hours before the final meeting he calls up a perfect stranger and hires him to go with him as a bodyguard.'

'Not exactly as a bodyguard,' I said. 'I didn't even tell him I had a gun. Just for company.'

'Where did he hear of you?'

'First he said a mutual friend. Then that he just picked my name out of the book.'

Randall poked gently among the stuff on the table and detached a white card with an air of touching something not quite clean. He pushed it along the wood.

'He had your card. Your business card.'

I glanced at the card. It had come out of his billfold, together with a number of other cards I hadn't bothered to examine back there in the hollow of Purissima Canyon. It was one of my cards all right. It looked rather dirty at that, for a man like Marriott. There was a round smear across one corner.

'Sure,' I said. 'I hand those out whenever I get a chance. Naturally.'

'Marriott let you carry the money,' Randall said. 'Eight thousand dollars. He was rather a trusting soul.'

I drew on my cigarette and blew the smoke towards the ceiling. The light hurt my eyes. The back of my head ached.

'I don't have the eight thousand dollars,' I said. 'Sorry.'

'No. You wouldn't be here, if you had the money. Or would you?' There was a cold sneer on his face now, but it looked artificial.

'I'd do a lot for eight thousand dollars,' I said. 'But if I wanted to kill a man with a sap, I'd only hit him twice at the most – on the back of the head.'

He nodded slightly. One of the dicks behind him spit into the wastebasket.

'That's one of the puzzling features. It looks like an amateur job, but of course it might be meant to look like an amateur job. The money was not Marriott's, was it?'

'I don't know. I got the impression not, but that was just an impression. He wouldn't tell me who the lady in the case was.'

'We don't know anything about Marriott – yet,' Randall said slowly. 'I suppose it's at least possible he meant to steal the eight thousand himself.'

'Huh?' I felt surprised. I probably looked surprised. Nothing changed in Randall's smooth face.

'Did you count the money?'

'Of course not. He just gave me a package. There was money in it and it looked like a lot. He said it was eight grand. Why would he want to steal it from me when he already had it before I came on the scene?'

Randall looked at a corner of the ceiling and drew his mouth down at the corners. He shrugged.

'Go back a bit,' he said. 'Somebody had stuck up Marriott and a lady and taken this jade necklace and stuff and had later offered to sell it back for what seems like a pretty small amount, in view of its supposed value. Marriott was to handle the payoff. He thought of handling it alone and we don't know whether the other parties made a point of that or whether it was mentioned. Usually in cases like that they are rather fussy. But Marriott evidently decided it was all right to have you along. Both of you figured you were dealing with an organized gang and that they would play ball within the limits of their trade. Marriott was scared. That would be natural enough. He wanted company. You were the company. But you are a complete stranger to him, just a name on a card handed to him by some unknown party, said by him to be a mutual friend. Then at the last minute Marriott decides to have you carry the money and do the talking while he hides in the car. You say that was your idea, but he may have been hoping you would suggest it, and if you didn't suggest it, he would have had the idea himself.'

'He didn't like the idea at first,' I said.

Randall shrugged again. 'He pretended not to like the idea – but he gave in. So finally he gets a call and off you go to the place he describes. All this is coming from Marriott. None of it is known to you independently. When you get there, there seems to be nobody about. You are supposed to drive down into that hollow, but it doesn't look to be room

72

enough for the big car. It wasn't, as a matter of fact, because the car was pretty badly scratched on the left side. So you get out and walk down into the hollow, see and hear nothing, wait a few minutes, come back to the car and then somebody in the car socks you on the back of the head. Now suppose Marriott wanted that money and wanted to make you the fall guy – wouldn't he have acted just the way he did?'

'It's a swell theory,' I said. 'Marriott socked me, took the money, then he got sorry and beat his brains out, after first burying the money under a bush.'

Randall looked at me woodenly. 'He had an accomplice of course. Both of you were supposed to be knocked out, and the accomplice would beat it with the money. Only the accomplice double-crossed Marriott by killing him. He didn't have to kill you because you didn't know him.'

I looked at him with admiration and ground out my cigarette stub in a wooden tray that had once had a glass lining in it but hadn't any more.

'It fits the facts – so far as we know them,' Randall said calmly. 'It's no sillier than any other theory we could think up at the moment.'

'It doesn't fit one fact – that I was socked from the car, does it? That would make me suspect Marriott of having socked me – other things being equal. Although I didn't suspect him after he was killed.'

'The way you were socked fits best of all,' Randall said. 'You didn't tell Marriott you had a gun, but he may have seen the bulge under your arm or at least suspected you had a gun. In that case he would want to hit you when you suspected nothing. And you wouldn't suspect anything from the back of the car.'

'Okey,' I said. 'You win. It's a good theory, always supposing the money was not Marriott's and that he wanted to steal it and that he had an accomplice. So his plan is that we both wake up with bumps on our heads and the money is gone and we say so sorry and I go home and forget all about it. Is that how it ends? I mean is that how he expected it to end? It had to look good to him too, didn't it?'

Randall smiled wryly. 'I don't like it myself. I was just trying it out. It fits the facts – as far as I know them, which is not far.'

'We don't know enough to even start theorizing,' I said. 'Why not assume he was telling the truth and that he perhaps recognized one of the stick-up men?'

'You say you heard no struggle, no cry?'

'No. But he could have been grabbed quickly, by the throat. Or he could have been too scared to cry out when they jumped him. Say they were watching from the bushes and saw me go down the hill. I went some distance, you know. A good hundred feet. They go over to look into the car and see Marriott. Somebody sticks a gun in his face and makes him get out – quietly. Then he's sapped down. But something he says, or some way he looks, makes them think he has recognized somebody.'

'In the dark?'

'Yes,' I said. 'It must have been something like that. Some voices stay in your mind. Even in the dark people are recognized.'

Randall shook his head. 'If this was an organized gang of jewel thieves, they wouldn't kill without a lot of provocation.' He stopped suddenly and his eyes got a glazed look. He closed his mouth very slowly, very tight. He had an idea. 'Hijack,' he said.

I nodded. 'I think that's an idea.'

'There's another thing,' he said. 'How did you get here?'

'I drove my car.'

'Where was your car?'

'Down at Montemar Vista, in the parking lot by the sidewalk café.'

He looked at me very thoughtfully. The two dicks behind him looked at me suspiciously. The drunk in the cells tried to yodel, but his voice cracked and that discouraged him. He began to cry.

'I walked back to the highway,' I said. 'I flagged a car. A girl was driving it alone. She stopped and took me down.'

'Some girl,' Randall said. 'It was late at night, on a lonely road, and she stopped.'

'Yeah. Some of them will do that. I didn't get to know her, but she seemed nice.' I stared at them, knowing they didn't believe me and wondering why I was lying about it.

'It was a small car,' I said. 'A Chevvy coupé. I didn't get the licence number.'

'Haw, he didn't get the licence number,' one of the dicks said and spat into the wastebasket again.

Randall leaned forward and stared at me carefully. 'If you're holding anything back with the idea of working on this case yourself to make yourself a little publicity, I'd forget it, Marlowe. I don't like all the points in your story and I'm going to give you the night to think it over. To-morrow I'll probably ask you for a sworn statement. In the meantime let me give you a tip. This is a murder and a police job and we wouldn't want your help, even if it was good. All we want from you is facts. Get me?'

'Sure. Can I go home now? I don't feel any too well.'

'You can go home now.' His eyes were icy.

I got up and started towards the door in a dead silence. When I had gone four steps Randall cleared his throat and said carelessly:

'Oh, one small point. Did you notice what kind of cigarettes Marriott smoked?'

I turned. 'Yes. Brown ones. South American, in a French enamel case.'

He leaned forward and pushed the embroidered silk case

out of the pile of junk on the table and then pulled it towards him.

'Ever see this one before?'

'Sure. I was just looking at it.'

'I mean, earlier this evening.'

'I believe I did,' I said. 'Lying around somewhere. Why?'

'You didn't search the body?'

'Okey,' I said. 'Yes, I looked through his pockets. That was in one of them. I'm sorry. Just professional curiosity. I didn't disturb anything. After all he was my client.'

Randall took hold of the embroidered case with both hands and opened it. He sat looking into it. It was empty. The three cigarettes were gone.

I bit hard on my teeth and kept the tired look on my face. It was not easy.

'Did you see him smoke a cigarette out of this?'

'No.'

Randall nodded coolly. 'It's empty as you see. But it was in his pocket just the same. There's a little dust in it. I'm going to have it examined under a microscope. I'm not sure, but I have an idea it's marijuana.'

I said: 'If he had any of those, I should think he would have smoked a couple to-night. He needed something to cheer him up.'

Randall closed the case carefully and pushed it away.

'That's all,' he said. 'And keep your nose clean.'

I went out.

The fog had cleared off outside and the stars were as bright as artificial stars of chromium on a sky of black velvet. I drove fast. I needed a drink badly and the bars were closed.

13

I got up at nine, drank three cups of black coffee, bathed the
back of my head with ice-water and read the two morning
papers that had been thrown against the apartment door.
There was a paragraph and a bit about Moose Malloy, in
Part II, but Nulty didn't get his name mentioned. There was
nothing about Lindsay Marriott, unless it was on the society
page.

I dressed and ate two soft-boiled eggs and drank a fourth
cup of coffee and looked myself over in the mirror. I still
looked a little shadowy under the eyes. I had the door open
to leave when the phone rang.

It was Nulty. He sounded mean.

'Marlowe?'

'Yeah. Did you get him?'

'Oh sure. We got him.' He stopped to snarl. 'On the Ventura line, like I said. Boy, did we have fun! Six foot six, built
like a coffer dam, on his way to Frisco to see the Fair. He had
five quarts of hooch in the front seat of the rent car, and he
was drinking out of another one as he rode along, doing a
quiet seventy. All we had to go up against him with was two
county cops with guns and blackjacks.'

He paused and I turned over a few witty sayings in my
mind, but none of them seemed amusing at the moment.
Nulty went on:

'So he done exercises with the cops and when they was
tired enough to go to sleep, he pulled one side off their car,
threw the radio into the ditch, opened a fresh bottle of hooch,
and went to sleep hisself. After a while the boys snapped out
of it and bounced blackjacks off his head for about ten minutes

77

before he noticed it. When he began to get sore they got handcuffs on him. It was easy. We got him in the icebox now, drunk driving, drunk in auto, assaulting police officer in performance of duty, two counts, malicious damage to official property, attempted escape from custody, assault less than mayhem, disturbing the peace, and parking on a stage highway. Fun, ain't it?'

'What's the gag?' I asked. 'You didn't tell me all that just to gloat.'

'It was the wrong guy,' Nulty said savagely. 'This bird is named Stoyanoffsky and he lives in Hemet and he just got through working as a sandhog on the San Jack tunnel. Got a wife and four kids. Boy, is she sore. What you doing on Malloy?'

'Nothing. I have a headache.'

'Any time you get a little free time——'

'I don't think so,' I said. 'Thanks just the same. When is the inquest on the nigger coming up?'

'Why bother?' Nulty sneered, and hung up.

I drove down to Hollywood Boulevard and put my car in the parking space beside the building and rode up to my floor. I opened the door of the little reception room which I always left unlocked, in case I had a client and the client wanted to wait.

Miss Anne Riordan looked up from a magazine and smiled at me.

She was wearing a tobacco brown suit with a high-necked white sweater inside it. Her hair by daylight was pure auburn and on it she wore a hat with a crown the size of a whisky glass and a brim you could have wrapped the week's laundry in. She wore it at an angle of approximately forty-five degrees, so that the edge of the brim just missed her shoulder. In spite of that it looked smart. Perhaps because of that.

She was about twenty-eight years old. She had a rather narrow forehead of more height than is considered elegant.

Her nose was small and inquisitive, her upper lip a shade too long and her mouth more than a shade too wide. Her eyes were grey-blue with flecks of gold in them. She had a nice smile. She looked as if she had slept well. It was a nice face, a face you get to like. Pretty, but not so pretty that you would have to wear brass knuckles every time you took it out.

'I didn't know just what your office hours were,' she said. 'So I waited. I gather that your secretary is not here to-day.'

'I don't have a secretary.'

I went across and unlocked the inner door, then switched on the buzzer that rang on the outer door. 'Let's go into my private thinking parlour.'

She passed in front of me with a vague scent of very dry sandalwood and stood looking at the five green filing cases, the shabby rust-red rug, the half-dusted furniture, and the not too clean net curtains.

'I should think you would want somebody to answer the phone,' she said. 'And once in a while to send your curtains to the cleaners.'

'I'll send them out come St Swithin's Day. Have a chair. I might miss a few unimportant jobs. And a lot of leg art. I save money.'

'I see,' she said demurely, and placed a large suede bag carefully on the corner of the glass-topped desk. She leaned back and took one of my cigarettes. I burned my finger with a paper match lighting it for her.

She blew a fan of smoke and smiled through it. Nice teeth, rather large.

'You probably didn't expect to see me again so soon. How is your head?'

'Poorly. No, I didn't.'

'Were the police nice to you?'

'About the way they always are.'

'I'm not keeping you from anything important, am I?'

'No.'

'All the same I don't think you're very pleased to see me.'

I filled a pipe and reached for the packet of paper matches. I lit the pipe carefully. She watched that with approval. Pipe smokers were solid men. She was going to be disappointed in me.

'I tried to leave you out of it,' I said. 'I don't know why exactly. It's no business of mine any more anyhow. I ate my dirt last night and banged myself to sleep with a bottle and now it's a police case: I've been warned to leave it alone.'

'The reason you left me out of it,' she said calmly, 'was that you didn't think the police would believe just mere idle curiosity took me down into that hollow last night. They would suspect some guilty reason and hammer at me until I was a wreck.'

'How do you know I didn't think the same thing?'

'Cops are just people,' she said irrelevantly.

'They start out that way, I've heard.'

'Oh – cynical this morning.' She looked around the office with an idle but raking glance. 'Do you do pretty well in here? I mean financially? I mean, do you make a lot of money – with this kind of furniture?'

I grunted.

'Or should I try minding my own business and not asking impertinent questions?'

'Would it work, if you tried it?'

'Now we're both doing it. Tell me, why did you cover up for me last night? Was it on account of I have reddish hair and a beautiful figure?'

I didn't say anything.

'Let's try this one,' she said cheerfully. 'Would you like to know who that jade necklace belonged to?'

I could feel my face getting stiff. I thought hard but I couldn't remember for sure. And then suddenly I could. I hadn't said a word to her about a jade necklace.

I reached for the matches and relit my pipe. 'Not very much,' I said. 'Why.'

'Because I know.'

'Uh-huh.'

'What do you do when you get real talkative – wiggle your toes?'

'All right,' I growled. 'You came here to tell me. Go ahead and tell me.'

Her blue eyes widened and for a moment I thought they looked a little moist. She took her lower lip between her teeth and held it that way while she stared down at the desk. Then she shrugged and let go of her lip and smiled at me candidly.

'Oh I know I'm just a damned inquisitive wench. But there's a strain of bloodhound in me. My father was a cop. His name was Cliff Riordan and he was police chief of Bay City for seven years. I suppose that's what's the matter.'

'I seem to remember. What happened to him?'

'He was fired. It broke his heart. A mob of gamblers headed by a man named Laird Brunette elected themselves a mayor. So they put Dad in charge of the Bureau of Records and Identification, which in Bay City is about the size of a tea-bag. So Dad quit and pottered around for a couple of years and then died. And Mother died soon after him. So I've been alone for two years.'

'I'm sorry,' I said.

She ground out her cigarette. It had no lipstick on it. 'The only reason I'm boring you with this is that it makes it easy for me to get along with policemen. I suppose I ought to have told you last night. So this morning I found out who had charge of the case and went to see him. He was a little sore at you at first.'

'That's all right,' I said. 'If I had told him the truth on all points, he still wouldn't have believed me. All he will do is chew one of my ears off.'

She looked hurt. I got up and opened the other window.

The noise of the traffic from the boulevard came in in waves, like nausea. I felt lousy. I opened the deep drawer of the desk and got the office bottle out and poured myself a drink.

Miss Riordan watched me with disapproval. I was no longer a solid man. She didn't say anything. I drank the drink and put the bottle away again and sat down.

'You didn't offer me one,' she said coolly.

'Sorry. It's only eleven o'clock or less. I didn't think you looked the type.'

Her eyes crinkled at the corners. 'Is that a compliment?'

'In my circle, yes.'

She thought that over. It didn't mean anything to her. It didn't mean anything to me either when I thought it over. But the drink made me feel a lot better.

She leaned forward and scraped her gloves slowly across the glass of the desk. 'You wouldn't want to hire an assistant, would you? Not if it only cost you a kind word now and then?'

'No.'

She nodded. 'I thought probably you wouldn't. I'd better just give you my information and go on home.'

I didn't say anything. I lit my pipe again. It makes you look thoughtful when you are not thinking.

'First of all, it occurred to me that a jade necklace like that would be a museum piece and would be well known,' she said.

I held the match in the air, still burning and watching the flame crawl close to my fingers. Then I blew it out softly and dropped it in the tray and said:

'I didn't say anything to you about a jade necklace.'

'No, but Lieutenant Randall did.'

'Somebody ought to sew buttons on his face.'

'He knew my father. I promised not to tell.'

'You're telling me.'

'You knew already, silly.'

Her hand suddenly flew up as if it was going to fly to her mouth, but it only rose half-way and then fell back slowly and her eyes widened. It was a good act, but I knew something else about her that spoiled it.

'You *did* know, didn't you?' She breathed the words hushedly.

'I thought it was diamonds. A bracelet, a pair of earrings, a pendant, three rings, one of the rings with emeralds too.'

'Not funny,' she said. 'Not even fast.'

'Fei Tsui jade. Very rare. Carved beads about six carats apiece, sixty of them. Worth eighty thousand dollars.'

'You have such nice brown eyes,' she said. 'And you think you're tough.'

'Well, who does it belong to and how did you find out?'

'I found out very simply. I thought the best jeweller in town would probably know, so I went and asked the manager of Block's. I told him I was a writer and wanted to do an article on rare jade – you know the line.'

'So he believed your red hair and your beautiful figure.'

She flushed clear to the temples. 'Well, he told me anyway. It belongs to a rich lady who lives in Bay City, in an estate on the canyon. Mrs Lewin Lockridge Grayle. Her husband is an investment banker or something, enormously rich, worth about twenty millions. He used to own a radio station in Beverly Hills, Station KFDK, and Mrs Grayle used to work there. He married her five years ago. She's a ravishing blonde. Mr Grayle is elderly, liverish, stays home and takes calomel while Mrs Grayle goes places and has a good time.'

'This manager of Block's,' I said. 'He's a fellow that gets around.'

'Oh, I didn't get all that from him, silly. Just about the necklace. The rest I got from Giddy Gertie Arbogast.'

I reached into the deep drawer and brought the office bottle up again.

'You're not going to turn out to be one of those drunken detectives, are you?' she asked anxiously.

'Why not? They always solve their cases and they never even sweat. Get on with the story.'

'Giddy Gertie is the society editor of the *Chronicle*. I've known him for years. He weighs two hundred and wears a Hitler moustache. He got out his morgue file on the Grayles. Look.'

She reached into her bag and slid a photograph across the desk, a five-by-three glazed still.

It was a blonde. A blonde to make a bishop kick a hole in a stained-glass window. She was wearing street clothes that looked black and white, and a hat to match and she was a little haughty, but not too much. Whatever you needed, wherever you happened to be – she had it. About thirty years old.

I poured a fast drink and burned my throat getting it down. 'Take it away,' I said. 'I'll start jumping.'

'Why, I got it for you. You'll want to see her, won't you?'

I looked at it again. Then I slid it under the blotter. 'How about to-night at eleven?'

'Listen, this isn't just a bunch of gag lines, Mr Marlowe. I called her up. She'll see you. On business.'

'It may start out that way.'

She made an impatient gesture, so I stopped fooling around and got my battle-scarred frown back on my face. 'What will she see me about?'

'Her necklace, of course. It was like this. I called her up and had a lot of trouble getting to talk to her, of course, but finally I did. Then I gave her the song and dance I had given the nice man at Block's and it didn't take. She sounded as if she had a hangover. She said something about talking to her secretary, but I managed to keep her on the phone and ask her if it was true she had a Fei Tsui jade necklace. After a while she said, yes. I asked if I might see it. She said, what for? I said my piece over again and it didn't take any better than the first time.

I could hear her yawning and bawling somebody outside the mouthpiece for putting me on. Then I said I was working for Philip Marlowe. She said "So what?" Just like that.'

'Incredible. But all the society dames talk like tramps nowadays.'

'I wouldn't know,' Miss Riordan said sweetly. 'Probably some of them *are* tramps. So I asked her if she had a phone with no extension and she said what business was it of mine. But the funny thing was she hadn't hung up on me.'

'She had the jade on her mind and she didn't know what you were leading up to. And she may have heard from Randall already.'

Miss Riordan shook her head. 'No. I called him later and he didn't know who owned the necklace until I told him. He was quite surprised that I had found out.'

'He'll get used to you,' I said. 'He'll probably have to. What then?'

'So I said to Mrs Grayle: 'You'd still like it back, wouldn't you?' Just like that. I didn't know any other way to say. I had to say something that would jar her a bit. It did. She gave me another number in a hurry. And I called that and I said I'd like to see her. She seemed surprised. So I had to tell her the story. She didn't like it. But she had been wondering why she hadn't heard from Marriott. I guess she thought he had gone south with the money or something. So I'm to see her at two o'clock. Then I'll tell her about you and how nice and discreet you are and how you would be a good man to help her get it back, if there's any chance and so on. She's already interested.'

I didn't say anything. I just stared at her. She looked hurt. 'What's the matter? Did I do right?'

'Can't you get it through your head that this is a police case now and that I've been warned to stay off it?'

'Mrs Grayle has a perfect right to employ you, if she wants to.'

'To do what?'

85

She snapped and unsnapped her bag impatiently. 'Oh, my goodness – a woman like that – with her looks – can't you see——' She stopped and bit her lip. 'What kind of man was Marriott?'

'I hardly knew him. I thought he was a bit of a pansy. I didn't like him very well.'

'Was he a man who would be attractive to women?'

'Some women. Others would want to spit.'

'Well, it looks as if he might have been attractive to Mrs Grayle. She went out with him.'

'She probably goes out with a hundred men. There's very little chance to get the necklace now.'

'Why?'

I got up and walked to the end of the office and slapped the wall with the flat of my hand, hard. The clacking typewriter on the other side stopped for a moment, and then went on. I looked down through the open window into the shaft between my building and the Mansion House Hotel. The coffee shop smell was strong enough to build a garage on. I went back to my desk, dropped the bottle of whisky back into the drawer, shut the drawer and sat down again. I lit my pipe for the eighth or ninth time and looked carefully across the half-dusted glass to Miss Riordan's grave and honest little face.

You could get to like that face a lot. Glamoured up blondes were a dime a dozen, but that was a face that would wear. I smiled at it.

'Listen, Anne. Killing Marriott was a dumb mistake. The gang behind this hold-up would never pull anything like that. What must have happened was that some gowed-up runt they took along for a gun-holder lost his head. Marriott made a false move and some punk beat him down and it was done so quickly nothing could be done to prevent it. Here is an organized mob with inside information on jewels and the movements of the women that wear them. They ask moderate returns and they would play ball. But here also is a back alley murder that doesn't fit at all. My idea is that whoever did it is a dead man hours ago, with weights on his ankles, deep in the Pacific Ocean. And either the jade went down with him or else they have some idea of its real value and they have cached it away in a place where it will stay for a long time – maybe for years before they dare bring it out again. Or, if the gang is big enough, it may show up on the other side of the world. The eight thousand they asked seems pretty low if they really knew the value of the jade. But it would be hard to sell. I'm sure of one thing. They never meant to murder anybody.'

Anne Riordan was listening to me with her lips slightly parted and a rapt expression on her face, as if she was looking at the Dalai Lama.

She closed her mouth slowly and nodded once. 'You're wonderful,' she said softly. 'But you're nuts.'

She stood up and gathered her bag to her. 'Will you go to see her or won't you?'

'Randall can't stop me – if it comes from her.'

'All right. I'm going to see another society editor and get some more dope on the Grayles if I can. About her love life. She would have one, wouldn't she?'

The face framed in auburn hair was wistful.

'Who hasn't?' I sneered.

'*I* never had. Not really.'

I reached up and shut my mouth with my hand. She gave me a sharp look and moved towards the door.

'You've forgotten something,' I said.

She stopped and turned. 'What?' She looked all over the top of the desk.

'You know damn well what.'

She came back to the desk and leaned across it earnestly. 'Why would they kill the man that killed Marriott, if they don't go in for murder?'

'Because he would be the type that would get picked up

some time and would talk – when they took his dope away from him. I mean they wouldn't kill a customer.'

'What makes you so sure the killer took dope?'

'I'm not sure. I just said that. Most punks do.'

'Oh.' She straightened up and nodded and smiled. 'I guess you mean these,' she said and reached quickly into her bag and laid a small tissue bag package on the desk.

I reached for it, pulled a rubber band off it carefully and opened up the paper. On it lay three long thick Russian cigarettes with paper mouthpieces. I looked at her and didn't say anything.

'I know I shouldn't have taken them,' she said almost breathlessly. 'But I knew they were jujus. They usually come in plain papers but lately around Bay City they have been putting them out like this. I've seen several. I thought it was kind of mean for the poor man to be found dead with marijuana cigarettes in his pocket.'

'You ought to have taken the case too,' I said quietly. 'There was dust in it. And it being empty was suspicious.'

'I couldn't – with you there. I – I almost went back and did. But I didn't quite have the courage. Did it get you in wrong?'

'No,' I lied. 'Why should it?'

'I'm glad of that,' she said wistfully.

'Why didn't you throw them away?'

She thought about it, her bag clutched to her side, her wide-brimmed absurd hat tilted so that it hid one eye.

'I guess it must be because I'm a cop's daughter,' she said at last. 'You just don't throw away evidence.' Her smile was frail and guilty and her cheeks were flushed. I shrugged.

'Well——' the word hung in the air, like smoke in a closed room. Her lips stayed parted after saying it. I let it hang. The flush on her face deepened.

'I'm horribly sorry. I shouldn't have done it.'

I passed that too.

She went very quickly to the door and out.

14

I poked at one of the long Russian cigarettes with a finger, then laid them in a neat row, side by side and squeaked my chair. You just don't throw away evidence. So they were evidence. Evidence of what? That a man occasionally smoked a stick of tea, a man who looked as if any touch of the exotic would appeal to him. On the other hand lots of tough guys smoked marijuana, also lots of band musicians and high school kids, and nice girls who had given up trying. American hashish. A weed that would grow anywhere. Unlawful to cultivate now. That meant a lot in a country as big as the U.S.A.

I sat there and puffed my pipe and listened to the clacking typewriter behind the wall of my office and the bong-bong of the traffic lights changing on Hollywood Boulevard and spring rustling in the air, like a paper bag blowing along a concrete sidewalk.

They were pretty big cigarettes, but a lot of Russians are, and marijuana is a coarse leaf. Indian hemp. American hashish. Evidence. God, what hats the women wear. My head ached. Nuts.

I got my penknife out and opened the small sharp blade, the one I didn't clean my pipe with, and reached for one of them. That's what a police chemist would do. Slit one down the middle and examine the stuff under a microscope, to start with. There might just happen to be something unusual about it. Not very likely, but what the hell, he was paid by the month.

I slit one down the middle. The mouthpiece part was pretty tough to slit. Okey, I was a tough guy, I slit it anyway. See can you stop me.

Out of the mouthpiece shiny segments of rolled thin cardboard partly straightened themselves and had printing on them. I sat up straight and pawed for them. I tried to spread them out on the desk in order, but they slid around on the desk. I grabbed another of the cigarettes and squinted inside the mouthpiece. Then I went to work with the blade of the pocket knife in a different way. I pinched the cigarette down to the place where the mouthpieces began. The paper was thin all the way, you could feel the grain of what was underneath. So I cut the mouthpiece off carefully and then still more carefully cut through the mouthpiece longways, but only just enough. It opened out and there was another card underneath, rolled up, not touched this time.

I spread it out fondly. It was a man's calling card. Thin pale ivory, just off white. Engraved on that were delicately shaded words. In the lower left-hand corner a Stillwood Heights telephone number. In the lower right-hand corner the legend, 'By Appointment Only.' In the middle, a little larger, but still discreet: 'Jules Amthor.' Below, a little smaller: 'Psychic Consultant.'

I took hold of the third cigarette. This time, with a lot of difficulty, I teased the card out without cutting anything. It was the same. I put it back where it had been.

I looked at my watch, put my pipe in an ashtray, and then had to look at my watch again to see what time it was. I rolled the two cut cigarettes and the cut card in part of the tissue paper, the one that was complete with card inside in another part of the tissue paper and locked both little packages away in my desk.

I sat looking at the card. Jules Amthor, Psychic Consultant, By Appointment Only, Stillwood Heights phone number, no address. Three like that rolled inside three sticks of tea, in a Chinese or Japanese silk cigarette case with an imitation tortoise-shell frame, a trade article that might have cost thirty-five to seventy-five cents in any Oriental store,

Hooey Phooey Sing – Long Sing Tung, that kind of place, where a nice-mannered Jap hisses at you, laughing heartily when you say that the Moon of Arabia incense smells like the girls in Frisco Sadie's back parlour.

And all this in the pocket of a man who was very dead, and who had another and genuinely expensive cigarette case containing cigarettes which he actually smoked.

He must have forgotten it. It didn't make sense. Perhaps it hadn't belonged to him at all. Perhaps he had picked it up in a hotel lobby. Forgotten he had it on him. Forgotten to turn it in. Jules Amthor, Psychic Consultant.

The phone rang and I answered it absently. The voice had the cool hardness of a cop who thinks he is good. It was Randall. He didn't bark. He was the icy type.

'So you didn't know who that girl was last night? And she picked you up on the boulevard and you walked over to there. Nice lying, Marlowe.'

'Maybe you have a daughter and you wouldn't like news camera-men jumping out of bushes and popping flashbulbs in her face.'

'You lied to me.'

'It was a pleasure.'

He was silent a moment, as if deciding something. 'We'll let that pass,' he said. 'I've seen her. She came in and told me her story. She's the daughter of a man I knew and respected, as it happens.'

'She told you,' I said, 'and you told her.'

'I told her a little,' he said coldly. 'For a reason. I'm calling you for the same reason. This investigation is going to be under cover. We have a chance to break this jewel gang and we're going to do it.'

'Oh, it's a gang murder this morning. Okey.'

'By the way, that was marijuana dust in that funny cigarette case – the one with the dragons on it. Sure you didn't see him smoke one out of it?'

'Quite sure. In my presence he smoked only the others. But he wasn't in my presence all the time.'

'I see. Well, that's all. Remember what I told you last night. Don't try getting ideas about this case. All we want from you is silence. Otherwise——'

He paused. I yawned into the mouthpiece.

'I heard that,' he snapped. 'Perhaps you think I'm not in a position to make that stick. I am. One false move out of you and you'll be locked up as a material witness.'

'You mean the papers are not to get the case?'

'They'll get the murder – but they won't know what's behind it.'

'Neither do you,' I said.

'I've warned you twice now,' he said. 'The third time is out.'

'You're doing a lot of talking,' I said, 'for a guy that holds cards.'

I got the phone hung in my face for that. Okey, the hell with him, let him work at it.

I walked around the office a little to cool off, made myself a short drink, looked at my watch again and didn't see what time it was, and sat down at the desk once more.

Jules Amthor, Psychic Consultant. Consultations By Appointment Only. Give him enough time and pay him enough money and he'll cure anything from a jaded husband to a grasshopper plague. He would be an expert in frustrated love affairs, women who slept alone and didn't like it, wandering boys and girls who didn't write home, sell the property now or hold it for another year, will this part hurt me with my public or make me seem more versatile? Men would sneak in on him too, big strong guys that roared like lions around their offices and were all cold mush under their vests. But mostly it would be women, fat women that panted and thin women that burned, old women that dreamed and young women that thought they might have Electra complexes, women of all sizes, shapes and ages, but with one thing in common — money. No Thursdays at the County Hospital for Mr Jules Amthor. Cash on the line for his. Rich bitches who had to be dunned for their milk bills would pay him right now.

A fakeloo artist, a hoopla spreader, and a lad who had his card rolled up inside sticks of tea, found on a dead man.

This was going to be good. I reached for the phone and asked the O-operator for the Stillwood Heights number.

15

A woman's voice answered, a dry, husky-sounding foreign voice: ' 'Allo.'

'May I talk to Mr Amthor?'

'Ah, no. I regret. I am ver-ry sor-ry. Amthor never speaks upon the telephone. I am hees secretary. Weel I take the message?'

'What's the address out there? I want to see him.'

'Ah, you weesh to consult Amthor professionally? He weel be ver-ry pleased. But he ees ver-ry beesy. When you weesh to see him?'

'Right away. Some time to-day.'

'Ah,' the voice regretted, 'that cannot be. The next week per'aps. I weel look at the book.'

'Look,' I said, 'never mind the book. You 'ave the pencil?'

'But certainly I 'ave the pencil. I——'

'Take this down. My name is Philip Marlowe. My address is 615 Cahuenga Building, Hollywood. That's on Hollywood Boulevard near Ivar. My phone number is Glenview 7537.' I spelled the hard ones and waited.

'Yes, Meester Marlowe. I 'ave that.'

'I want to see Mr Amthor about a man named Marriott.' I spelled that too. 'It is very urgent. It is a matter of life and death. I want to see him fast. F-a-s-t – fast. Sudden, in other words. Am I clear?'

'You talk ver-ry strange,' the foreign voice said.

'No.' I took hold of the phone standard and shook it. 'I feel fine. I always talk like that. This is a very queer business. Mr Amthor will positively want to see me. I'm a private detective. But I don't want to go to the police until I've seen him.'

'Ah,' the voice got as cool as a cafeteria dinner. 'You are of the police, no?'

'Listen,' I said. 'I am of the police, no. I am a private detective. Confidential. But it is very urgent just the same. You call me back, no? You 'ave the telephone number, yes?'

'Si. I 'ave the telephone number. Meester Marriott – he ees sick?'

'Well, he's not up and around,' I said. 'So you know him?'

'But no. You say a matter of life and death. Amthor he cure many people——'

'This is one time he flops,' I said. 'I'll be waiting for a call.'

I hung up and lunged for the office bottle. I felt as if I had been through a meat grinder. Ten minutes passed. The phone rang. The voice said:

'Amthor he weel see you at six o'clock.'

'That's fine. What's the address?'

'He weel send a car.'

'I have a car of my own. Just give me——'

'He weel send a car,' the voice said coldly, and the phone clicked in my ear.

I looked at my watch once more. It was more than time for lunch. My stomach burned from the last drink. I wasn't hungry. I lit a cigarette. It tasted like a plumber's handkerchief. I nodded across the office at Mr Rembrandt, then I reached for my hat and went out. I was half-way to the elevator before the thought hit me. It hit me without any reason or sense, like a dropped brick. I stopped and leaned against the marbled wall and pushed my hat around on my head and suddenly I laughed.

A girl passing me on the way from the elevators back to her work turned and gave me one of those looks which are supposed to make your spine feel like a run in a stocking. I waved my hand at her and went back to my office and grabbed the phone. I called up a man I knew who worked on the Lot Books of a title company.

'Can you find a property by the address alone?' I asked him.

'Sure. We have a cross-index. What is it?'

'1644 West 54th Place. I'd like to know a little something about the condition of the title.'

'I'd better call you back. What's that number?'

He called back in about three minutes.

'Get your pencil out,' he said. 'It's Lot 8 of Block 11 of Caraday's Addition to the Maplewood Tract Number 4. The owner of record, subject to certain things, is Jessie Pierce Florian, widow.'

'Yeah. What things?'

'Second half taxes, two ten-year street improvement bonds, one storm drain assessment bond also ten year, none of these delinquents, also a first trust deed of $2600.'

'You mean one of those things where they can sell you out on ten minutes' notice?'

'Not quite that quick, but a lot quicker than a mortgage. There's nothing unusual about it except the amount. It's high for that neighbourhood, unless it's a new house.'

'It's a very old house and in bad repair,' I said. 'I'd say fifteen hundred would buy the place.'

'Then it's distinctly unusual, because the refinancing was done only four years ago.'

'Okey, who holds it? Some investment company?'

'No. An individual. Man named Lindsay Marriott, a single man. Okey?'

I forget what I said to him or what thanks I made. They

probably sounded like words. I sat there, just staring at the wall.

My stomach suddenly felt fine. I was hungry. I went down to the Mansion House Coffee Shop and ate lunch and got my car out of the parking lot next to my building.

I drove south and east, towards West 54th Place. I didn't carry any liquor with me this time.

16

The block looked just as it had looked the day before. The street was empty except for an ice truck, two Fords in driveways and a swirl of dust going around a corner. I drove slowly past No. 1644 and parked farther along and studied the houses on either side of mine. I walked back and stopped in front of it, looking at the tough palm tree and the drab unwatered scrap of lawn. The house seemed empty, but probably wasn't. It just had that look. The lonely rocker on the front porch stood just where it had stood yesterday. There was a throw-away paper on the walk. I picked it up and slapped it against my leg and then I saw the curtain move next door, in the near front window.

Old Nosey again. I yawned and tilted my hat down. A sharp nose almost flattened itself against the inside of the glass. White hair above it, and eyes that were just eyes from where I stood. I strolled along the sidewalk and the eyes watched me. I turned in towards her house. I climbed the wooden steps and rang the bell.

The door snapped open as if it had been on a spring. She was a tall old bird with a chin like a rabbit. Seen from close her eyes were as sharp as lights on still water. I took my hat off.

'Are you the lady who called the police about Mrs Florian?' She stared at me coolly and missed nothing about me, probably not even the mole on my right shoulder blade.

'I ain't sayin' I am, young man, and I ain't sayin' I ain't. Who are you?' It was a high twangy voice, made for talking over an eight party line.

'I'm a detective.'

'Land's sakes. Why didn't you say so? What's she done now? I ain't seen a thing and I ain't missed a minute. Henry done all the goin' to the store for me. Ain't been a sound out of there.'

She snapped the screen door unhooked and drew me in. The hall smelled of furniture oil. It had a lot of dark furniture that had once been in good style. Stuff with inlaid panels and scollops at the corners. We went into a front room that had cotton lace antimacassars pinned on everything you could stick a pin into.

'Say, didn't I see you before?' she asked suddenly, a note of suspicion crawling around in her voice. 'Sure enough I did. You was the man that——'

'That's right. And I'm still a detective. Who's Henry?'

'Oh, he's just a little coloured boy that goes errands for me. Well, what you want, young man?' She patted a clean red and white apron and gave me the beady eye. She clicked her store teeth a couple of times for practice.

'Did the officers come here yesterday after they went to Mrs Florian's house?'

'What officers?'

'The uniformed officers,' I said patiently.

'Yes, they was here a minute. They didn't know nothing.'

'Describe the big man to me – the one that had a gun and made you call up.'

She described him, with complete accuracy. It was Malloy all right.

'What kind of car did he drive?'

'A little car. He couldn't hardly get into it.'

'That's all you can say? This man's a murderer!'

Her mouth gaped, but her eyes were pleased. 'Land's sakes, I wish I could tell you, young man. But I never knew much about cars. Murder, eh? Folks ain't safe a minute in this town. When I come here twenty-two years ago we didn't lock our doors hardly. Now it's gangsters and crooked police and politicians fightin' each other with machine guns, so I've heard. Scandalous is what it is, young man.'

'Yeah. What do you know about Mrs Florian?'

The small mouth puckered. 'She ain't neighbourly. Plays her radio loud late nights. Sings. She don't talk to anybody.' She leaned forward a little. 'I'm not positive, but my opinion is she drinks liquor.'

'She have many visitors?'

'She don't have no visitors at all.'

'You'd know, of course, Mrs——'

'Mrs Morrison. Land's sakes, yes. What else have I got to do but look out of the windows?'

'I bet it's fun. Mrs Florian has lived here a long time?'

'About ten years, I reckon. Had a husband once. Looked like a bad one to me. He died.' She paused and thought. 'I guess he died natural,' she added. 'I never heard different.'

'Left her money?'

Her eyes receded and her chin followed them. She sniffed hard. 'You been drinkin' liquor,' she said coldly.

'I just had a tooth out. The dentist gave it to me.'

'I don't hold with it.'

'It's bad stuff, except for medicine,' I said.

'I don't hold with it for medicine neither.'

'I think you're right,' I said. 'Did he leave her money? Her husband?'

'I wouldn't know.' Her mouth was the size of a prune and as smooth. I had lost out.

'Has anybody at all been there since the officers?'

'Ain't seen.'

'Thank you very much, Mrs Morrison. I won't trouble

you any more now. You've been very kind and helpful.'

I walked out of the room and opened the door. She followed me and cleared her throat and clicked her teeth a couple more times.

'What number should I call?' she asked, relenting a little.

'University 4-5000. Ask for Lieutenant Nulty. What does she live on – relief?'

'This ain't a relief neighbourhood,' she said coldly.

'I bet that side piece was the admiration of Sioux Falls once,' I said, gazing at a carved sideboard that was in the hall because the dining-room was too small for it. It had curved ends, thin carved legs, was inlaid all over, and had a painted basket of fruit on the front.

'Mason City,' she said softly. 'Yessir, we had a nice home once, me and George. Best there was.'

I opened the screen door and stepped through it and thanked her again. She was smiling now. Her smile was as sharp as her eyes.

'Gets a registered letter first of every month,' she said suddenly.

I turned and waited. She leaned towards me. 'I see the mailman go up to the door and get her to sign. First day of every month. Dresses up then and goes out. Don't come home till all hours. Sings half the night. Times I could have called the police it was so loud.'

I patted the thin malicious arm.

'You're one in a thousand, Mrs Morrison,' I said. I put my hat on, tipped it to her and left. Half-way down the walk I thought of something and swung back. She was still standing inside the screen door, with the house door open behind her. I went back up on the steps.

'To-morrow's the first,' I said. 'First of April. April Fool's Day. Be sure to notice whether she gets her registered letter, will you, Mrs Morrison?'

The eyes gleamed at me. She began to laugh – a high-pitched old woman's laugh. 'April Fool's Day,' she tittered. 'Maybe she won't get it.'

I left her laughing. The sound was like a hen having hiccups.

17

Nobody answered my ring or knock next door. I tried again. The screen door wasn't hooked. I tried the house door. It was unlocked. I stepped inside.

Nothing was changed, not even the smell of gin. There were still no bodies on the floor. A dirty glass stood on the small table beside the chair where Mrs Florian had sat yesterday. The radio was turned off. I went over to the davenport and felt down behind the cushions. The same dead soldier and another one with him now.

I called out. No answer. Then I thought I heard a long slow unhappy breathing that was half groaning. I went through the arch and sneaked into the little hall-way. The bedroom door was partly open and the groaning sound came from behind it. I stuck my head in and looked.

Mrs Florian was in bed. She was lying flat on her back with a cotton comforter pulled up to her chin. One of the little fluffballs on the comforter was almost in her mouth. Her long yellow face was slack, half dead. Her dirty hair straggled on the pillow. Her eyes opened slowly and looked at me with no expression. The room had a sickening smell of sleep, liquor and dirty clothes. A sixty-nine cent alarm clock ticked on the peeling grey-white paint of the bureau. It ticked loud enough to shake the walls. Above it a mirror showed a distorted view of the woman's face. The trunk from which she had taken the photos was still open.

I said: 'Good afternoon, Mrs Florian. Are you sick?'

She worked her lips together slowly, rubbed one over the other, then slid a tongue out and moistened them and worked her jaws. Her voice came from her mouth sounding like a worn-out phonograph record. Her eyes showed recognition now, but not pleasure.

'You get him?'

'The Moose?'

'Sure.'

'Not yet. Soon, I hope.'

She screwed her eyes up and then snapped them open as if trying to get rid of a film over them.

'You ought to keep your house locked up,' I said. 'He might come back.'

'You think I'm scared of the Moose, huh?'

'You acted like it when I was talking to you yesterday.'

She thought about that. Thinking was weary work. 'Got any liquor?'

'No, I didn't bring any to-day, Mrs Florian. I was a little low on cash.'

'Gin's cheap. It hits.'

'I might go out for some in a little while. So you're not afraid of Malloy?'

'Why would I be?'

'Okey, you're not. What *are* you afraid of?'

Light snapped into her eyes, held for a moment, and faded out again. 'Aw beat it. You coppers give me an ache in the fanny.'

I said nothing. I leaned against the door frame and put a cigarette in my mouth and tried to jerk it up far enough to hit my nose with it. This is harder than it looks.

'Coppers,' she said slowly, as if talking to herself, 'will never catch that boy. He's good and he's got dough and he's got friends. You're wasting your time, copper.'

'Just the routine,' I said. 'It was practically a self-defence anyway. Where would he be?'

She snickered and wiped her mouth on the cotton comforter.

'Soap now,' she said. 'Soft stuff. Copper smart. You guys still think it gets you something.'

'I liked the Moose,' I said.

Interest flickered in her eyes. 'You known him?'

'I was with him yesterday – when he killed the nigger over on Central.'

She opened her mouth wide and laughed her head off without making any more sound than you would make cracking a breadstick. Tears ran out of her eyes and down her face.

'A big strong guy,' I said. 'Soft-hearted in spots too. Wanted his Velma pretty bad.'

The eyes veiled. 'Thought it was her folks was looking for her,' she said softly.

'They are. But she's dead, you said. Nothing there. Where did she die?'

'Dalhart, Texas. Got a cold and went to the chest and off she went.'

'You were there?'

'Hell, no. I just heard.'

'Oh. Who told you, Mrs Florian?'

'Some hoofer. I forget the name right now. Maybe a good stiff drink might help some. I feel like Death Valley.'

'And you look like a dead mule,' I thought, but didn't say it out loud. 'There's just one more thing,' I said, 'then I'll maybe run out for some gin. I looked up the title to your house, I don't know just why.'

She was rigid under the bedclothes, like a wooden woman. Even her eyelids were frozen half down over the clogged iris of her eyes. Her breath stilled.

'There's a rather large trust deed on it,' I said. 'Considering the low value of property around here. It's held by a man named Lindsay Marriott.'

Her eyes blinked rapidly, but nothing else moved. She stared.

'I used to work for him,' she said at last. 'I used to be a servant in his family. He kind of takes care of me a little.'

I took the unlighted cigarette out of my mouth and looked at it aimlessly and stuck it back in.

'Yesterday afternoon, a few hours after I saw you, Mr Marriott called me up at my office. He offered me a job.'

'What kind of job?' Her voice croaked now, badly.

I shrugged. 'I can't tell you that. Confidential. I went to see him last night.'

'You're a clever son of a bitch,' she said thickly and moved a hand under the bedclothes.

I stared at her and said nothing.

'Copper-smart,' she sneered.

I ran a hand up and down the door frame. It felt slimy. Just touching it made me want to take a bath.

'Well, that's all,' I said smoothly. 'I was just wondering how come. Might be nothing at all. Just a coincidence. It just looked as if it might mean something.'

'Copper-smart,' she said emptily. 'Not a real copper at that. Just a cheap shamus.'

'I suppose so,' I said. 'Well, good-bye, Mrs Florian. By the way, I don't think you'll get a registered letter to-morrow morning.'

She threw the bedclothes aside and jerked upright with her eyes blazing. Something glittered in her right hand. A small revolver, a Banker's Special. It was old and worn, but looked business-like.

'Tell it,' she snarled. 'Tell it fast.'

I looked at the gun and the gun looked at me. Not too steadily. The hand behind it began to shake, but the eyes still blazed. Saliva bubbled at the corners of her mouth.

'You and I could work together,' I said.

The gun and her jaw dropped at the same time. I was inches

from the door. While the gun was still dropping, I slid through it and beyond the opening.

'Think it over,' I called back.

There was no sound, no sound of any kind.

I went fast back through the hall and dining-room and out of the house. My back felt queer as I went down the walk. The muscles crawled.

Nothing happened. I went along the street and got into my car and drove away from there.

The last day of March and hot enough for summer. I felt like taking my coat off as I drove. In front of the 77th Street Station, two prowl car men were scowling at a bent front fender. I went in through the swing doors and found a uniformed lieutenant behind the railing looking over the charge sheet. I asked him if Nulty was upstairs. He said he thought he was, was I a friend of his. I said yes. He said okey, go on up, so I went up the worn stairs and along the corridor and knocked at the door. The voice yelled and I went in.

He was picking his teeth, sitting in one chair with his feet on the other. He was looking at his left thumb, holding it up in front of his eyes and at arm's length. The thumb looked all right to me, but Nulty's stare was gloomy, as if he thought it wouldn't get well.

He lowered it to his thigh and swung his feet to the floor and looked at me instead of at his thumb. He wore a dark grey suit and a mangled cigar end was waiting on the desk for him to get through with the toothpick.

I turned the felt seat cover that lay on the other chair with its straps not fastened to anything, sat down, and put a cigarette in my face.

'You,' Nulty said, and looked at his toothpick, to see if it was chewed enough.

'Any luck?'

'Malloy? I ain't on it any more.'

'Who is?'

'Nobody ain't. Why? The guy's lammed. We got him on the teletype and they got readers out. Hell, he'll be in Mexico long gone.'

'Well, all he did was kill a negro,' I said. 'I guess that's only a misdemeanour.'

'You still interested? I thought you was workin'?' His pale eyes moved damply over my face.

'I had a job last night, but it didn't last. Have you still got that Pierrot photo?'

He reached around and pawed under his blotter. He held it out. It still looked pretty. I stared at the face.

'This is really mine,' I said. 'If you don't need it for the file, I'd like to keep it.'

'Should be in the file, I guess,' Nulty said. 'I forgot about it. Okey, keep it under your hat. I passed the file in.'

I put the photo in my breast pocket and stood up. 'Well, I guess that's all,' I said, a little too airily.

'I smell something,' Nulty said coldly.

I looked at the piece of rope on the edge of his desk. His eyes followed my look. He threw the toothpick on the floor and stuck the chewed cigar in his mouth.

'Not this either,' he said.

'It's a vague hunch. If it grows more solid, I won't forget you.'

'Things is tough. I need a break, pal.'

'A man who works as hard as you deserves one,' I said.

He struck a match on his thumbnail, looked pleased because it caught the first time, and started inhaling smoke from the cigar.

'I'm laughing,' Nulty said sadly, as I went out.

The hall was quiet, the whole building was quiet. Down in front the prowl car men were still looking at their bent tender. I drove back to Hollywood.

The phone was ringing as I stepped into the office. I leaned down over the desk and said, 'Yes?'

'Am I addressing Mr Philip Marlowe?'

'Yes, this is Marlowe.'

'This is Mrs Grayle's residence. Mrs Lewin Lockridge Grayle. Mrs Grayle would like to see you here as soon as convenient.'

'Where?'

'The address is Number 862 Aster Drive, in Bay City. May I say you will arrive within the hour?'

'Are you Mr Grayle?'

'Certainly not, sir. I am the butler.'

'That's me you hear ringing the door bell,' I said.

18

It was close to the ocean and you could feel the ocean in the air but you couldn't see water from the front of the place. Aster Drive had a long smooth curve there and the houses on the inland side were just nice houses, but on the canyon side they were great silent estates, with twelve foot walls and wrought iron gates and ornamental hedges; and inside, if you could get inside, a special brand of sunshine, very quiet, put up in noise-proof containers just for the upper classes.

A man in a dark blue Russian tunic and shiny black puttees and flaring breeches stood in the half-open gates. He was a dark, good-looking lad, with plenty of shoulders and shiny smooth hair and the peak on his rakish cap made a soft shadow over his eyes. He had a cigarette in the corner of his mouth and he held his head tilted a little, as if he liked to keep the smoke out of his nose. One hand had a smooth black gauntlet on it and the other was bare. There was a heavy ring on his third finger.

There was no number in sight, but this should be 862. I stopped my car and leaned out and asked him. It took him a long time to answer. He had to look me over very carefully. Also the car I was driving. He came over to me and as he came he carelessly dropped his ungloved hand towards his hip. It was the kind of carelessness that was meant to be noticed.

He stopped a couple of feet away from my car and looked me over again.

'I'm looking for the Grayle residence,' I said.

'This is it. Nobody in.'

'I'm expected.'

He nodded. His eyes gleamed like water. 'Name?'

'Philip Marlowe.'

'Wait there.' He strolled, without hurry, over to the gates and unlocked an iron door set into one of the massive pillars. There was a telephone inside. He spoke briefly into it, snapped the door shut, and came back to me.

'You have some identification?'

I let him look at the licence on the steering post. 'That doesn't prove anything,' he said. 'How do I know it's your car?'

I pulled the key out of the ignition and threw the door open and got out. That put me about a foot from him. He had a nice breath. Haig and Haig at least.

'You've been at the sideboy again,' I said.

He smiled. His eyes measured me. I said:

'Listen, I'll talk to the butler over that phone and he'll know my voice. Will that pass me in or do I have to ride on your back?'

'I just work here,' he said softly. 'If I didn't——' he let the rest hang in the air, and kept on smiling.

'You're a nice lad,' I said and patted his shoulder. 'Dartmouth or Dannemora?'

'Christ,' he said. 'Why didn't you say you were a cop?'

We both grinned. He waved his hand and I went in through the half-open gate. The drive curved and tall moulded hedges of dark green completely screened it from the street and from the house. Through a green gate I saw a Jap gardener at work weeding a huge lawn. He was pulling a piece of weed out of the vast velvet expanse and sneering at it the way Jap gardeners do. Then the tall hedge closed in again and I didn't see anything more for a hundred feet. Then the hedge ended in a wide circle in which half a dozen cars were parked.

One of them was a small coupé. There were a couple of very nice two-tone Buicks of the latest model, good enough to go for the mail in. There was a black limousine, with dull nickel louvres and hubcaps the size of bicycle wheels. There was a long sport phaeton with the top down. A short very wide all-weather concrete driveway led from these to the side entrance of the house.

Off to the left, beyond the parking space there was a sunken garden with a fountain at each of the four corners. The entrance was barred by a wrought-iron gate with a flying Cupid in the middle. There were busts on light pillars and a stone seat with crouching griffins at each end. There was an oblong pool with stone water-lilies in it and a big stone bull-frog sitting on one of the leaves. Still farther a rose colonnade led to a thing like an altar, hedged in at both sides, yet not so completely but that the sun lay in an arabesque along the steps of the altar. And far over to the left there was a wild garden, not very large, with a sundial in the corner near an angle of wall that was built to look like a ruin. And there were flowers. There were a million flowers.

The house itself was not so much. It was smaller than Buckingham Palace, rather grey for California, and probably had fewer windows than the Chrysler Building.

I sneaked over to the side entrance and pressed a bell and somewhere a set of chimes made a deep mellow sound like church bells.

A man in a striped vest and gilt buttons opened the door, bowed, took my hat and was through for the day. Behind him in dimness, a man in striped knife-edge pants and a black coat and wing collar with grey striped tie leaned his grey head forward about half an inch and said: 'Mr Marlowe? If you will come this way, please——'

We went down a hall. It was a very quiet hall. Not a fly buzzed in it. The floor was covered with Oriental rugs and there were paintings along the walls. We turned a corner and there was more hall. A French window showed a gleam of blue water far off and I remembered almost with a shock that we were near the Pacific Ocean and that this house was on the edge of one of the canyons.

The butler reached a door and opened it against voices and stood aside and I went in. It was a nice room with large chesterfields and lounging chairs done in pale yellow leather arranged around a fireplace in front of which, on the glossy but not slippery floor, lay a rug as thin as silk and as old as Æsop's aunt. A jet of flowers glistened in a corner, another on a low table, the walls were of dull painted parchment, there was comfort, space, cosiness, a dash of the very modern and a dash of the very old, and three people sitting in a sudden silence watching me cross the floor.

One of them was Anne Riordan, looking just as I had seen her last, except that she was holding a glass of amber fluid in her hand. One was a tall thin sad-faced man with a stony chin and deep eyes and no colour in his face but an unhealthy yellow. He was a good sixty, or rather a bad sixty. He wore a dark business suit, a red carnation, and looked subdued.

The third was the blonde. She was dressed to go out, in a pale greenish blue. I didn't pay much attention to her clothes. They were what the guy designed for her and she would go to the right man. The effect was to make her look very young and to make her lapis lazuli eyes look very blue. Her hair was of the gold of old paintings and had been fussed with just enough but not too much. She had a full set of curves which nobody had been able to improve on. The dress was rather plain except for a clasp of diamonds at the throat. Her hands were not small, but they had shape, and the nails were the usual jarring note – almost magenta. She was giving me one of her smiles. She looked as if she smiled easily, but her eyes had a still look, as if they thought slowly and carefully. And her mouth was sensual.

'So nice of you to come,' she said. 'This is my husband. Mix Mr Marlowe a drink, honey.'

Mr Grayle shook hands with me. His hand was cold and a little moist. His eyes were sad. He mixed a Scotch and soda and handed it to me.

Then he sat down in a corner and was silent. I drank half of the drink and grinned at Miss Riordan. She looked at me with a sort of absent expression, as if she had another clue.

'Do you think you can do anything for us?' the blonde asked slowly, looking down into her glass. 'If you think you can, I'd be delighted. But the loss is rather small, compared with having any more fuss with gangsters and awful people.'

'I don't know very much about it really,' I said.

'Oh, I hope you can.' She gave me a smile I could feel in my hip pocket.

I drank the other half of my drink. I began to feel rested. Mrs Grayle rang a bell set into the arm of the leather chester-field and a footman came in. She half pointed to the tray. He looked around and mixed two drinks. Miss Riordan was still playing cute with the same one and apparently Mr Grayle didn't drink. The footman went out.

Mrs Grayle and I held our glasses. Mrs Grayle crossed her legs, a little carelessly.

'I don't know whether I can do anything,' I said. 'I doubt it. What is there to go on?'

'I'm sure you can.' She gave me another smile. 'How far did Lin Marriott take you into his confidence?'

She looked sideways at Miss Riordan. Miss Riordan just couldn't catch the look. She kept right on sitting. She looked sideways the other way. Mrs Grayle looked at her husband. 'Do you have to bother with this, honey?'

Mr Grayle stood up and said he was very glad to have met me and that he would go and lie down for a while. He didn't feel very well. He hoped I would excuse him. He was so polite I wanted to carry him out of the room just to show my appreciation.

He left. He closed the door softly, as if he was afraid to wake a sleeper. Mrs Grayle looked at the door for a moment and then put the smile back on her face and looked at me.

'Miss Riordan is in your complete confidence, of course.'

'Nobody's in my complete confidence, Mrs Grayle. She happens to know about this case – what there is to know.'

'Yes.' She drank a sip or two, then finished her glass at a swallow and set it aside.

'To hell with this polite drinking,' she said suddenly. 'Let's get together on this. You're a very good-looking man to be in your sort of racket.'

'It's a smelly business,' I said.

'I didn't quite mean that. Is there any money in it – or is that impertinent?'

'There's not much money in it. There's a lot of grief. But there's a lot of fun, too. And there's always a chance of a big case.'

'How does one get to be a private detective? You don't mind my sizing you up a little? And push that table over here, will you? So I can reach the drinks.'

I got up and pushed the huge silver tray on a stand across the glossy floor to her side. She made two more drinks. I still had half of my second.

'Most of us are ex-cops,' I said. 'I worked for the D.A. for a while. I got fired.'

She smiled nicely. 'Not for incompetence, I'm sure.'

'No, for talking back. Have you had any more phone calls?'

'Well——' She looked at Anne Riordan. She waited. Her look said things.

Anne Riordan stood up. She carried her glass, still full, over to the tray and set it down. 'You probably won't run short,' she said. 'But if you do – and thanks very much for talking to me, Mrs Grayle. I won't use anything. You have my word for it.'

'Heavens, you're not leaving,' Mrs Grayle said with her smile.

Anne Riordan took her lower lip between her teeth and held it there for a moment as if making up her mind whether to bite it off and spit it out or leave it on a while longer.

'Sorry, afraid I'll have to. I don't work for Mr Marlowe, you know. Just a friend. Good-bye, Mrs Grayle.'

The blonde gleamed at her. 'I hope you'll drop in again soon. Any time.' She pressed the bell twice. That got the butler. He held the door open.

Miss Riordan went out quickly and the door closed. For quite a while after it closed, Mrs Grayle stared at it with a faint smile. 'It's much better this way, don't you think?' she said after an interval of silence. I nodded. 'You're probably wondering how she knows so much if she's just a friend,' I said. 'She's a curious little girl. Some of it she dug out herself, like who you were and who owned the jade necklace. Some of it just happened. She came by last night to that dell where Marriott was killed. She was out riding. She happened to see a light and came down there.'

'Oh.' Mrs Grayle lifted a glass quickly and made a face. 'It's horrible to think of. Poor Lin. He was rather a heel. Most of one's friends are. But to die like that is awful.' She shuddered. Her eyes got large and dark.

'So it's all right about Miss Riordan. She won't talk. Her father was chief of police here for a long time,' I said.

'Yes. So she told me. You're not drinking.'

'I'm doing what *I* call drinking.'

'You and I should get along. Did Lin – Mr Marriott – tell you how the hold-up happened?'

'Between here and the Trocadero somewhere. He didn't say exactly. Three or four men.'

She nodded her golden gleaming head. 'Yes. You know there was something rather funny about that hold-up. They gave me back one of my rings, rather a nice one, too.'

'He told me that.'

'Then again I hardly ever wore the jade. After all, it's a museum piece, probably not many like it in the world, a very rare type of jade. Yet they snapped at it. I wouldn't expect them to think it had any value much, would you?'

'They'd know you wouldn't wear it otherwise. Who knew about its value?'

She thought. It was nice to watch her thinking. She still had her legs crossed, and still carelessly.

'All sorts of people, I suppose.'

'But they didn't know you would be wearing it that night? Who knew that?'

She shrugged her pale blue shoulders. I tried to keep my eyes where they belonged.

'My maid. But she's had a hundred chances. And I trust her——'

'Why?'

'I don't know. I just trust some people. I trust you.'

'Did you trust Marriott?'

Her face got a little hard. Her eyes a little watchful. 'Not in some things. In others, yes. There are degrees.' She had a nice way of talking, cool, half-cynical, and yet not hard-boiled. She rounded her words well.

'All right – besides the maid. The chauffeur?'

She shook her head, no. 'Lin drove me that night, in his own car. I don't think George was around at all. Wasn't it Thursday?'

'I wasn't there. Marriott said four or five days before in

telling me about it. Thursday would have been an even week from last night.'

'Well, it was Thursday.' She reached for my glass and her fingers touched mine a little, and were soft to the touch. 'George gets Thursday evening off. That's the usual day, you know.' She poured a fat slug of mellow-looking Scotch into my glass and squirted in some fizz-water. It was the kind of liquor you think you can drink for ever and all you do is get reckless. She gave herself the same treatment.

'Lin told you my name?' she asked softly, the eyes still watchful.

'He was careful not to.'

'Then he probably misled you a little about the time. Let's see what we have. Maid and chauffeur out. Out of consideration as accomplices, I mean.'

'They're not out by me.'

'Well, at least I'm trying,' she laughed. 'Then there's Newton, the butler. He might have seen it on my neck that night. But it hangs down rather low and I was wearing a white fox evening wrap; no, I don't think he could have seen it.'

'I bet you looked a dream,' I said.

'You're not getting a little tight, are you?'

'I've been known to be soberer.'

She put her head back and went off into a peal of laughter. I have only known four women in my life who could do that and still look beautiful. She was one of them.

'Newton is okey,' I said. 'His type don't run with hoodlums. That's just guessing, though. How about the footman?'

She thought and remembered, then shook her head. 'He didn't see me.'

'Anybody ask you to wear the jade?'

Her eyes instantly got more guarded. 'You're not fooling me a damn bit,' she said.

She reached for my glass to refill it. I let her have it, even though it still had an inch to go. I studied the lovely lines of her neck.

When she had filled the glasses and we were playing with them again I said, 'Let's get the record straight and then I'll tell you something. Describe the evening.'

She looked at her wrist watch, drawing a full length sleeve back to do it. 'I ought to be——'

'Let him wait.'

Her eyes flashed at that. I liked them that way. 'There's such a thing as being just a little too frank,' she said.

'Not in my business. Describe the evening. Or have me thrown out on my ear. One or the other. Make your lovely mind up.'

'You'd better sit over here beside me.'

'I've been thinking that a long time,' I said. 'Ever since you crossed your legs, to be exact.'

She pulled her dress down. 'These damn things are always up around your neck.'

I sat beside her on the yellow leather chesterfield. 'Aren't you a pretty fast worker?' she asked quietly.

I didn't answer her.

'Do you do much of this sort of thing?' she asked with a sidelong look.

'Practically none. I'm a Tibetan monk, in my spare time.'

'Only you don't have any spare time.'

'Let's focus,' I said. 'Let's get what's left of our minds – or mine – on the problem. How much are you going to pay me?'

'Oh, that's the problem. I thought you were going to get my necklace back. Or try to.'

'I have to work in my own way. This way.' I took a long drink and it nearly stood me on my head. I swallowed a little air.

'And investigate a murder,' I said.

'That has nothing to do with it. I mean that's a police affair, isn't it?'

'Yeah – only the poor guy paid me a hundred bucks to

take care of him – and I didn't. Makes me feel guilty. Makes me want to cry. Shall I cry?'

'Have a drink.' She poured us some more Scotch. It didn't seem to affect her any more than water affects Boulder Dam.

'Well, where have we got to?' I said, trying to hold my glass so that the whisky would stay inside it. 'No maid, no chauffeur, no butler, no footman. We'll be doing our own laundry next. How did the hold-up happen? Your version might have a few details Marriott didn't give me.'

She leaned forward and cupped her chin in her hand. She looked serious without looking silly-serious.

'We went to a party in Brentwood Heights. Then Lin suggested we run over to the Troc for a few drinks and a few dances. So we did. They were doing some work on Sunset and it was very dusty. So coming back Lin dropped down to Santa Monica. That took us past a shabby-looking hotel called the Hotel Indio, which I happened to notice for some silly meaningless reason. Across the street from it was a beer joint and a car was parked in front of that.'

'Only one car – in front of a beer joint?'

'Yes. Only one. It was a very dingy place. Well, this car started up and followed us and of course I thought nothing of that either. There was no reason to. Then before we got to where Santa Monica turns into Arguello Boulevard, Lin said, "Let's go over the other road" and turned up some curving residential street. Then all of a sudden a car rushed by us and grazed the fender and then pulled over to stop. A man in an overcoat and scarf and hat low on his face came back to apologize. It was a white scarf bunched out and it drew my eyes. It was about all I really saw of him except that he was tall and thin. As soon as he got close – and I remembered afterwards that he didn't walk in our headlights at all——'

'That's natural. Nobody likes to look into headlights. Have a drink. My treat this time.'

She was leaning forward, her fine eyebrows – not daubs of

paint – drawn together in a frown of thought. I made two drinks. She went on:

'As soon as he got close to the side where Lin was sitting he jerked the scarf up over his nose and a gun was shining at us. "Stick-up," he said. "Be very quiet and everything will be jake." Then another man came over on the other side.'

'In Beverly Hills,' I said, 'the best policed four square miles in California.'

She shrugged. 'It happened just the same. They asked for my jewellery and bag. The man with the scarf did. The one on my side never spoke at all. I passed the things across Lin and the man gave me back my bag and one ring. He said to hold off calling the police and insurance people for a while. They would make us a nice smooth easy deal. He said they found it easier to work on a straight percentage. He seemed to have all the time in the world. He said they could work through the insurance people, if they had to, but that meant cutting in a shyster, and they preferred not to. He sounded like a man with some education.'

'It might have been Dressed-Up Eddie,' I said. 'Only he got bumped off in Chicago.'

She shrugged. We had a drink. She went on.

'Then they left and we went home and I told Lin to keep quiet about it. The next day I got a call. We have two phones, one with extensions and one in my bedroom with no extensions. The call was on this. It's not listed, of course.'

I nodded. 'They can buy the number for a few dollars. It's done all the time. Some movie people have to change their numbers every month.'

We had a drink.

'I told the man calling to take it up with Lin and he would represent me and if they were not too unreasonable, we might deal. He said okey, and from then on I guess they just stalled long enough to watch us a little. Finally, as you know, we agreed on eight thousand dollars and so forth.'

'Could you recognize any of them?'

'Of course not.'

'Randall know all this?'

'Of course. Do we have to talk about it any more? It bores me.' She gave me the lovely smile.

'Did he make any comment?'

She yawned. 'Probably. I forget.'

I sat with my empty glass in my hand and thought. She took it away from me and started to fill it again.

I took the refilled glass out of her hand and transferred it to my left and took hold of her left hand with my right. It felt smooth and soft and warm and comforting. It squeezed mine. The muscles in it were strong. She was a well built woman, and no paper flower.

'I think he had an idea,' she said. 'But he didn't say what it was.'

'Anybody would have an idea out of all that,' I said.

She turned her head slowly and looked at me. Then she nodded. 'You can't miss it, can you?'

'How long have you known him?'

'Oh, years. He used to be an announcer at the station my husband owned. K.F.D.K. That's where I met him. That's where I met my husband too.'

'I knew that. But Marriott lived as if he had money. Not riches, but comfortable money.'

'He came into some and quit radio business.'

'Do you know for a fact he came into money – or was that just something he said?'

She shrugged. She squeezed my hand.

'Or it may not have been very much money and he may have gone through it pretty fast,' I squeezed her hand back. 'Did he borrow from you?'

'You're a little old-fashioned, aren't you?' She looked down at the hand I was holding.

'I'm still working. And your Scotch is as good it keeps me half-sober. Not that I'd have to be drunk——'

'Yes.' She drew her hand out of mine and rubbed it. 'You must have quite a clutch — in your spare time. Lin Marriott was a high-class blackmailer, of course. That's obvious. He lived on women.'

'He had something on you?'

'Should I tell you?'

'It probably wouldn't be wise.'

She laughed. 'I will, anyhow. I got a little tight at his house once and passed out. I seldom do. He took some photos of me — with my clothes up to my neck.'

'The dirty dog,' I said. 'Have you got any of them handy?'

She slapped my wrist. She said softly:

'What's your name?'

'Phil. What's yours?'

'Helen. Kiss me.'

She fell softly across my lap and I bent down over her face and began to browse on it. She worked her eyelashes and made butterfly kisses on my cheeks. When I got to her mouth it was half open and burning and her tongue was a darting snake between her teeth.

The door opened and Mr Grayle stepped quietly into the room. I was holding her and didn't have a chance to let go. I lifted my face and looked at him. I felt as cold as Finnegan's feet, the day they buried him.

The blonde in my arms didn't move, didn't even close her lips. She had a half-dreamy, half-sarcastic expression on her face.

Mr Grayle cleared his throat slightly and said: 'I beg your pardon, I'm sure,' and went quietly out of the room. There was an infinite sadness in his eyes.

I pushed her away and stood up and got my handkerchief out and mopped my face.

She lay as I had left her, half sideways along the davenport, the skin showing in a generous sweep above one stocking.

'Who was that?' she asked thickly.

'Mr Grayle.'

'Forget him.'

I went away from her and sat down in the chair I had sat in when I first came into the room.

After a moment she straightened herself out and sat up and looked at me steadily.

'It's all right. He understands. What the hell can he expect?'

'I guess he knows.'

'Well, I tell you it's all right. Isn't that enough? He's a sick man. What the hell——'

'Don't go shrill on me. I don't like shrill women.'

She opened a bag lying beside her and took out a small hand-kerchief and wiped her lips, then looked at her face in a mirror.

'I guess you're right,' she said. 'Just too much Scotch. To-night at the Belvedere Club. Ten o'clock.' She wasn't looking at me. Her breath was fast.

'Is that a good place?'

'Laird Brunette owns it. I know him pretty well.'

'Right,' I said. I was still cold. I felt nasty, as if I had picked a poor man's pocket.

She got a lipstick out and touched her lips very lightly and then looked at me along her eyes. She tossed the mirror. I caught it and looked at my face. I worked at it with my hand-kerchief and stood up to give her back the mirror.

She was leaning back, showing all her throat, looking at me lazily down her eyes.

'What's the matter?'

'Nothing. Ten o'clock at the Belvedere Club. Don't be too magnificent. All I have is a dinner suit. In the bar?'

She nodded, her eyes still lazy.

I went across the room and out, without looking back. The footman met me in the hall and gave me my hat, looking like the Great Stone Face.

19

I walked down the curving driveway and lost myself in the shadow of the tall trimmed hedges and came to the gates. Another man was holding the fort now, a husky in plain clothes, an obvious bodyguard. He let me out with a nod.

A horn tooted. Miss Riordan's coupé was drawn up behind my car. I went over there and looked in at her. She looked cool and sarcastic.

She sat there with her hands on the wheel, gloved and slim. She smiled.

'I waited. I suppose it was none of my business. What did you think of her?'

'I bet she snaps a mean garter.'

'Do you always have to say things like that?' She flushed bitterly. 'Sometimes I hate men. Old men, young men, football players, opera tenors, smart millionaires, beautiful men who are gigolos and almost-heels who are – private detectives.'

I grinned at her sadly. 'I know I talk too smart. It's in the air nowadays. Who told you he was a gigolo?'

'Who?'

'Don't be obtuse. Marriott.'

'Oh, it was a cinch guess. I'm sorry. I don't mean to be nasty. I guess you can snap her garter any time you want to, without much of a struggle. But there's one thing you can be sure of – you're a late comer to the show.'

The wide curving street dozed peacefully in the sun. A beautifully painted panel truck slid noiselessly to a stop before a house across the street, then backed a little and went up the driveway to a side entrance. On the side of the panel truck was painted the legend: 'Bay City Infant Service.'

Anne Riordan leaned towards me, her grey-blue eyes hurt and clouded. Her slightly too long upper lip pouted and then pressed back against her teeth. She made a sharp little sound with her breath.

'Probably you'd like me to mind my own business, is that it? And not have ideas you don't have first. I thought I was helping a little.'

'I don't need any help. The police don't want any from me. There's nothing I can do for Mrs Grayle. She has a yarn about a beer parlour where a car started from and followed them, but what does that amount to? It was a crummy dive on Santa Monica. This was a high class mob. There was somebody in it that could even tell Fei Tsui jade when he saw it.'

'If he wasn't tipped off.'

'There's that too,' I said, and fumbled a cigarette out of a package. 'Either way there's nothing for me in it.'

'Not even about psychics?'

I stared rather blankly. 'Psychics?'

'My God,' she said softly. 'And I thought you were a detective.'

'There's a hush on part of this,' I said. 'I've got to watch my step. This Grayle packs a lot of dough in his pants. And law is where you buy it in this town. Look at the funny way the cops are acting. No build-up, no newspaper handout, no chance for the innocent stranger to step in with the trifling clue that turns out to be all important. Nothing but silence and warnings to me to lay off. I don't like it at all.'

'You got most of the lipstick off,' Anne Riordan said. 'I mentioned psychics. Well, good-bye. It was nice to know you – in a way.'

She pressed her starter button and jammed her gears in and was gone in a swirl of dust.

I watched her go. When she was gone I looked across the

street. The man from the panel truck that said Bay City Infant Service came out of the side door of the house dressed in a uniform so white and stiff and gleaming that it made me feel clean just to look at it. He was carrying a carton of some sort. He got into his panel truck and drove away.

I figured he had just changed a diaper.

I got into my own car and looked at my watch before starting up. It was almost five.

The Scotch, as good enough Scotch will, stayed with me all the way back to Hollywood. I took the red lights as they came.

'There's a nice little girl,' I told myself out loud, in the car, 'for a guy that's interested in a nice little girl.' Nobody said anything. 'But I'm not,' I said. Nobody said anything to that either. 'Ten o'clock at the Belvedere Club,' I said. Somebody said: 'Phooey.'

It sounded like my voice.

It was a quarter to six when I reached my office again. The building was very quiet. The typewriter beyond the party wall was stilled. I lit a pipe and sat down to wait.

20

The Indian smelled. He smelled clear across the little reception room when the buzzer sounded and I opened the door between to see who it was. He stood just inside the corridor door looking as if he had been cast in bronze. He was a big man from the waist up and he had a big chest. He looked like a bum.

He wore a brown suit of which the coat was too small for his shoulders and his trousers were probably a little tight under the armpits. His hat was at least two sizes too small and had been perspired in freely by somebody it fitted better than it fitted him. He wore it about where a house wears a wind vane. His collar had the snug fit of a horse-collar and was of about the same shade of dirty brown. A tie dangled outside his buttoned jacket, a black tie which had been tied with a pair of pliers in a knot the size of a pea. Around his bare and magnificent throat, above the dirty collar, he wore a wide piece of black ribbon, like an old woman trying to freshen up her neck.

He had a big flat face and a high-bridged fleshy nose that looked as hard as the prow of a cruiser. He had lidless eyes, drooping jowls, the shoulders of a blacksmith and the short and apparently awkward legs of a chimpanzee. I found out later that they were only short.

If he had been cleaned up a little and dressed in a white nightgown, he would have looked like a very wicked Roman senator.

His smell was the earthy smell of primitive man, and not the slimy dirt of cities.

'Huh,' he said. 'Come quick. Come now.'

I backed into my office and wiggled my finger at him and he followed me making as much noise as a fly makes walking on the wall. I sat down behind my desk and squeaked my swivel chair professionally and pointed to the customer's chair on the other side. He didn't sit down. His small black eyes were hostile.

'Come where?' I said.

'Huh. Me Second Planting. Me Hollywood Indian.'

'Have a chair, Mr Planting.'

He snorted and his nostrils got very wide. They had been wide enough for mouseholes to start with.

'Name Second Planting. Name no Mister Planting.'

'What can I do for you?'

He lifted his voice and began to intone in a deep-chested sonorous boom. 'He say come quick. Great white father say come quick. He say me bring you in fiery chariot. He say——'

'Yeah. Cut out the pig Latin,' I said. 'I'm no schoolmarm at the snake dances.'

'Nuts,' the Indian said.

We sneered at each other across the desk for a moment. He sneered better than I did. Then he removed his hat with massive disgust and turned it upside down. He rolled a finger around under the sweatband. That turned the sweatband up into view, and it had not been misnamed. He removed a paper clip from the edge and threw a fold of tissue paper on the desk. He pointed at it angrily, with a well-chewed fingernail. His lank hair had a shelf around it, high up, from the too-tight hat.

I unfolded the piece of tissue paper and found a card inside. The card was no news to me. There had been three exactly like it in the mouthpieces of three Russian-appearing cigarettes.

I played with my pipe, stared at the Indian and tried to ride him with my stare. He looked as nervous as a brick wall.

'Okey, what does he want?'

'He want you come quick. Come now. Come in fiery——'

'Nuts,' I said.

The Indian liked that. He closed his mouth slowly and winked an eye solemnly and then almost grinned.

'Also it will cost him a hundred bucks as a retainer,' I added, trying to look as if that was a nickel.

'Huh?' Suspicious again. Stick to basic English.

'Hundred dollars,' I said. 'Iron men. Fish. Bucks to the number of one hundred. Me no money, me no come. Savvy?' I began to count a hundred with both hands.

'Huh. Big shot,' the Indian sneered.

He worked under his greasy hatband and threw another fold of tissue paper on the desk. I took it and unwound it. It contained a brand new hundred dollar bill.

The Indian put his hat back on his head without bothering to tuck the hatband back in place. It looked only slightly more comic that way. I sat staring at the hundred dollar bill, with my mouth open.

'Psychic is right,' I said at last. 'A guy that smart I'm afraid of.'

'Not got all day,' the Indian remarked, conversationally.

I opened my desk and took out a Colt .38 automatic of the type known as Super Match. I hadn't worn it to visit Mrs Lewin Lockridge Grayle. I stripped my coat off and strapped the leather harness on and tucked the automatic down inside it and strapped the lower strap and put my coat back on again.

This meant as much to the Indian as if I had scratched my neck.

'Gottum car,' he said. 'Big car.'

'I don't like big cars any more,' I said. 'I gottum own car.'

'You come my car,' the Indian said threateningly.

'I come your car,' I said.

I locked the desk and office up, switched the buzzer off and went out, leaving the reception room door unlocked as usual.

We went along the hall and down in the elevator. The Indian smelled. Even the elevator operator noticed it.

21

The car was a dark blue seven-passenger sedan, a Packard of the latest model, custom-built. It was the kind of car you wear your rope pearls in. It was parked by a fire-hydrant and a dark foreign-looking chauffeur with a face of carved wood was behind the wheel. The interior was upholstered in quilted grey chenille. The Indian put me in the back. Sitting there alone I felt like a high-class corpse, laid out by an undertaker with a lot of good taste.

The Indian got in beside the chauffeur and the car turned

in the middle of the block and a cop across the street said: 'Hey,' weakly, as if he didn't mean it, and then bent down quickly to tie his shoe.

We went west, dropped over to Sunset and slid fast and noiseless along that. The Indian sat motionless beside the chauffeur. An occasional whiff of his personality drifted back to me. The driver looked as if he was half asleep but he passed the fast boys in the convertible sedans as though they were being towed. They turned on all the green lights for him. Some drivers are like that. He never missed one.

We curved through the bright mile or two of the Strip, past the antique shops with famous screen names on them, past the windows full of point lace and ancient pewter, past the gleaming new night clubs with famous chefs and equally famous gambling rooms, run by polished graduates of the Purple Gang, past the Georgian-Colonial vogue, now old hat, past the handsome modernistic buildings in which the Hollywood flesh-peddlers never stop talking money, past a drive-in lunch which somehow didn't belong, even though the girls wore white silk blouses and drum majorettes' shakos and nothing below the hips but glazed kid Hessian boots. Past all this and down a wide smooth curve to the bridle path of Beverly Hills and lights to the south, all colours of the spectrum and crystal clear in an evening without fog, past the shadowed mansions up on the hills to the north, past Beverly Hills altogether and up into the twisting foothill boulevard and the sudden cool dusk and the drift of wind from the sea.

It had been a warm afternoon, but the heat was gone. We whipped past a distant cluster of lighted buildings and an endless series of lighted mansions, not too close to the road. We dipped down to skirt a huge green polo field with another equally huge practice field beside it, soared again to the top of a hill and swung mountainward up a steep hill road of clean concrete that passed orange groves, some rich man's pet because this is not orange country, and then little by little the lighted windows of the millionaires' homes were gone and the road narrowed and this was Stillwood Heights.

The smell of sage drifted up from a canyon and made me think of a dead man and a moonless sky. Straggly stucco houses were moulded flat to the side of the hill, like bas-reliefs. Then there were no more houses, just the still dark foothills with an early star or two above them, and the concrete ribbon of road and a sheer drop on one side into a tangle of scrub oak and manzanita where sometimes you can hear the call of the quails if you stop and keep still and wait. On the other side of the road was a raw clay bank at the edge of which a few unbeatable wild flowers hung on like naughty children that won't go to bed.

Then the road twisted into a hairpin turn and the big tyres scratched over loose stones, and the car tore less soundlessly up a long driveway lined with the wild geraniums. At the top of this, faintly lighted, lonely as a lighthouse, stood an eyrie, an eagle's nest, an angular building of stucco and glass brick, raw and modernistic and yet not ugly and altogether a swell place for a psychic consultant to hang out his shingle. Nobody would be able to hear any screams.

The car turned beside the house and a light flicked on over a black door set into the heavy wall. The Indian climbed out grunting and opened the rear door of the car. The chauffeur lit a cigarette with an electric lighter and a harsh smell of tobacco came back to me softly in the evening. I got out.

We went over to the black door. It opened of itself, slowly, almost with menace. Beyond it a narrow hallway probed back into the house. Light glowed from the glass brick walls.

The Indian growled, 'Huh. You go in, big shot.'

'After you, Mr Planting.'

He scowled and went in and the door closed after us as silently and mysteriously as it had opened. At the end of the narrow hallway we squeezed into a little elevator and the Indian closed the door and pressed a button. We rose softly, without sound. Such smelling as the Indian had done before was a mooncast shadow to what he was doing now.

The elevator stopped, the door opened. There was light and I stepped out into a turret room where the day was still trying to be remembered. There were windows all around it. Far off the sea flickered. Darkness prowled slowly on the hills. There were panelled walls where there were no windows, and rugs on the floor with the soft colours of old Persians, and there was a reception desk that looked as if it had been made of carvings stolen from an ancient church. And behind the desk a woman sat and smiled at me, a dry tight withered smile that would turn to powder if you touched it.

She had sleek coiled hair and a dark, thin, wasted Asiatic face. There were heavy coloured stones in her ears and heavy rings on her fingers, including a moonstone and an emerald in a silver setting that may have been a real emerald but somehow managed to look as phony as a dime store slave bracelet. And her hands were dry and dark and not young and not fit for rings.

She spoke. The voice was familiar. 'Ah, Meester Marlowe, so ver-ry good of you to come. Amthor he weel be so ver-ry pleased.'

I laid the hundred dollar bill the Indian had given me down on the desk. I looked behind me. The Indian had gone down again in the elevator.

'Sorry. It was a nice thought, but I can't take this.'

'Amthor he – he weesh to employ you, is it not?' She smiled again. Her lips rustled like tissue paper.

'I'd have to find out what the job is first.'

She nodded and got up slowly from behind the desk. She swished before me in a tight dress that fitted her like a mermaid's skin and showed that she had a good figure if you like them four sizes bigger below the waist.

'I weel conduct you,' she said.

She pressed a button in the panelling and a door slid open

noiselessly. There was a milky glow beyond it. I looked back at her smile before I went through. It was older than Egypt now. The door slid silently shut behind me.

There was nobody in the room.

It was octagonal, draped in black velvet from floor to ceiling, with a high remote black ceiling that may have been of velvet too. In the middle of a coal-black lustreless rug stood an octagonal white table, just large enough for two pairs of elbows and in the middle of it a milk-white globe on a black stand. The light came from this. How, I couldn't see. On either side of the table there was a white octagonal stool which was a smaller edition of the table. Over against one wall there was one more such stool. There were no windows. There was nothing else in the room, nothing at all. On the walls there was not even a light fixture. If there were other doors, I didn't see them. I looked back at the one by which I had come in. I couldn't see that either.

I stood there for perhaps fifteen seconds with the faint obscure feeling of being watched. There was probably a peephole somewhere, but I couldn't spot it. I gave up trying. I listened to my breath. The room was so still that I could hear it going through my nose, softly, like little curtains rustling.

Then an invisible door on the far side of the room slid open and a man stepped through and the door closed behind him. The man walked straight to the table with his head down and sat on one of the octagonal stools and made a sweeping motion with one of the most beautiful hands I have ever seen.

'Please be seated. Opposite me. Do not smoke and do not fidget. Try to relax, completely. Now how may I serve you?'

I sat down, got a cigarette into my mouth and rolled it along my lips without lighting it. I looked him over. He was thin, tall and straight as a steel rod. He had the palest finest white hair I ever saw. It could have been strained through silk gauze. His skin was as fresh as a rose petal. He might have been thirty-five or sixty-five. He was ageless. His hair was brushed straight back from as good a profile as Barrymore ever had. His eyebrows were coal black, like the walls and ceiling and floor. His eyes were deep, far too deep. They were the depthless drugged eyes of the somnambulist. They were like a well I read about once. It was nine hundred years old, in an old castle. You could drop a stone into it and wait. You could listen and wait and then you would give up waiting and laugh and then just as you were ready to turn away a faint, minute splash would come back up to you from the bottom of that well, so tiny, so remote that you could hardly believe a well like that possible.

His eyes were deep like that. And they were also eyes without expression, without soul, eyes that could watch lions tear a man to pieces and never change, that could watch a man impaled and screaming in the hot sun with his eyelids cut off.

He wore a double-breasted black business suit that had been cut by an artist. He stared vaguely at my fingers.

'Please do not fidget,' he said. 'It breaks the waves, disturbs my concentration.'

'It makes the ice melt, the butter run and the cat squawk,' I said.

He smiled the faintest smile in the world. 'You didn't come here to be impertinent, I'm sure.'

'You seem to forget why I did come. By the way, I gave that hundred dollar bill back to your secretary. I came, as you may recall, about some cigarettes. Russian cigarettes filled with marijuana. With your card rolled in the hollow mouthpieces.'

'You wish to find out why that happened?'

'Yeah. I ought to be paying you the hundred dollars.'

'That will not be necessary. The answer is simple. There are things I do not know. This is one of them.'

For a moment I almost believed him. His face was as smooth as an angel's wing.

'Then why send me a hundred dollars – and a tough Indian that stinks – and a car? By the way, does the Indian have to stink? If he's working for you, couldn't you sort of get him to take a bath?'

'He is a natural medium. They are rare – like diamonds, and like diamonds, are sometimes found in dirty places. I understand you are a private detective?'

'Yes.'

'I think you are a very stupid person. You look stupid. You are in a stupid business. And you came here on a stupid mission.'

'I get it,' I said. 'I'm stupid. It sank in after a while.'

'And I think I need not detain you any longer.'

'You're not detaining me,' I said. 'I'm detaining you. I want to know why those cards were in those cigarettes.'

He shrugged the smallest shrug that could be shrugged. 'My cards are available to anybody. I do not give my friends marijuana cigarettes. Your question remains stupid.'

'I wonder if this would brighten it up any. The cigarettes were in a cheap Chinese or Japanese case of imitation tortoise-shell. Ever see anything like that?'

'No. Not that I recall.'

'I can brighten it up a little more. The case was in the pocket of a man named Lindsay Marriott. Ever hear of him?'

He thought. 'Yes. I tried at one time to treat him for camera shyness. He was trying to get into pictures. It was a waste of time. Pictures did not want him.'

'I can guess that,' I said. 'He would photograph like Isadora Duncan. I've still got the big one left. Why did you send me the C-note?'

'My dear Mr Marlowe,' he said coldly, 'I am no fool. I am in a very sensitive profession. I am a quack. That is to say I do things which the doctors in their small frightened selfish guild cannot accomplish. I am in danger at all times – from people like you. I merely wish to estimate the danger before dealing with it.'

'Pretty trivial in my case, huh?'

'It hardly exists,' he said politely and made a peculiar motion with his left hand which made my eyes jump at it. Then he put it down very slowly on the white table and looked down at it. Then he raised his depthless eyes again and folded his arms.

'Your hearing——'

'I smell it now,' I said. 'I wasn't thinking of him.'

I turned my head to the left. The Indian was sitting on the third white stool against the black velvet.

He had some kind of a white smock on him over his other clothes. He was sitting without a movement, his eyes closed, his head bent forward a little, as if he had been asleep for an hour. His dark strong face was full of shadows.

I looked back at Amthor. He was smiling his minute smile.

'I bet that makes the dowagers shed their false teeth,' I said. 'What does he do for real money – sit on your knee and sing French songs?'

He made an impatient gesture. 'Get to the point, please.'

'Last night Marriott hired me to go with him on an expedition that involved paying some money to some crooks at a spot they picked. I got knocked on the head. When I came out of it Marriott had been murdered.'

Nothing changed much in Amthor's face. He didn't scream or run up the walls. But for him the reaction was sharp. He unfolded his arms and refolded them the other way. His mouth looked grim. Then he sat like a stone lion outside the Public Library.

'The cigarettes were found on him,' I said.

He looked at me coolly. 'But not by the police, I take it. Since the police have not been here.'

'Correct.'

'The hundred dollars,' he said very softly, 'was hardly enough.'

'That depends what you expect to buy with it.'

'You have these cigarettes with you?'

'One of them. But they don't prove anything. As you said,

anybody could get your cards. I'm just wondering why they were where they were. Any ideas?'

'How well did you know Mr Marriott?' he asked softly.

'Not at all. But I had ideas about him. They were so obvious they stuck out.'

Amthor tapped lightly on the white table. The Indian still slept with his chin on his huge chest, his heavy-lidded eyes tight shut.

'By the way, did you ever meet a Mrs Grayle, a wealthy lady who lives in Bay City?'

He nodded absently. 'Yes, I treated her centres of speech. She had a very slight impediment.'

'You did a sweet job on her,' I said. 'She talks as good as I do now.'

That failed to amuse him. He still tapped on the table. I listened to the taps. Something about them I didn't like. They sounded like a code. He stopped, folded his arms again and leaned back against the air.

'What I like about this job everybody knows everybody,' I said. 'Mrs Grayle knew Marriott too.'

'How did you find that out?' he asked slowly.

I didn't say anything.

'You will have to tell the police – about those cigarettes,' he said.

I shrugged.

'You are wondering why I do not have you thrown out,' Amthor said pleasantly. 'Second Planting could break your neck like a celery stalk. I am wondering myself. You seem to have some sort of theory. Blackmail I do not pay. It buys nothing – and I have many friends. But naturally there are certain elements which would like to show me in a bad light. Psychiatrists, sex specialists, neurologists, nasty little men with rubber hammers and shelves loaded with the literature of aberrations. And of course they are all – doctors. While I am still a – quack. What is your theory?'

I tried to stare him down, but it couldn't be done. I felt myself licking my lips.

He shrugged lightly. 'I can't blame you for wanting to keep it to yourself. This is a matter that I must give thought to. Perhaps you are a much more intelligent man than I thought. I also make mistakes. In the meantime——' He leaned forward and put a hand on each side of the milky globe.

'I think Marriott was a blackmailer of women,' I said. 'And finger man for a jewel mob. But who told him what women to cultivate – so that he would know their comings and goings, get intimate with them, make love to them, make them load up with the ice and take them out, and then slip to a phone and tell the boys where to operate?'

'That,' Amthor said carefully, 'is your picture of Marriott – and of me. I am slightly disgusted.'

I leaned forward until my face was not more than a foot from his. 'You're in a racket. Dress it up all you please and it's still a racket. And it wasn't just the cards, Amthor. As you say, anybody could get those. It wasn't the marijuana. You wouldn't be in a cheap line like that – not with your chances. But on the back of each card there is a blank space. And on blank spaces, or even on written ones, there is sometimes invisible writing.'

He smiled bleakly, but I hardly saw it. His hands moved over the milky bowl.

The light went out. The room was as black as Carrie Nation's bonnet.

22

I kicked my stool back and stood up and jerked the gun out of the holster under my arm. But it was no good. My coat was buttoned and I was too slow. I'd have been too slow anyway, if it came to shooting anybody.

There was a soundless rush of air and an earthy smell. In the complete darkness the Indian hit me from behind and pinned my arms to my sides. He started to lift me. I could have got the gun out still and fanned the room with blind shots, but I was a long way from friends. It didn't seem as if there was any point in it.

I let go of the gun and took hold of his wrists. They were greasy and hard to hold. The Indian breathed gutterally and set me down with a jar that lifted the top of my head. He had my wrists now, instead of me having his. He twisted them behind me fast and a knee like a corner stone went into my back. He bent me. I can be bent. I'm not the City Hall. He bent me.

I tried to yell, for no reason at all. Breath panted in my throat and couldn't get out. The Indian threw me sideways and got a body scissors on me as I fell. He had me in a barrel. His hands went to my neck. Sometimes I wake up in the night. I feel them there and I smell the smell of him. I feel the breath fighting and losing and the greasy fingers digging in. Then I get up and take a drink and turn the radio on.

I was just about gone when the light flared on again, blood red, on account of the blood in my eyeballs and at the back of them. A face floated around and a hand pawed me delicately, but the other hands stayed on my throat.

A voice said softly, 'Let him breathe – a little.'

The fingers slackened. I wrenched loose from them. Something that glinted hit me on the side of the jaw.

The voice said softly: 'Get him on his feet.'

The Indian got me on my feet. He pulled me back against the wall, holding me by both twisted wrists.

'Amateur,' the voice said softly and the shiny thing that was as hard and bitter as death hit me again, across the face. Something warm trickled. I licked at it and tasted iron and salt.

A hand explored my wallet. A hand explored all my pockets. The cigarette in tissue paper came out and was unwrapped. It went somewhere in the haze that was in front of me.

'There were three cigarettes?' the voice said gently, and the shining thing hit my jaw again.

'Three,' I gulped.

'Just where did you say the others were?'

'In my desk – at the office.'

The shiny thing hit me again. 'You are probably lying – but I can find out.' Keys shone with funny little red lights in front of me. The voice said: 'Choke him a little more.'

The iron fingers went into my throat. I was strained back against him, against the smell of him and the hard muscles of his stomach. I reached up and took one of his fingers and tried to twist it.

The voice said softly: 'Amazing. He's learning.'

The glinting thing swayed through the air again. It smacked my jaw, the thing that had once been my jaw.

'Let him go. He's tame,' the voice said.

The heavy strong arms dropped away and I swayed forward and took a step and steadied myself. Amthor stood smiling very slightly, almost dreamily in front of me. He held my gun in his delicate, lovely hand. He held it pointed at my chest.

'I could teach you,' he said in his soft voice. 'But to what purpose? A dirty little man in a dirty little world. One spot of brightness on you and you would still be that. Is it not so?' He smiled, so beautifully.

I swung at his smile with everything I had left.

It wasn't so bad considering. He reeled and blood came out of both his nostrils. Then he caught himself and straightened up and lifted the gun again.

'Sit down, my child,' he said softly. 'I have visitors coming. I am so glad you hit me. It helps a great deal.'

I felt for the white stool and sat down and put my head

137

down on the white table beside the milky globe which was now shining again softly. I stared at it sideways, my face on the table. The light fascinated me. Nice light, nice soft light.

Behind me and around me there was nothing but silence.

I think I went to sleep, just like that, with a bloody face on the table, and a thin beautiful devil with my gun in his hand watching me and smiling.

23

'All right,' the big one said. 'You can quit stalling now.'

I opened my eyes and sat up.

'Out in the other room, pally.'

I stood up, still dreamy. We went somewhere, through a door. Then I saw where it was – the reception room with the windows all around. It was black dark now outside.

The woman with the wrong rings sat at her desk. A man stood beside her.

'Sit here, pally.'

He pushed me down. It was a nice chair, straight but comfortable, but I wasn't in the mood for it. The woman behind the desk had a notebook open and was reading out loud from it. A short elderly man with a deadpan expression and a grey moustache was listening to her.

Amthor was standing by a window, with his back to the room, looking out at the placid line of the ocean, far off, beyond the pier lights, beyond the world. He looked at it as if he loved it. He half turned his head to look at me once, and I could see that the blood had been washed off his face, but his nose wasn't the nose I had first met, not by two sizes. That made me grin, cracked lips and all.

'You got fun, pally?'

I looked at what made the sound, what was in front of me

and what had helped me get where I was. He was a wind-blown blossom of some two hundred pounds with freckled teeth and the mellow voice of a circus barker. He was tough, fast and he ate red meat. Nobody could push him around. He was the kind of cop who spits on his blackjack every night instead of saying his prayers. But he had humorous eyes.

He stood in front of me splay-legged, holding my open wallet in his hand, making scratches on the leather with his right thumbnail, as if he just liked to spoil things. Little things, if they were all he had. But probably faces would give him more fun.

'Peeper, huh, pally? From the big bad burg, huh? Little spot of blackmail, huh?'

His hat was on the back of his head. He had dusty brown hair darkened by sweat on his forehead. His humorous eyes were flecked with red veins.

My throat felt as though it had been through a mangle. I reached up and felt it. That Indian. He had fingers like pieces of tool steel.

The dark woman stopped reading out of her notebook and closed it. The elderly smallish man with the grey moustache nodded and came over to stand behind the one who was talking to me.

'Cops?' I asked, rubbing my chin.

'What do *you* think, pally?'

Policeman's humour. The small one had a cast in one eye, and it looked half blind.

'Not L.A.,' I said, looking at him. 'That eye would retire him in Los Angeles.'

The big man handed me my wallet. I looked through it. I had all the money still. All the cards. It had everything that belonged in it. I was surprised.

'Say something, pally,' the big one said. 'Something that would make us get fond of you.'

'Give me back my gun.'

He leaned forward a little and thought. I could see him thinking. It hurt his corns. 'Oh, you want your gun, pally?' He looked sideways at the one with the grey moustache. 'He wants his gun,' he told him. He looked at me again. 'And what would you want your gun for, pally?'

'I want to shoot an Indian.'

'Oh, you want to shoot an Indian, pally.'

'Yeah – just one Indian, pop.'

He looked at the one with the moustache again. 'This guy is very tough,' he told him. 'He wants to shoot an Indian.'

'Listen, Hemingway, don't repeat everything I say,' I said.

'I think the guy is nuts,' the big one said. 'He just called me Hemingway. Do you think he is nuts?'

The one with the moustache bit a cigar and said nothing. The tall beautiful man at the window turned slowly and said softly: 'I think possibly he is a little unbalanced.'

'I can't think of any reason why he should call me Hemingway,' the big one said. 'My name ain't Hemingway.'

The older man said: 'I didn't see a gun.'

They looked at Amthor. Amthor said: 'It's inside. I have it. I'll give it to you, Mr Blane.'

The big man leaned down from his hips and bent his knees a little and breathed in my face. 'What for did you call me Hemingway, pally?'

'There are ladies present.'

He straightened up again. 'You see.' He looked at the one with the moustache. The one with the moustache nodded and then turned and walked away, across the room. The sliding door opened. He went in and Amthor followed him.

There was silence. The dark woman looked down at the top of her desk and frowned. The big man looked at my right eyebrow and slowly shook his head from side to side, wonderingly.

The door opened again and the man with the moustache came back. He picked a hat up from somewhere and handed it to me. He took my gun out of his pocket and handed it to me. I knew by the weight it was empty. I tucked it under my arm and stood up.

The big man said: 'Let's go, pally. Away from here. I think maybe a little air will help you to get straightened out.'

'Okey, Hemingway.'

'He's doing that again,' the big man said sadly. 'Calling me Hemingway on account of there are ladies present. Would you think that would be some kind of dirty crack in his book?'

The man with the moustache said, 'Hurry up.'

The big man took me by the arm and we went over to the little elevator. It came up. We got into it.

24

At the bottom of the shaft we got out and walked along the narrow hallway and out of the black door. It was crisp clear air outside, high enough to be above the drift of foggy spray from the ocean. I breathed deeply.

The big man still had hold of my arm. There was a car standing there, a plain dark sedan, with private plates.

The big man opened the front door and complained: 'It ain't really up to your class, pally. But a little air will set you up fine. Would that be all right with you? We wouldn't want to do anything that you wouldn't like us to do, pally.'

'Where's the Indian?'

He shook his head a little and pushed me into the car. I got into the right side of the front seat. 'Oh, yeah, the Indian,' he said. 'You got to shoot him with a bow and arrow. That's the law. We got him in the back of the car.'

I looked in the back of the car. It was empty.

'Hell, he ain't there,' the big one said. 'Somebody must of

glommed him off. You can't leave nothing in a unlocked car any more.'

'Hurry up,' the man with the moustache said, and got into the back seat. Hemingway went around and pushed his hard stomach behind the wheel. He started the car. We turned and drifted off down the driveway lined with wild geraniums. A cold wind lifted off the sea. The stars were too far off. They said nothing.

We reached the bottom of the drive and turned out on to the concrete mountain road and drifted without haste along that.

'How come you don't have a car with you, pally?'

'Amthor sent for me.'

'Why would that be, pally?'

'It must have been he wanted to see me.'

'This guy is good,' Hemingway said. 'He figures things out.'

He spit out of the side of the car and made a turn nicely and let the car ride its motor down the hill. 'He says you called him up on the phone and tried to put the bite on him. So he figures he better have a look-see what kind of guy he is doing business with – if he is doing business. So he sends his own car.'

'On account of he knows he is going to call some cops he knows and I won't need mine to get home with,' I said. 'Okey, Hemingway.'

'Yeah, that again. Okey. Well, he has a dictaphone under his table and his secretary takes it all down and when we come she reads it back to Mister Blane here.'

I turned and looked at Mister Blane. He was smoking a cigar, peacefully, as though he had his slippers on. He didn't look at me.

'Like hell she did,' I said. 'More likely a stock bunch of notes they had all fixed up for a case like that.'

'Maybe you would like to tell us why you wanted to see this guy,' Hemingway suggested politely.

'You mean while I still have part of my face?'

'Aw, we ain't those kind of boys at all,' he said, with a large gesture.

'You know Amthor pretty well, don't you, Hemingway?'

'Mr Blane kind of knows him. Me, I just do what the orders is.'

'Who the hell is Mister Blane?'

'That's the gentleman in the back seat.'

'And besides being in the back seat who the hell is he?'

'Why, Jesus, everybody knows Mr Blane.'

'All right,' I said, suddenly feeling very weary.

There was a little more silence, more curves, more winding ribbons of concrete, more darkness, and more pain.

The big man said: 'Now that we are all between pals and no ladies present we really don't give so much time to why you went back up there, but this Hemingway stuff is what really has me down.'

'A gag,' I said. 'An old, old gag.'

'Who is this Hemingway person at all?'

'A guy that keeps saying the same thing over and over until you begin to believe it must be good.'

'That must take a hell of a long time,' the big man said. 'For a private dick you certainly have a wandering kind of mind. Are you still wearing your own teeth?'

'Yeah, with a few plugs in them.'

'Well, you certainly have been lucky, pally.'

The man in the back seat said: 'This is all right. Turn right at the next.'

'Check.'

Hemingway swung the sedan into a narrow dirt road that edged along the flank of a mountain. We drove along that about a mile. The smell of the sage became overpowering.

'Here,' the man in the back seat said.

Hemingway stopped the car and set the brake. He leaned across me and opened the door.

'Well, it's nice to have met you, pally. But don't come back. Anyways not on business. Out.'

'I walk home from here?'

The man in the back seat said: 'Hurry up.'

'Yeah, you walk home from here, pally. Will that be all right with you?'

'Sure, it will give me time to think a few things out. For instance you boys are not L.A. cops. But one of you is a cop, maybe both of you. I'd say you are Bay City cops. I'm wondering why you were out of your territory.'

'Ain't that going to be kind of hard to prove, pally?'

'Good-night, Hemingway.'

He didn't answer. Neither of them spoke. I started to get out of the car and put my foot on the running board and leaned forward, still a little dizzy.

The man in the back seat made a sudden flashing movement that I sensed rather than saw. A pool of darkness opened at my feet and was far, far deeper than the blackest night.

I dived into it. It had no bottom.

25

The room was full of smoke.

The smoke hung straight up in the air, in thin lines, straight up and down like a curtain of small clear beads. Two windows seemed to be open in an end wall, but the smoke didn't move. I had never seen the room before. There were bars across the windows.

I was dull, without thought. I felt as if I had slept for a year. But the smoke bothered me. I lay on my back and thought about it. After a long time I took a deep breath that hurt my lungs.

I yelled: 'Fire!'

That made me laugh. I didn't know what was funny about it but I began to laugh. I lay there on the bed and laughed. I didn't like the sound of the laugh. It was the laugh of a nut.

The one yell was enough. Steps thumped rapidly outside the room and a key was jammed into a lock and the door swung open. A man jumped in sideways and shut the door after him. His right hand reached towards his hip.

He was a short thick man in a white coat. His eyes had a queer look, black and flat. There were bulbs of grey skin at the outer corners of them.

I turned my head on the hard pillow and yawned.

'Don't count that one, Jack. It slipped out,' I said.

He stood there scowling, his right hand hovering towards his right hip. Greenish malignant face and flat black eyes and grey white skin and nose that seemed just a shell.

'Maybe you want some more strait-jacket,' he sneered.

'I'm fine, Jack. Just fine. Had a long nap. Dreamed a little, I guess. Where am I?'

'Where you belong.'

'Seems like a nice place,' I said. 'Nice people, nice atmosphere. I guess I'll have me a short nap again.'

'Better be just that,' he snarled.

He went out. The door shut. The lock clicked. The steps growled into nothing.

He hadn't done the smoke any good. It still hung there in the middle of the room, all across the room. Like a curtain. It didn't dissolve, didn't float off, didn't move. There was air in the room, and I could feel it on my face. But the smoke couldn't feel it. It was a grey web woven by a thousand spiders. I wondered how they had got them to work together.

Cotton flannel pyjamas. The kind they have in the County Hospital. No front, not a stitch more than is essential. Coarse, rough material. The neck chafed my throat. My throat was still sore. I began to remember things. I reached up and felt the throat muscles. They were still sore. Just one Indian, pop.

Okey, Hemingway. So you want to be a detective? Earn good money. Nine easy lessons. We provide badge. For fifty cents extra we send you a truss.

The throat felt sore but the fingers feeling it didn't feel anything. They might just as well have been a bunch of bananas. I looked at them. They looked like fingers. No good. Mail order fingers. They must have come with the badge and the truss. And the diploma.

It was night. The world outside the windows was a black world. A glass porcelain bowl hung from the middle of the ceiling on three brass chains. There was light in it. It had little coloured lumps around the edge, orange and blue alternately. I stared at them. I was tired of the smoke. As I stared they began to open up like little portholes and heads popped out. Tiny heads, but alive, heads like the heads of small dolls, but alive. There was a man in a yachting cap with a Johnnie Walker nose and a fluffy blonde in a picture hat and a thin man with a crooked bow tie. He looked like a waiter in a beach-town fly-trap. He opened his lips and sneered: 'Would you like your steak rare or medium, sir?'

I closed my eyes tight and winked them hard and when I opened them again it was just a sham porcelain bowl on three brass chains.

But the smoke still hung motionless in the moving air.

I took hold of the corner of a rough sheet and wiped the sweat off my face with the numb fingers the correspondence school had sent me after the nine easy lessons, one half in advance, Box Two Million Four Hundred and Sixty Eight Thousand Nine Hundred and Twenty Four, Cedar City, Iowa. Nuts. Completely nuts.

I sat up on the bed and after a while I could reach the floor with my feet. They were bare and they had pins and needles in them. Notions counter on the left, madam. Extra large safety-pins on the right. The feet began to feel the floor. I stood up. Too far up. I crouched over, breathing hard and held the side of the bed and a voice that seemed to come from under the bed said over and over again: 'You've got the dt's ... you've got the dt's ... you've got the dt's.'

I started to walk, wobbling like a drunk. There was a bottle of whisky on a small white enamel table between the two barred windows. It looked like a good shape. It looked about half full. I walked towards it. There are a lot of nice people in the world, in spite. You can crab over the morning paper and kick the shins of the guy in the next seat at the movies and feel mean and discouraged and sneer at the politicians, but there are a lot of nice people in the world just the same. Take the guy that left that half bottle of whisky there. He had a heart as big as one of Mae West's hips.

I reached it and put both my still half-numb hands down on it and hauled it up to my mouth, sweating as if I was lifting one end of the Golden Gate Bridge.

I took a long untidy drink. I put the bottle down again, with infinite care. I tried to lick underneath my chin.

The whisky had a funny taste. While I was realizing that it had a funny taste I saw a wash-bowl jammed into the corner of the wall. I made it. I just made it. I vomited. Dizzy Dean never threw anything harder.

Time passed – an agony of nausea and staggering and dazedness and clinging to the edge of the bowl and making animal sounds for help.

It passed. I staggered back to the bed and lay down on my back again and lay there panting, watching the smoke. The smoke wasn't quite so clear. Not quite so real. Maybe it was just something back of my eyes. And then quite suddenly it wasn't there at all and the light from the porcelain ceiling fixture etched the room sharply.

I sat up again. There was a heavy wooden chair against the wall near the door. There was another door besides the door the man in the white coat had come in at. A closet door, probably. It might even have my clothes in it. The floor was covered with green and grey linoleum in squares. The walls were painted white. A clean room. The bed on which I sat was a narrow iron hospital bed, lower than they usually are, and there were thick leather straps with buckles attached to the sides, about where a man's wrists and ankles would be.

It was a swell room – to get out of.

I had feeling all over my body now, soreness in my head and throat and in my arm. I couldn't remember about the arm. I rolled up the sleeve of the cotton pyjama thing and looked at it fuzzily. It was covered with pin pricks on the skin all the way from the elbow to the shoulder. Around each was a small discoloured patch, about the size of a quarter.

Dope. I had been shot full of dope to keep me quiet. Perhaps scopolamine too, to make me talk. Too much dope for the time. I was having the French fits coming out of it. Some do, some don't. It all depends how you are put together. Dope.

That accounted for the smoke and the little heads around the edge of the ceiling light and the voices and the screwy thoughts and the straps and bars and the numb fingers and feet. The whisky was probably part of somebody's forty-eight hour liquor cure. They had just left it around so that I wouldn't miss anything.

I stood up and almost hit the opposite wall with my stomach. That made me lie down and breathe very gently for quite a long time. I was tingling all over now and sweating. I could feel little drops of sweat form on my forehead and then slide slowly and carefully down the side of my nose to the corner of my mouth. My tongue licked at them foolishly.

I sat up once more and planted my feet on the floor and stood up.

'Okey, Marlowe,' I said between my teeth. 'You're a tough guy. Six feet of iron man. One hundred and ninety pounds stripped and with your face washed. Hard muscles and no glass jaw. You can take it. You've been sapped down twice, had your throat choked and been beaten half silly on the jaw with a gun barrel. You've been shot full of hop and kept under it until you're as crazy as two waltzing mice. And what does all that amount to? Routine. Now let's see you do something really tough, like putting your pants on.'

I lay down on the bed again.

Time passed again. I don't know how long. I had no watch. They don't make that kind of time in watches anyway.

I sat up. This was getting to be stale. I stood up and started to walk. No fun walking. Makes your heart jump like a nervous cat. Better lie down and go back to sleep. Better take it easy for a while. You're in bad shape, pally. Okey, Hemingway, I'm weak. I couldn't knock over a flower-vase. I couldn't break a fingernail.

Nothing doing. I'm walking. I'm tough. I'm getting out of here.

I lay down on the bed again.

The fourth time was a little better. I got across the room and back twice. I went over to the wash-bowl and rinsed it out and leaned on it and drank water out of the palm of my hand. I kept it down. I waited a little and drank more. Much better.

I walked. I walked. I walked.

Half an hour of walking and my knees were shaking but my head was clear. I drank more water, a lot of water. I almost cried into the bowl while I was drinking it.

I walked back to the bed. It was a lovely bed. It was made of rose-leaves. It was the most beautiful bed in the world. They had got it from Carole Lombard. It was too soft for her. It was worth the rest of my life to lie down in it for two minutes. Beautiful soft bed, beautiful sleep, beautiful eyes closing and lashes falling and the gentle sound of breathing and darkness and rest sunk in deep pillows. ...

I walked.

They built the Pyramids and got tired of them and pulled

them down and ground the stone up to make concrete for Boulder Dam and they built that and brought the water to the Sunny Southland and used it to have a flood with.

I walked all through it. I couldn't be bothered.

I stopped walking. I was ready to talk to somebody.

26

The closet door was locked. The heavy chair was too heavy for me. It was meant to be. I stripped the sheets and pad off the bed and dragged the mattress to one side. There was a mesh spring underneath fastened top and bottom by coil springs of black enamelled metal about nine inches long. I went to work on one of them. It was the hardest work I ever did. Ten minutes later I had two bleeding fingers and a loose spring. I swung it. It had a nice balance. It was heavy. It had a whip to it.

And when this was all done I looked across at the whisky bottle and it would have done just as well, and I had forgotten all about it.

I drank some more water. I rested a little, sitting on the side of the bare springs. Then I went over to the door and put my mouth against the hinge side and yelled:

'Fire! Fire! Fire!'

It was a short wait and a pleasant one. He came running hard along the hallway outside and his key jammed viciously into the lock and twisted hard.

The door jumped open. I was flat against the wall on the opening side. He had the sap out this time, a nice little tool about five inches long, covered with woven brown leather. His eyes popped at the stripped bed and then began to swing around.

I giggled and socked him. I laid the coil spring on the

side of his head and he stumbled forward. I followed him down to his knees. I hit him twice more. He made a moaning sound. I took the sap out of his limp hand. He whined.

I used my knee on his face. It hurt my knee. He didn't tell me whether it hurt his face. While he was still groaning I knocked him cold with the sap.

I got the key from the outside of the door and locked it from the inside and went through him. He had more keys. One of them fitted my closet. In it my clothes hung. I went through my pockets. The money was gone from my wallet. I went back to the man with the white coat. He had too much money for his job. I took what I had started with and heaved him on to the bed and strapped him wrist and ankle and stuffed half a yard of sheet into his mouth. He had a smashed nose. I waited long enough to make sure he could breathe through it.

I was sorry for him. A simple hard-working little guy trying to hold his job down and get his weekly pay cheque. Maybe with a wife and kids. Too bad. And all he had to help him was a sap. It didn't seem fair. I put the doped whisky down where he could reach it, if his hands hadn't been strapped.

I patted his shoulder. I almost cried over him.

All my clothes, even my gun harness and gun, but no shells in the gun, hung in the closet. I dressed with fumbling fingers, yawning a great deal.

The man on the bed rested. I left him there and locked him in.

Outside was a wide silent hallway with three closed doors. No sounds came from behind any of them. A wine-coloured carpet crept down the middle and was as silent as the rest of the house. At the end there was a jog in the hall and then another hall at right angles and the head of a big old-fashioned staircase with white oak bannisters. It curved graciously down into the dim hall below. Two stained-glass inner doors ended the lower hall. It was tessellated and thick rugs lay on it. A crack of light seeped past the edge of an almost closed door. But no sound at all.

An old house, built as once they built them and don't build them any more. Standing probably on a quiet street with a rose arbour at the side and plenty of flowers in front. Gracious and cool and quiet in the bright California sun. And inside it who cares, but don't let them scream too loud.

I had my foot out to go down the stairs when I heard a man cough. That jerked me around and I saw there was a half-open door along the other hallway at the end. I tiptoed along the runner. I waited, close to the partly open door, but not in it. A wedge of light lay at my feet on the carpet. The man coughed again. It was a deep cough, from a deep chest. It sounded peaceful and at ease. It was none of my business. My business was to get out of there. But any man whose door could be open in that house interested me. He would be a man of position, worth tipping your hat to. I sneaked a little into the wedge of light. A newspaper rustled.

I could see part of a room and it was furnished like a room, not like a cell. There was a dark bureau with a hat on it and some magazines. Windows with lace curtains, a good carpet.

Bed springs creaked heavily. A big guy, like his cough. I reached out fingertips and pushed the door an inch or two. Nothing happened. Nothing ever was slower than my head craning in. I saw the room now, the bed, and the man on it, the ash-tray heaped with stubs that overflowed on to a night table and from that to the carpet. A dozen mangled newspapers all over the bed. One of them in a pair of huge hands before a huge face. I saw the hair above the edge of the green paper. Dark, curly – black even – and plenty of it. A line of white skin under it. The paper moved a little more and I didn't breathe and the man on the bed didn't look up.

He needed a shave. He would always need a shave. I had seen him before, over on Central Avenue, in a negro dive called Florian's. I had seen him in a loud suit with white golf balls on the coat and a whisky sour in his hand. And I had seen him with an Army Colt looking like a toy in his fist, stepping softly through a broken door. I had seen some of his work and it was the kind of work that stays done.

He coughed again and rolled his buttocks on the bed and yawned bitterly and reached sideways for a frayed pack of cigarettes on the night table. One of them went into his mouth. Light flared at the end of his thumb. Smoke came out of his nose.

'Ah,' he said, and the paper went up in front of his face again.

I left him there and went back along the side hall. Mr Moose Malloy seemed to be in very good hands. I went back to the stairs and down.

A voice murmured behind the almost closed door. I waited for the answering voice. None. It was a telephone conversation. I went over close to the door and listened. It was a low voice, a mere murmur. Nothing carried that meant anything. There was finally a dry clicking sound. Silence continued inside the room after that.

This was the time to leave, to go far away. So I pushed the door open and stepped quietly in.

27

It was an office, not small, not large, with a neat professional look. A glass-doored bookcase with heavy books inside. A first aid cabinet on the wall. A white enamel and glass sterilizing cabinet with a lot of hypodermic needles and syringes inside it being cooked. A wide flat desk with a blotter on it, a bronze paper cutter, a pen set, an appointment book, very little else, except the elbows of a man who sat brooding, with his face in his hands.

Between the spread yellow fingers I saw hair the colour of wet brown sand, so smooth that it appeared to be painted on his skull. I took three more steps and his eyes must have looked beyond the desk and seen my shoes move. His head came up and he looked at me. Sunken colourless eyes in a parchment-like face. He unclasped his hands and leaned back slowly and looked at me with no expression at all.

Then he spread his hands with a sort of helpless but disapproving gesture and when they came to rest again, one of them was very close to the corner of the desk.

I took two steps more and showed him the blackjack. His index and second finger still moved towards the corner of the desk.

'The buzzer,' I said, 'won't buy you anything tonight. I put your tough boy to sleep.'

His eyes got sleepy. 'You have been a very sick man, sir. A very sick man. I can't recommend your being up and about yet.'

I said: 'The right hand.' I snapped the blackjack at it. It coiled into itself like a wounded snake.

I went around the desk grinning without there being anything to grin at. He had a gun in the drawer of course. They always have a gun in the drawer and they always get it too late, if they get it at all. I took it out. It was a .38 automatic, a standard model not as good as mine, but I could use its ammunition. There didn't seem to be any in the drawer. I started to break the magazine out of his.

He moved vaguely, his eyes still sunken and sad.

'Maybe you've got another buzzer under the carpet,' I said. 'Maybe it rings in the Chief's office down at headquarters. Don't use it. Just for an hour I'm a very tough guy. Anybody comes in that door is walking into a coffin.'

'There is no buzzer under the carpet,' he said. His voice had the slightest possible foreign accent.

I got his magazine out and my empty one and changed them. I ejected the shell that was in the chamber of his gun and let it lie. I jacked one up into the chamber of mine and went back to the other side of the desk again.

There was a spring lock on the door. I backed towards it and pushed it shut and heard the lock click. There was also a bolt. I turned that.

I went back to the desk and sat in a chair. It took my last ounce of strength.

'Whisky,' I said.

He began to move his hands around.

'Whisky,' I said.

He went to the medicine cabinet and got a flat bottle with a green revenue stamp on it and a glass.

'Two glasses,' I said. 'I tried your whisky once. I damn near hit Catalina Island with it.'

He brought two small glasses and broke the seal and filled the two glasses.

'You first,' I said.

He smiled faintly and raised one of the glasses.

'Your health, sir—what remains of it.' He drank. I drank. I reached for the bottle and stood it near me and waited for the heat to get to my heart. My heart began to pound, but it was back up in my chest again, not hanging on a shoelace.

'I had a nightmare,' I said. 'Silly idea. I dreamed I was tied to a cot and shot full of dope and locked in a barred room. I got very weak. I slept. I had no food. I was a sick man. I was knocked on the head and brought into a place where they did that to me. They took a lot of trouble. I'm not that important.'

He said nothing. He watched me. There was a remote speculation in his eyes, as if he wondered how long I would live.

'I woke up and the room was full of smoke,' I said. 'It was

just a hallucination, irritation of the optic nerve or whatever a guy like you would call it. Instead of pink snakes I had smoke. So I yelled and a toughie in a white coat came in and showed me a blackjack. It took me a long time to get ready to take it away from him. I got his keys and my clothes and even took my money out of his pocket. So here I am. All cured. What were you saying?'

'I made no remark,' he said.

'Remarks want you to make them,' I said. 'They have their tongues hanging out waiting to be said. This thing here——' I waved the blackjack lightly, 'is a persuader. I had to borrow it from a guy.'

'Please give it to me at once,' he said with a smile you would get to love. It was like the executioner's smile when he comes to your cell to measure you for the drop. A little friendly, a little paternal, and a little cautious at the same time. You would get to love it if there was any way you could live long enough.

I dropped the blackjack into his palm, his left palm.

'Now the gun, please,' he said softly. 'You have been a very sick man, Mr Marlowe. I think I shall have to insist that you go back to bed.'

I stared at him.

'I am Dr Sonderborg,' he said, 'and I don't want any nonsense.'

He laid the blackjack down on the desk in front of him. His smile was as stiff as a frozen fish. His long fingers made movements like dying butterflies.

'The gun, please,' he said softly. 'I advise strongly——'

'What time is it, warden?'

He looked mildly surprised. I had my wrist watch on now but it had run down.

'It is almost midnight. Why?'

'What day is it?'

'Why, my dear sir — Sunday evening, of course.'

I steadied myself on the desk and tried to think and held the gun close enough to him so that he might try and grab it.

'That's over forty-eight hours. No wonder I had fits. Who brought me here?'

He stared at me and his left hand began to edge towards the gun. He belonged to the Wandering Hand Society. The girls would have had a time with him.

'Don't make me get tough,' I whined. 'Don't make me lose my beautiful manners and my flawless English. Just tell me how I got here.'

He had courage. He grabbed for the gun. It wasn't where he grabbed. I sat back and put it in my lap.

He reddened and grabbed for the whisky and poured himself another drink and downed it fast. He drew a deep breath and shuddered. He didn't like the taste of liquor. Dopers never do.

'You will be arrested at once, if you leave here,' he said sharply. 'You were properly committed by an officer of the law——'

'Officers of the law can't do it.'

That jarred him, a little. His yellowish face began to work.

'Shake it up and pour it,' I said. 'Who put me in here, why and how? I'm in a wild mood to-night. I want to go dance in the foam. I hear the banshees calling. I haven't shot a man in a week. Speak out, Dr Fell. Pluck the antique viol, let the soft music float.'

'You are suffering from narcotic poisoning,' he said coldly. 'You very nearly died. I had to give you digitalis three times. You fought, you screamed, you had to be restrained.' His words were coming so fast they were leap-frogging themselves. 'If you leave my hospital in this condition, you will get into serious trouble.'

'Did you say you were a doctor – a medical doctor?'

'Certainly. I am Dr Sonderborg, as I told you.'

'You don't scream and fight from narcotic poisoning, doc.

You just lie in a coma. Try again. And skim it. All I want is the cream. Who put me in your private funny house?'

'But——'

'But me no buts. I'll make a sop of you. I'll drown you in a butt of Malmsey wine. I wish I had a butt of Malmsey wine myself to drown in. Shakespeare. He knew his liquor too. Let's have a little of our medicine.' I reached for his glass and poured us a couple more. 'Get on with it, Karloff.'

'The police put you in here.'

'What police?'

'The Bay City police naturally.' His restless yellow fingers twisted his glass. 'This is Bay City.'

'Oh. Did this police have a name?'

'A Sergeant Galbraith, I believe. Not a regular patrol car officer. He and another officer found you wandering outside the house in a dazed condition on Friday night. They brought you in because this place was close. I thought you were an addict who had taken an overdose. But perhaps I was wrong.'

'It's a good story. I couldn't prove it wrong. But why keep me here?'

He spread his restless hands. 'I have told you again and again that you were a very sick man and still are. What would you expect me to do?'

'I must owe you some money then.'

He shrugged. 'Naturally. Two hundred dollars.'

I pushed my chair back a little. 'Dirt cheap. Try and get it.'

'If you leave here,' he said sharply, 'you will be arrested at once.'

I leaned back over the desk and breathed in his face. 'Not just for going out of here, Karloff. Open that wall safe.'

He stood up in a smooth lunge. 'This has gone quite far enough.'

'You won't open it?'

'I most certainly will not open it.'

'This is a gun I'm holding.'

He smiled, narrowly and bitterly.

'It's an awful big safe.' I said. 'New too. This is a fine gun. You won't open it?'

Nothing changed in his face.

'Damn it,' I said. 'When you have a gun in your hand, people are supposed to do anything you tell them to. It doesn't work, does it?'

He smiled. His smile held a sadistic pleasure. I was slipping back. I was going to collapse.

I staggered at the desk and he waited, his lips parted softly.

I stood leaning there for a long moment, staring into his eyes. Then I grinned. The smile fell off his face like a soiled rag. Sweat stood out on his forehead.

'So long,' I said. 'I leave you to dirtier hands than mine.'

I backed to the door and opened it and went out.

The front doors were unlocked. There was a roofed porch. The garden hummed with flowers. There was a white picket fence and a gate. The house was on a corner. It was a cool, moist night, no moon.

The sign on the corner said Descanso Street. Houses were lighted down the block. I listened for sirens. None came. The other sign said Twenty-third Street. I ploughed over to Twenty-fifth Street and started towards the eight-hundred block. No. 819 was Anne Riordan's number. Sanctuary.

I had walked a long time before I realized that I was still holding the gun in my hand. And I had heard no sirens.

I kept on walking. The air did me good, but the whisky was dying, and it writhed as it died. The block had fir trees along it, and brick houses, and looked like a house on Capitol Hill in Seattle more than Southern California.

There was a light still in No. 819. It had a white porte-cochere, very tiny, pressed against a tall cypress hedge. There were rose bushes in front of the house. I went up the walk. I listened before I pushed the bell. Still no sirens wailing. The bell chimed and after a little while a voice croaked through one of those electrical contraptions that let you talk with your front door locked.

'What is it, please?'

'Marlowe.'

Maybe her breath caught, maybe the electrical thing just made that sound being shut off.

The door opened wide and Miss Anne Riordan stood there in a pale green slack suit looking at me. Her eyes went wide and scared. Her face under the glare of the porchlight was suddenly pale.

'My God,' she wailed. 'You look like Hamlet's father!'

28

The living-room had a tan figured rug, white and rose chairs, a black marble fireplace with very tall brass andirons, high bookcases built back into the walls, and rough cream drapes against the lowered venetian blinds.

There was nothing womanish in the room except a full-length mirror with a clear sweep of floor in front of it.

I was half-sitting and half-lying in a deep chair with my legs on a footstool. I had had two cups of black coffee, then I had had a drink, then I had had two soft-boiled eggs and a slice of toast broken into them, then some more black coffee with brandy laced in it. I had had all this in the breakfast room, but I couldn't remember what it looked like any more. It was too long ago.

I was in good shape again. I was almost sober and my stomach was bunting towards third base instead of trying for the centre-field flagpole.

Anne Riordan sat opposite me, leaning forward, her neat chin cupped in her neat hand, her eyes dark and shadowy under the fluffed out reddish-brown hair. There was a pencil stuck through her hair. She looked worried. I had told her some of it, but not all. Especially about Moose Malloy I had not told her.

'I thought you were drunk,' she said. 'I thought you had to be drunk before you came to see me. I thought you had been out with that blonde. I thought – I don't know what I thought.'

'I bet you didn't get all this writing,' I said, looking around. 'Not even if you got paid for what you thought you thought.'

'And my dad didn't get it grafting on the cops either,' she said. 'Like that fat slob they have for chief of police nowadays.'

'It's none of my business,' I said.

She said: 'We had some lots at Del Rey. Just sand lots they suckered him for. And they turned out to be oil lots.'

I nodded and drank out of the nice crystal glass I was holding. What was in it had a nice warm taste.

'A fellow could settle down here,' I said. 'Move right in. Everything set for him.'

'If he was that kind of fellow. And anybody wanted him to,' she said.

'No butler,' I said. 'That makes it tough.'

She flushed. 'But you – you'd rather get your head beaten to a pulp and your arm riddled with dope needles and your chin used for a backboard in a basketball game. God knows there's enough of it.'

I didn't say anything. I was too tired.

'At least,' she said, 'you had the brains to look in those mouthpieces. The way you talked over on Aster Drive I thought you had missed the whole thing.'

'Those cards don't mean anything.'

Her eyes snapped at me. 'You sit there and tell me that after the man had you beaten up by a couple of crooked policemen and thrown in a two-day liquor cure to teach you to mind your own business? Why the thing stands out so far you could break off a yard of it and still have enough left for a baseball bat.'

'I ought to have said that one,' I said. 'Just my style. Crude. What sticks out?'

'That this elegant psychic person is nothing but a high-class mobster. He picks the prospects and milks the minds and then tells the rough boys to go out and get the jewels.'

'You really think that?'

She stared at me. I finished my glass and got my weak look on my face again. She ignored it.

'Of course I think it,' she said. 'And so do you.'

'I think it's a little more complicated than that.'

Her smile was cosy and acid at the same time. 'I beg your pardon. I forgot for the moment you were a detective. It *would* have to be complicated, wouldn't it? I suppose there's a sort of indecency about a simple case.'

'It's more complicated than that,' I said.

'All right. I'm listening.'

'I don't know. I just think so. Can I have one more drink?'

She stood up. 'You know, you'll have to taste water sometime, just for the hell of it.' She came over and took my glass. 'This is going to be the last.' She went out of the room and somewhere ice cubes tinkled and I closed my eyes and listened to the small unimportant sounds. I had no business coming here. If they knew as much about me as I suspected, they might come here looking. That would be a mess.

She came back with the glass and her fingers cold from holding the cold glass touched mine and I held them for a moment and then let them go slowly as you let go of a dream when you wake with the sun in your face and you have been in an enchanted valley.

She flushed and went back to her chair and sat down and made a lot of business of arranging herself in it.

She lit a cigarette, watching me drink.

'Amthor's a pretty ruthless sort of lad,' I said. 'But I don't somehow see him as the brain guy of a jewel mob. Perhaps I'm wrong. If he was and he thought I had something on him, I don't think I'd have got out of that dope hospital alive. But he's a man who has things to fear. He didn't get really tough until I began to babble about invisible writing.'

She looked at me evenly. 'Was there some?'

I grinned. 'If there was, I didn't read it.'

'That's a funny way to hide nasty remarks about a person, don't you think? In the mouthpieces of cigarettes. Suppose they were never found.'

'I think the point is that Marriott feared something and that if anything happened to him, the cards *would* be found. The police would go over anything in his pockets with a fine-tooth comb. That's what bothers me. If Amthor's a crook, nothing would have been left to find.'

'You mean if Amthor murdered him – or had him murdered? But what Marriott knew about Amthor may not have had any direct connection with the murder.'

I leaned back and pressed my back into the chair and finished my drink and made believe I was thinking that over. I nodded.

'But the jewel robbery had a connection with the murder. And we're assuming Amthor had a connection with the jewel robbery.'

Her eyes were a little sly. 'I bet you feel awful,' she said. 'Wouldn't you like to go to bed?'

'Here?'

She flushed to the roots of her hair. Her chin stuck out. 'That was the idea. I'm not a child. Who the devil cares what I do or when or how?'

I put my glass aside and stood up. 'One of my rare moments of delicacy is coming over me,' I said. 'Will you drive me to a taxi stand, if you're not too tired?'

'You damned sap,' she said angrily. 'You've been beaten to

a pulp and shot full of God knows how many kinds of narcotics and I suppose all you need is a night's sleep to get up bright and early and start out being a detective again.'

'I thought I'd sleep a little late.'

'You ought to be in a hospital, you damn fool!'

I shuddered. 'Listen,' I said. 'I'm not very clear-headed tonight and I don't think I ought to linger around here too long. I haven't a thing on any of these people that I could prove, but they seem to dislike me. Whatever I might say would be my word against the law, and the law in this town seems to be pretty rotten.'

'It's a nice town,' she said sharply, a little breathlessly. 'You can't judge——'

'Okey, it's a nice town. So is Chicago. You could live there a long time and not see a Tommy-gun. Sure, it's a nice town. It's probably no crookeder than Los Angeles. But you can only buy a piece of a big city. You can buy a town this size all complete, with the original box and tissue paper. That's the difference. And that makes me want out.'

She stood up and pushed her chin at me. 'You'll go to bed now and right here. I have a spare bedroom and you can turn right in and——'

'Promise to lock your door?'

She flushed and bit her lip. 'Sometimes I think you're a world-beater,' she said, 'and sometimes I think you're the worst heel I ever met.'

'On either count would you run me over to where I can get a taxi?'

'You'll stay here,' she snapped. 'You're not fit. You're a sick man.'

'I'm not too sick to have my brain picked,' I said nastily.

She ran out of the room so fast she almost tripped over the two steps from the living-room up to the hall. She came back in nothing flat with a long flannel coat on over her slack suit and no hat and her reddish hair looking as mad as her face.

She opened a side door and threw it away from her, bounced through it and her steps clattered on the driveway. A garage door made a faint sound lifting. A car door opened and slammed shut again. The starter ground and the motor caught and the lights flared past the open French door of the living-room.

I picked my hat out of a chair and switched off a couple of lamps and saw that the French door had a Yale lock. I looked back a moment before I closed the door. It was a nice room. It would be a nice room to wear slippers in.

I shut the door and the little car slid up beside me and I went around behind it to get in.

She drove me all the way home, tight-lipped, angry. She drove like a fury. When I got out in front of my apartment house she said good-night in a frosty voice and swirled the little car in the middle of the street and was gone before I could get my keys out of my pocket.

They locked the lobby door at eleven. I unlocked it and passed into the always musty lobby and along to the stairs and the elevator. I rode up to my floor. Bleak light shone along it. Milk bottles stood in front of service doors. The red fire door loomed at the back. It had an open screen that let in a lazy trickle of air that never quite swept the cooking smell out. I was home in a sleeping world, a world as harmless as a sleep-ing cat.

I unlocked the door of my apartment and went in and sniffed the smell of it, just standing there, against the door for a little while before I put the light on. A homely smell, a smell of dust and tobacco smoke, the smell of a world where men live, and keep on living.

I undressed and went to bed. I had nightmares and woke out of them sweating. But in the morning I was a well man again.

29

I was sitting on the side of my bed in my pyjamas, thinking about getting up, but not yet committed. I didn't feel very well, but I didn't feel as sick as I ought to, not as sick as I would feel if I had a salaried job. My head hurt and felt large and hot and my tongue was dry and had gravel on it and my throat was stiff and my jaw was not untender. But I had had worse mornings.

It was a grey morning with high fog, not yet warm but likely to be. I heaved up off the bed and rubbed the pit of my stomach where it was sore from vomiting. My left foot felt fine. It didn't have an ache in it. So I had to kick the corner of the bed with it.

I was still swearing when there was a sharp tap at the door, the kind of bossy knock that makes you want to open the door two inches, emit the succulent raspberry and slam it again.

I opened it a little wider than two inches. Detective-Lieutenant Randall stood there, in a brown gabardine suit, with a pork-pie lightweight felt on his head, very neat and clean and solemn and with a nasty look in his eye.

He pushed the door lightly and I stepped away from it. He came in and closed it and looked around. 'I've been looking for you for two days,' he said. He didn't look at me. His eyes measured the room.

'I've been sick.'

He walked around with a light springy step, his creamy grey hair shining, his hat under his arm now, his hands in his pockets. He wasn't a very big man for a cop. He took one hand out of his pocket and placed the hat carefully on top of some magazines.

'Not here,' he said.

'In a hospital.'

'Which hospital?'

'A pet hospital.'

He jerked as if I had slapped his face. Dull colour showed behind his skin.

'A little early in the day, isn't it – for that sort of thing?'

I didn't say anything. I lit a cigarette. I took one draw on it and sat down on the bed again, quickly.

'No cure for lads like you, is there?' he said. 'Except to throw you in the sneezer.'

'I've been a sick man and I haven't had my morning coffee. You can't expect a very high grade of wit.'

'I told you not to work on this case.'

'You're not God. You're not even Jesus Christ.' I took another drag on the cigarette. Somewhere down inside me felt raw, but I liked it a little better.

'You'd be amazed how much trouble I could make you.'

'Probably.'

'Do you know why I haven't done it so far?'

'Yeah.'

'Why?' He was leaning over a little, sharp as a terrier, with that stony look in his eyes they all get sooner or later.

'You couldn't find me.'

He leaned back and rocked on his heels. His face shone a little. 'I thought you were going to say something else,' he said. 'And if you said it, I was going to smack you on the button.'

'Twenty million dollars wouldn't scare you. But you might get orders.'

He breathed hard, with his mouth a little open. Very slowly he got a packet of cigarettes out of his pocket and tore the wrapper. His fingers were trembling a little. He put a cigarette between his lips and went over to my magazine table for a match folder. He lit the cigarette carefully, put the match in the ash-tray and not on the floor, and inhaled.

'I gave you some advice over the telephone the other day,' he said. 'Thursday.'

'Friday.'

'Yes – Friday. It didn't take. I can understand why. But I didn't know at that time you had been holding out evidence. I was just recommending a line of action that seemed like a good idea in this case.'

'What evidence?'

He stared at me silently.

'Will you have some coffee?' I asked. 'It might make you human.'

'No.'

'*I* will.' I stood up and started for the kitchenette.

'Sit down,' Randall snapped. 'I'm far from through.'

I kept on going out to the kitchenette, ran some water into the kettle and put it on the stove. I took a drink of cold water from the tap, then another. I came back with a third glass in my hand to stand in the doorway and look at him. He hadn't moved. The veil of his smoke was almost a solid thing to one side of him. He was looking at the floor.

'Why was it wrong to go to Mrs Grayle when she sent for me?' I asked.

'I wasn't talking about that.'

'Yeah, but you were just before.'

'She didn't send for you.' His eyes lifted and had the stony look still. And the flush still dyed his sharp cheekbones. 'You forced yourself on her and talked about scandal and practically blackmailed yourself into a job.'

'Funny. As I remember it, we didn't even talk job. I didn't think there was anything in her story. I mean, anything to get my teeth into. Nowhere to start. And of course I supposed she had already told it to you.'

'She had. That beer joint on Santa Monica is a crook hideout. But that doesn't mean anything. I couldn't get a thing there. The hotel across the street smells too. Nobody we want. Cheap punks.'

'She tell you I forced myself on her?'

He dropped his eyes a little. 'No.'

I grinned. 'Have some coffee?'

'No.'

I went back into the kitchenette and made the coffee and waited for it to drip. Randall followed me out this time and stood in the doorway himself.

'This jewel gang has been working in Hollywood and around for a good ten years to my knowledge,' he said. 'They went too far this time. They killed a man. I think I know why.'

'Well, if it's a gang job and you break it, that will be the first gang murder solved since I lived in the town. And I could name and describe at least a dozen.'

'It's nice of you to say that, Marlowe.'

'Correct me if I'm wrong.'

'Damn it,' he said irritably. 'You're not wrong. There were a couple solved for the record, but they were just rappers. Some punk took it for the high pillow.'

'Yeah. Coffee?'

'If I drink some, will you talk to me decently, man to man, without wise-cracking?'

'I'll try. I don't promise to spill all my ideas.'

'I can do without those,' he said acidly.

'That's a nice suit you're wearing.'

The flush dyed his face again. 'This suit cost twenty-seven-fifty,' he snapped.

'Oh, Christ, a sensitive cop,' I said, and went back to the stove.

'That smells good. How do you make it?'

I poured. 'French drip. Coarse ground coffee. No filter papers.' I got the sugar from the closet and the cream from the refrigerator. We sat down on opposite sides of the nook.

'Was that a gag, about your being sick, in a hospital?'

'No gag. I ran into a little trouble – down in Bay City. They took me in. Not the cooler, a private dope and liquor cure.'

His eyes got distant. 'Bay City, eh? You like it the hard way, don't you, Marlowe?'

'It's not that I like it the hard way. It's that I get it that way. But nothing like this before. I've been sapped twice, the second time by a police officer or a man who looked like one and claimed to be one. I've been beaten with my own gun and choked by a tough Indian. I've been thrown unconscious into this dope hospital and kept there locked up and part of the time probably strapped down. And I couldn't prove any of it, except that I actually do have quite a nice collection of bruises and my left arm has been needled plenty.'

He stared hard at the corner of the table. 'In Bay City,' he said slowly.

'The name's like a song. A song in a dirty bathtub.'

'What were you doing down there?'

'I didn't go down there. These cops took me over the line. I went to see a guy in Stillwood Heights. That's in L.A.'

'A man named Jules Amthor,' he said quietly. 'Why did you swipe those cigarettes?'

I looked into my cup. The damned little fool, 'It looked funny, him – Marriott – having that extra case. With reefers in it. It seems they make them up like Russian cigarettes down in Bay City with hollow mouthpieces and the Romanoff arms and everything.'

He pushed his empty cup at me and I refilled it. His eyes were going over my face line by line, corpuscle by corpuscle, like Sherlock Holmes with his magnifying glass or Thorndyke with his pocket lens.

'You ought to have told me,' he said bitterly. He sipped and wiped his lips with one of those fringed things they give you in apartment houses for napkins. 'But you didn't swipe them. The girl told me.'

'Aw well, hell,' I said. 'A guy never gets to do anything in this country any more. Always women.'

'She likes you,' Randall said, like a polite F.B.I. man in a movie, a little sad, but very manly. 'Her old man was as straight a cop as ever lost a job. She had no business taking those things. She likes you.'

'She's a nice girl. Not my type.'

'You don't like them nice?' He had another cigarette going. The smoke was being fanned away from his face by his hand.

'I like smooth shiny girls, hard-boiled and loaded with sin.'

'They take you to the cleaners,' Randall said indifferently.

'Sure. Where else have I ever been? What do you call this session?'

He smiled his first smile of the day. He probably allowed himself four.

'I'm not getting much out of you,' he said.

'I'll give you a theory, but you are probably way ahead of me on it. This Marriott was a blackmailer of women, because Mrs Grayle just about told me so. But he was something else. He was the finger man for the jewel mob. The society finger, the boy who would cultivate the victims and set the stage. He would cultivate women he could take out, get to know them pretty well. Take this hold-up a week from Thursday. It smells. If Marriott hadn't been driving the car, or hadn't taken Mrs Grayle to the Troc or hadn't gone home the way he did, past that beer parlour, the hold-up couldn't have been brought off.'

'The chauffeur could have been driving,' Randall said reasonably. 'But that wouldn't have changed things much. Chauffeurs are not getting themselves pushed in the face with lead bullets by hold-up men – for ninety a month. But there couldn't be many stick-ups with Marriott alone with women or things would get talked about.'

'The whole point of this kind of racket is that things are

not talked about,' I said. 'In consideration for that the stuff is sold back cheap.'

Randall leaned back and shook his head. 'You'll have to do better than that to interest me. Women talk about anything. It would get around that this Marriott was a kind of tricky guy to go out with.'

'It probably did. That's why they knocked him off.'

Randall stared at me woodenly. His spoon was stirring air in an empty cup. I reached over and he waved the pot aside. 'Go on with that one,' he said.

'They used him up. His usefulness was exhausted. It was about time for him to get talked about a little, as you suggest. But you don't quit in those rackets and you don't get your time. So this last hold-up was just that for him – the last. Look, they really asked very little for the jade considering its value. And Marriott handled the contact. But all the same Marriott was scared. At the last moment he thought he had better not go alone. And he figured a little trick that if anything did happen to him, something on him would point to a man, a man quite ruthless and clever enough to be the brains of that sort of mob, and a man in an unusual position to get information about rich women. It was a childish sort of trick but it did actually work.'

Randall shook his head. 'A gang would have stripped him, perhaps even have taken the body out to sea and dumped it.'

'No. They wanted the job to look amateurish. They wanted to stay in business. They probably have another finger lined up,' I said.

Randall still shook his head. 'The man these cigarettes pointed to is not the type. He has a good racket of his own. I've inquired. What did you think of him?'

His eyes were too blank, much too blank. I said: 'He looked pretty damn deadly to me. And there's no such thing as too much money, is there? And after all his psychic racket is a temporary racket for any one place. He has a vogue and everybody goes to him and after a while the vogue dies down and the business is licking its shoes. That is, if he's a psychic and nothing else. Just like movie stars. Give him five years. He could work it that long. But give him a couple of ways to use the information he must get out of these women and he's going to make a killing.'

'I'll look him up more thoroughly,' Randall said with the blank look. 'But right now I'm more interested in Marriott. Let's go back farther – much farther. To how you got to know him.'

'He just called me up. Picked my name out of the phone book. He said so, at any rate.'

'He had your card.'

I looked surprised. 'Sure. I'd forgotten that.'

'Did you ever wonder why he picked *your* name – ignoring that matter of your short memory?'

I stared at him across the top of my coffee cup. I was beginning to like him. He had a lot behind his vest besides his shirt.

'So that's what you really came up for?' I said.

He nodded. 'The rest, you know, is just talk.' He smiled politely at me and waited.

I poured some more coffee.

Randall leaned over sideways and looked along the cream-coloured surface of the table. 'A little dust,' he said absently, then straightened up and looked me in the eye. 'Perhaps I ought to go at this in a little different way,' he said. 'For instance, I think your hunch about Marriott is probably right. There's twenty-three grand in currency in his safe-deposit box – which we had a hell of a time to locate, by the way. There are also some pretty fair bonds and a trust deed to a property on West Fifty-fourth Place.'

He picked a spoon up and rapped it lightly on the edge of his saucer and smiled. 'That interest you?' he asked mildly. 'The number was 1644 West Fifty-fourth Place.'

'Yeah,' I said thickly.

'Oh, there was quite a bit of jewellery in Marriott's box too – pretty good stuff. But I don't think he stole it. I think it was very likely given to him. That's one up for you. He was afraid to sell it – on account of the association of thought in his own mind.'

I nodded. 'He'd feel as if it was stolen.'

'Yes. Now that trust deed didn't interest me at all at first, but here's how it works. It's what you fellows are up against in police work. We get all the homicide and doubtful death reports from outlying districts. We're supposed to read them the same day. That's a rule, like you shouldn't search without a warrant or frisk a guy for a gun without reasonable grounds. But we break rules. We have to. I didn't get around to some of the reports until this morning. Then I read one about a killing of a negro on Central, last Thursday. By a tough ex-con. called Moose Malloy. And there was an identifying witness. And sink my putt, if you weren't the witness.'

He smiled, softly, his third smile. 'Like it?'

'I'm listening.'

'This was only this morning, understand. So I looked at the name of the man making the report and I knew him, Nulty. So I knew the case was a flop. Nulty is the kind of guy – well, were you ever up at Crestline?'

'Yeah.'

'Well, up near Crestline there's a place where a bunch of old box cars have been made into cabins. I have a cabin up there myself, but not a box car. These box cars were brought up on trucks, believe it or not, and there they stand without any wheels. Now Nulty is the kind of guy who would make a swell brakeman on one of those box cars.'

'That's not nice,' I said. 'A fellow officer.'

'So I called Nulty up and he hemmed and hawed around and spit a few times and then he said you had an idea about some girl called Velma something or other that Malloy was sweet on a long time ago and you went to see the widow of the guy that used to own the dive where the killing happened when it was a white joint, and where Malloy and the girl both worked at that time. And her address was 1644 West Fifty-fourth Place, the place Marriott had the trust deed on.'

'Yes?'

'So I just thought that was enough coincidence for one morning,' Randall said. 'And here I am. And so far I've been pretty nice about it.'

'The trouble is,' I said, 'it looks like more than it is. This Velma girl is dead, according to Mrs Florian. I have her photo.'

I went into the living-room and reached into my suit-coat and my hand was in mid-air when it began to feel funny and empty. But they hadn't even taken the photos. I got them out and took them to the kitchen and tossed the Pierrot girl down in front of Randall. He studied it carefully.

'Nobody I ever saw,' he said. 'That another one?'

'No, this is a newspaper still of Mrs Grayle. Anne Riordan got it.'

He looked at it and nodded. 'For twenty million, I'd marry her myself.'

'There's something I ought to tell you,' I said. 'Last night I was so damn mad I had crazy ideas about going down there and trying to bust it alone. This hospital is at Twenty-third and Descanso in Bay City. It's run by a man named Sonderborg who says he's a doctor. He's running a crook hideout on the side. I saw Moose Malloy there last night. In a room.'

Randall sat very still, looking at me. 'Sure?'

'You couldn't mistake him. He's a big guy, enormous. He doesn't look like anybody you ever saw.'

He sat looking at me, without moving. Then very slowly he moved out from under the table and stood up.

'Let's go see this Florian woman.'

'How about Malloy?'

He sat down again. 'Tell me the whole thing, carefully.'

I told him. He listened without taking his eyes off my face.

I don't think he even winked. He breathed with his mouth slightly open. His body didn't move. His fingers tapped gently on the edge of the table. When I had finished he said:

'This Dr Sonderborg – what did he look like?'

'Like a doper, and probably a dope peddler.' I described him to Randall as well as I could.

He went quietly into the other room and sat down at the telephone. He dialled his number and spoke quietly for a long time. Then he came back. I had just finished making more coffee and boiling a couple of eggs and making two slices of toast and buttering them. I sat down to eat.

Randall sat down opposite me and leaned his chin in his hand. 'I'm having a state narcotics man go down there with a fake complaint and ask to look around. He may get some ideas. He won't get Malloy. Malloy was out of there ten minutes after you left last night. That's one thing you can bet on.'

'Why not the Bay City cops?' I put salt on my eggs.

Randall said nothing. When I looked up at him his face was red and uncomfortable.

'For a cop,' I said, 'you're the most sensitive guy I ever met.'

'Hurry up with that eating. We have to go.'

'I have to shower and shave and dress after this.'

'Couldn't you just go in your pyjamas?' he asked acidly.

'So the town is as crooked as all that?' I said.

'It's Laird Brunette's town. They say he put up thirty grand to elect a mayor.'

'The fellow that owns the Belvedere Club?'

'And the two gambling boats.'

'But it's in our county,' I said.

He looked down at his clean, shiny fingernails.

'We'll stop by your office and get those other two reefers,' he said. 'If they're still there.' He snapped his fingers. 'If you'll lend me your keys, I'll do it while you get shaved and dressed.'

'We'll go together,' I said. 'I might have some mail.'

He nodded and after a moment sat down and lit another cigarette. I shaved and dressed and we left in Randall's car.

I had some mail, but it wasn't worth reading. The two cut up cigarettes in the desk drawer had not been touched. The office had no look of having been searched.

Randall took the two Russian cigarettes and sniffed at the tobacco and put them away in his pocket.

'He got one card from you,' he mused. 'There couldn't have been anything on the back of that, so he didn't bother about the others. I guess Amthor is not very much afraid – just thought you were trying to pull something. Let's go.'

30

Old Nosey poked her nose an inch outside the front door, sniffed carefully as if there might be an early violet blooming, looked up and down the street with a raking glance, and nodded her white head. Randall and I took our hats off. In that neighbourhood that probably ranked you with Valentino. She seemed to remember me.

'Good morning, Mrs Morrison,' I said. 'Can we step inside a minute? This is Lieutenant Randall from Headquarters.'

'Land's sakes, I'm all flustered. I got a big ironing to do,' she said.

'We won't keep you a minute.'

She stood back from the door and we slipped past her into her hallway with the side piece from Mason City or wherever it was and from that into the neat living-room with the lace curtains at the windows. A smell of ironing came from the back of the house. She shut the door in between as carefully as if it was made of short pie crust.

She had a blue and white apron on this morning. Her eyes were just as sharp and her chin hadn't grown any.

She parked herself about a foot from me and pushed her face forward and looked into my eyes.

'She didn't get it.'

I looked wise. I nodded my head and looked at Randall and Randall nodded his head. He went to a window and looked at the side of Mrs Florian's house. He came back softly, holding his pork pie under his arm, debonair as a French count in a college play.

'She didn't get it,' I said.

'Nope, she didn't. Saturday was the first. April Fool's Day. He! He?' She stopped and was about to wipe her eyes with her apron when she remembered it was a rubber apron. That soured her a little. Her mouth got the pruny look.

'When the mailman come by and he didn't go up her walk she run out and called to him. He shook his head and went on. She went back in. She slammed the door so hard I figured a window'd break. Like she was mad.'

'I swan,' I said.

Old Nosey said to Randall sharply: 'Let me see your badge, young man. This young man had a whisky breath on him t'other day. I ain't never rightly trusted him.'

Randall took a gold and blue enamel badge out of his pocket and showed it to her.

'Looks like real police all right,' she admitted. 'Well, ain't nothing happened over Sunday. She went out for liquor. Come back with two square bottles.'

'Gin,' I said. 'That just gives you an idea. Nice folks don't drink gin.'

'Nice folks don't drink no liquor at all,' Old Nosey said pointedly.

'Yeah,' I said. 'Come Monday, that being to-day, and the mailman went by again. This time she was really sore.'

'Kind of smart guesser, ain't you, young man? Can't wait for folks to get their mouth open hardly.'

'I'm sorry, Mrs Morrison. This is an important matter to us——'

'This here young man don't seem to have no trouble keepin' his mouth in place.'

'He's married,' I said. 'He's had practice.'

Her face turned a shade of violet that reminded me, unpleasantly, of cyanosis. 'Get out of my house afore I call the police!' she shouted.

'There is a police officer standing before you, madam,' Randall said shortly. 'You are in no danger.'

'That's right there is,' she admitted. The violet tint began to fade from her face. 'I don't take to this man.'

'You have company, madam. Mrs Florian didn't get her registered letter to-day either — is that it?'

'No.' Her voice was sharp and short. Her eyes were furtive. She began to talk rapidly, too rapidly. 'People was there last night. I didn't even see them. Folks took me to the picture show. Just as we got back – no, just after they driven off – a car went away from next door. Fast without any lights. I didn't see the number.'

She gave me a sharp sidelong look from her furtive eyes. I wondered why they were furtive. I wandered to the window and lifted the lace curtain. An official blue-grey uniform was nearing the house. The man wearing it wore a heavy leather bag over his shoulder and had a vizored cap.

I turned away from the window, grinning.

'You're slipping,' I told her rudely. 'You'll be playing shortstop in a Class C league next year.'

'That's not smart,' Randall said coldly.

'Take a look out of the window.'

He did and his face hardened. He stood quite still looking at Mrs Morrison. He was waiting for something, a sound like nothing else on earth. It came in a moment.

It was the sound of something being pushed into the front door mail slot. It might have been a handbill, but it wasn't. There were steps going back down the walk, then along the street, and Randall went to the window again. The mailman didn't stop at Mrs Florian's house. He went on, his blue-grey back even and calm under the heavy leather pouch.

Randall turned his head and asked with deadly politeness: 'How many mail deliveries a morning are there in this district, Mrs Morrison?'

She tried to face it out. 'Just the one,' she said sharply – 'one mornings and one afternoons.'

Her eyes darted this way and that. The rabbit chin was trembling on the edge of something. Her hands clutched at the rubber frill that bordered the blue and white apron.

'The morning delivery just went by,' Randall said dreamily. 'Registered mail comes by the regular mailman?'

'She always got it Special Delivery,' the old voice cracked.

'Oh. But on Saturday she ran out and spoke to the mailman when he didn't stop at her house. And you said nothing about Special Delivery.'

It was nice to watch him working – on somebody else.

Her mouth opened wide and her teeth had the nice shiny look that comes from standing all night in a glass of solution. Then suddenly she made a squawking noise and threw the apron over her head and ran out of the room.

He watched the door through which she had gone. It was beyond the arch. He smiled. It was a rather tired smile.

'Neat, and not a bit gaudy,' I said. 'Next time you play the tough part. I don't like being rough with old ladies – even if they are lying gossips.'

He went on smiling. 'Same old story.' He shrugged. 'Police work. Phooey. She started with facts, as she knew facts. But they didn't come fast enough or seem exciting enough. So she tried a little lily-gilding.'

He turned and we went out into the hall. A faint noise of

sobbing came from the back of the house. For some patient man, long dead, that had been the weapon of final defeat, probably. To me it was just an old woman sobbing, but nothing to be pleased about.

We went quietly out of the house, shut the front door quietly and made sure that the screen door didn't bang. Randall put his hat on and sighed. Then he shrugged, spreading his cool well-kept hands out far from his body. There was a thin sound of sobbing still audible, back in the house.

The mailman's back was two houses down the street.

'Police work,' Randall said quietly, under his breath, and twisted his mouth.

We walked across the space to the next house. Mrs Florian hadn't even taken the wash in. It still jittered, stiff and yellowish on the wire line in the side yard. We went up on the steps and rang the bell. No answer. We knocked. No answer.

'It was unlocked last time,' I said.

He tried the door, carefully screening the movement with his body. It was locked this time. We went down off the porch and walked around the house on the side away from Old Nosey. The back porch had a hooked screen. Randall knocked on that. Nothing happened. He came back off the two almost paintless wooden steps and went along the disused and overgrown driveway and opened up a wooden garage. The doors creaked. The garage was full of nothing. There were a few battered old-fashioned trunks not worth breaking up for firewood. Rusted gardening tools, old cans, plenty of those, in cartons. On each side of the doors, in the angle of the wall a nice fat black widow spider sat in its casual untidy web. Randall picked up a piece of wood and killed them absently. He shut the garage up again, walked back along the weedy drive to the front and up the steps of the house on the other side from Old Nosey. Nobody answered his ring or knock.

He came back slowly, looking across the street over his shoulder.

'Back door's easiest,' he said. 'The old hen next door won't do anything about it now. She's done too much lying.'

He went up the two back steps and slid a knife blade neatly into the crack of the door and lifted the hook. That put us in the screen porch. It was full of cans and some of the cans were full of flies.

'Jesus, what a way to live!' he said.

The back door was easy. A five-cent skeleton key turned the lock. But there was a bolt.

'This jars me,' I said. 'I guess she's beat it. She wouldn't lock up like this. She's too sloppy.'

'Your hat's older than mine,' Randall said. He looked at the glass panel in the back door. 'Lend it to me to push the glass in. Or shall we do a neat job?'

'Kick it in. Who cares around here?'

'Here goes.'

He stepped back and lunged at the lock with his leg parallel to the floor. Something cracked idly and the door gave a few inches. We heaved it open and picked a piece of jagged cast metal off the linoleum and laid it politely on the woodstone drainboard, beside about nine empty gin bottles.

Flies buzzed against the closed windows of the kitchen. The place reeked. Randall stood in the middle of the floor, giving it the careful eye.

Then he walked softly through the swing door without touching it except low down with his toe and using that to push it far enough back so that it stayed open. The living-room was much as I had remembered it. The radio was off.

'That's a nice radio,' Randall said. 'Cost money. If it's paid for. Here's something.'

He went down on one knee and looked along the carpet. Then he went to the side of the radio and moved a loose cord with his foot. The plug came into view. He bent and studied the knobs on the radio front.

'Yeah,' he said. 'Smooth and rather large. Pretty smart, that. You don't get prints on a light cord, do you?'

'Shove it in and see if it's turned on.'

He reached around and shoved it into the plug in the baseboard. The light went on at once. We waited. The thing hummed for a while and then suddenly a heavy volume of sound began to pour out of the speaker. Randall jumped at the cord and yanked it loose again. The sound was snapped off sharp.

When he straightened his eyes were full of light.

We went swiftly into the bedroom. Mrs Jessie Pierce Florian lay diagonally across her bed, in a rumpled cotton house dress, with her head close to one end of the footboard. The corner post of the bed was smeared darkly with something the flies liked.

She had been dead long enough.

Randall didn't touch her. He stared down at her for a long time and then looked at me with a wolfish baring of his teeth.

'Brains on her face,' he said. 'That seems to be the theme song of this case. Only this was done with just a pair of hands. But Jesus, what a pair of hands. Look at the neck bruises, the spacing of the finger marks.'

'You look at them,' I said. I turned away. 'Poor old Nulty. It's not just a shine killing any more.'

31

A shiny black bug with a pink head and pink spots on it crawled slowly along the polished top of Randall's desk and waved a couple of feelers around, as if testing the breeze for a take-off. It wobbled a little as it crawled, like an old woman carrying too many parcels. A nameless dick sat at another desk and kept talking into an old-fashioned hushaphone telephone mouthpiece, so that his voice sounded like someone whispering in a tunnel. He talked with his eyes half closed, a big scarred hand on the desk in front of him holding a burning cigarette between the knuckles of the first and second fingers.

The bug reached the end of Randall's desk and marched straight off into the air. It fell on its back on the floor, waved a few thin worn legs in the air feebly and then played dead. Nobody cared, so it began waving the legs again and finally struggled over on its face. It trundled slowly off into a corner towards nothing, going nowhere.

The police loudspeaker box on the wall put out a bulletin about a hold-up on San Pedro south of Forty-fourth. The hold-up was a middle-aged man wearing a dark grey suit and grey felt hat. He was last seen running east on Forty-fourth and then dodging between two houses. 'Approach carefully,' the announcer said. 'This suspect is armed with a .32 caliber revolver and has just held up the proprietor of a Greek restaurant at Number 3966 South San Pedro.'

A flat click and the announcer went off the air and another one came on and started to read a hot car list, in a slow monotonous voice that repeated everything twice.

The door opened and Randall came in with a sheaf of letter size typewritten sheets. He walked briskly across the room and sat down across the desk from me and pushed some papers at me.

'Sign four copies,' he said.

I signed four copies.

The pink bug reached a corner of the room and put feelers out for a good spot to take off from. It seemed a little discouraged. It went along the baseboard towards another corner. I lit a cigarette and the dick at the hushaphone abruptly got up and went out of the office.

Randall leaned back in his chair, looking just the same as ever, just as cool, just as smooth, just as ready to be nasty or nice as the occasion required.

'I'm telling you a few things,' he said, 'just so you won't go having any more brainstorms. Just so you won't go masterminding all over the landscape any more. Just so maybe for Christ's sake you will let this one lay.'

I waited.

'No prints in the dump,' he said. 'You know which dump I mean. The cord was jerked to turn the radio off, but she turned it up herself probably. That's pretty obvious. Drunks like loud radios. If you have gloves on to do a killing and you turn up the radio to drown shots or something, you can turn it off the same way. But that wasn't the way it was done. And that woman's neck is broken. She was dead before the guy started to smack her head around. Now why did he start to smack her head around?'

'I'm just listening.'

Randall frowned. 'He probably didn't know he'd broken her neck. He was sore at her,' he said. 'Deduction.' He smiled sourly.

I blew some smoke and waved it away from my face.

'Well, why was he sore at her? There was a grand reward paid the time he was picked up at Florian's for the bank job in Oregon. It was paid to a shyster who is dead since, but the Florians likely got some of it. Malloy may have suspected that. Maybe he actually knew it. And maybe he was just trying to shake it out of her.'

I nodded. It sounded worth a nod. Randall went on:

'He took hold of her neck just once and his fingers didn't slip. If we get him, we might be able to prove by the spacing of the marks that his hands did it. Maybe not. The doc. figures it happened last night, fairly early. Motion picture time, anyway. So far we don't tie Malloy to the house last night, not by any neighbours. But it certainly looks like Malloy.'

'Yeah,' I said. 'Malloy all right. He probably didn't mean to kill her, though. He's just too strong.'

'That won't help him any,' Randall said grimly.

'I suppose not. I just make the point that Malloy does not appear to me to be a killer type. Kill if cornered – but not for pleasure or money – and not women.'

'Is that an important point?' he asked dryly.

'Maybe you know enough to know what's important. And what isn't. I don't.'

He stared at me long enough for a police announcer to have time to put out another bulletin about the hold-up of the Greek restaurant on South San Pedro. The suspect was now in custody. It turned out later that he was a fourteen-year-old Mexican armed with a water-pistol. So much for eye-witnesses.

Randall waited until the announcer stopped and went on:

'We got friendly this morning. Let's stay that way. Go home and lie down and have a good rest. You look pretty peaked. Just let me and the police department handle the Marriott killing and find Moose Malloy and so on.'

'I got paid on the Marriott business,' I said. 'I fell down on the job. Mrs Grayle has hired me. What do you want me to do – retire and live on my fat?'

He stared at me again. 'I know. I'm human. They give you guys licences, which must mean they expect you to do something with them besides hang them on the wall in your office. On the other hand any acting-captain with a grouch can break you.'

'Not with the Grayles behind me.'

He studied it. He hated to admit I could be even half right. So he frowned and tapped his desk.

'Just so we understand each other,' he said after a pause. 'If you crab this case, you'll be in a jam. It may be a jam you can wriggle out of this time. I don't know. But little by little you will build up a body of hostility in this department that will make it damn hard for you to do any work.'

'Every private dick faces that every day of his life – unless he's just a divorce man.'

'You can't work on murders.'

'You've said your piece. I heard you say it. I don't expect to go out and accomplish things a big police department can't accomplish. If I have any small private notions, they are just that – small and private.'

He leaned slowly across the desk. His thin restless fingers tap-tapped, like the poinsettia shoots tapping against Mrs Jessie Florian's front wall. His creamy grey hair shone. His cool steady eyes were on mine.

'Let's go on,' he said. 'With what there is to tell. Amthor's away on a trip. His wife – and secretary – doesn't know or won't say where. The Indian has also disappeared. Will you sign a complaint against these people?'

'No. I couldn't make it stick.'

He looked relieved. 'The wife says she never heard of you. As to these two Bay City cops, if that's what they were – that's out of my hands. I'd rather not have the thing any more complicated than it is. One thing I feel pretty sure of — Amthor had nothing to do with Marriott's death. The cigarettes with his card in them were just a plant.'

'Doc Sonderborg?'

He spread his hands. 'The whole shebang skipped. Men from the D.A.'s office went down there on the quiet. No contact with Bay City at all. The house is locked up and empty. They got in, of course. Some hasty attempt had been made to clean up, but there are prints – plenty of them. It will take a week to work out what we have. There's a wall safe they're working on now. Probably had dope in it – and other things. My guess is that Sonderborg will have a record, not local, somewhere else, for abortion, or treating gunshot wounds or altering finger tips or for illegal use of dope. If it comes under Federal statutes, we'll get a lot of help.'

'He said he was a medical doctor,' I said.

Randall shrugged. 'May have been once. May never have been convicted. There's a guy practising medicine near Palm Springs right now who was indicted as a dope peddler in

Hollywood five years ago. He was as guilty as hell – but the protection worked. He got off. Anything else worrying you?'

'What do you know about Brunette – for telling?'

'Brunette's a gambler. He's making plenty. He's making it an easy way.'

'All right,' I said, and started to get up. 'That sounds reasonable. But it doesn't bring us any nearer to this jewel heist gang that killed Marriott.'

'I can't tell you everything, Marlowe.'

'I don't expect it,' I said. 'By the way, Jessie Florian told me – the second time I saw her – that she had been a servant in Marriott's family once. That was why he was sending her money. Anything to support that?'

'Yes. Letters in his safety-deposit box from her thanking him and saying the same thing.' He looked as if he was going to lose his temper. '*Now* will you for God's sake go home and mind your own business?'

'Nice of him to take such care of the letters, wasn't it?'

He lifted his eyes until their glance rested on the top of my head. Then he lowered the lids until half the iris was covered. He looked at me like that for a long ten seconds. Then he smiled. He was doing an awful lot of smiling that day. Using up a whole week's supply.

'I have a theory about that,' he said. 'It's crazy, but it's human nature. Marriott was by the circumstances of his life a threatened man. All crooks are gamblers, more or less, and all gamblers are superstitious – more or less. I think Jessie Florian was Marriott's lucky piece. As long as he took care of her, nothing would happen to him.'

I turned my head and looked for the pink-headed bug. He had tried two corners of the room now and was moving off disconsolately towards a third. I went over and picked him up in my handkerchief and carried him back to the desk.

'Look,' I said. 'This room is eighteen floors above ground. And this little bug climbs all the way up here just to make a friend. Me. *My* luck piece.' I folded the bug carefully into the soft part of the handkerchief and tucked the handkerchief into my pocket. Randall was pie-eyed. His mouth moved, but nothing came out of it.

'I wonder whose lucky piece Marriott was,' I said.

'Not yours, pal.' His voice was acid – cold acid.

'Perhaps not yours either.' My voice was just a voice. I went out of the room and shut the door.

I rode the express elevator down to the Spring Street entrance and walked out on the front porch of City Hall and down some steps and over to the flower beds. I put the pink bug down carefully behind a bush.

I wondered, in the taxi going home, how long it would take him to make the Homicide Bureau again.

I got my car out of the garage at the back of the apartment house and ate some lunch in Hollywood before I started down to Bay City. It was a beautiful cool sunny afternoon down at the beach. I left Arguello Boulevard at Third Street and drove over to the City Hall.

32

It was a cheap looking building for so prosperous a town. It looked more like something out of the Bible belt. Bums sat unmolested in a long row on the retaining wall that kept the front lawn – now mostly Bermuda grass – from falling into the street. The building was of three stories and had an old belfry at the top, and the bell still hanging in the belfry. They had probably rung it for the volunteer fire brigade back in the good old chaw-and-spit days.

The cracked walk and the front steps led to open double doors in which a knot of obvious city hall fixers hung around waiting for something to happen so they could make something else out of it. They all had the well-fed stomachs, the careful eyes, the nice clothes and the reach-me-down manners. They gave me about four inches to get in.

Inside was a long dark hallway that had been mopped the day McKinley was inaugurated. A wooden sign pointed out the police department Information Desk. A uniformed man dozed behind a pint-sized PBX set into the end of a scarred wooden counter. A plain-clothes man with his coat off and his hog's leg looking like a fire plug against his ribs took one eye off his evening paper, bonged a spittoon ten feet away from him, yawned, and said the Chief's office was upstairs at the back.

The second floor was lighter and cleaner, but that didn't mean that it was clean and light. A door on the ocean side, almost at the end of the hall, was lettered: John Wax, Chief of Police. Enter.

Inside there was a low wooden railing and a uniformed man behind it working a typewriter with two fingers and one thumb. He took my card, yawned, said he would see, and managed to drag himself through a mahogany door marked John Wax, Chief of Police. Private. He came back and held the door in the railing for me.

I went on in and shut the door of the inner office. It was cool and large and had windows on three sides. A stained wood desk was set far back like Mussolini's, so that you had to walk across an expanse of blue carpet to get to it, and while you were doing that you would be getting the beady eye.

I walked to the desk. A tilted embossed sign on it read: John Wax, Chief of Police. I figured I might be able to remember the name. I looked at the man behind the desk. No straw was sticking to his hair.

He was a hammered-down heavyweight, with short pink hair and a pink scalp glistening through it. He had small, hungry, heavy-lidded eyes, as restless as fleas. He wore a suit of fawn-coloured flannel, a coffee-coloured shirt and tie, a diamond ring, a diamond-studded lodge pin in his lapel, and the required three stiff points of handkerchief coming up a little more than the required three inches from his outside breast pocket.

One of his plump hands was holding my card. He read it, turned it over and read the back, which was blank, read the front again, put it down on his desk and laid on it a paperweight in the shape of a bronze monkey, as if he was making sure he wouldn't lose it.

He pushed a pink paw at me. When I gave it back to him, he motioned to a chair.

'Sit down, Mr Marlowe. I see you are in our business more or less. What can I do for you?'

'A little trouble, Chief. You can straighten it out for me in a minute, if you care to.'

'Trouble,' he said softly. 'A little trouble.'

He turned in his chair and crossed his thick legs and gazed thoughtfully towards one of his pairs of windows. That let me seen handspun lisle socks and English brogues that looked as if they had been pickled in port wine. Counting what I couldn't see and not counting his wallet he had half a grand on him. I figured his wife had money.

'Trouble,' he said, still softly, 'is something our little city don't know much about, Mr Marlowe. Our city is small but very, very clean. I look out of my western windows and I see the Pacific Ocean. Nothing cleaner than that, is there?' He didn't mention the two gambling ships that were hull down on the brass waves just beyond the three-mile limit.

Neither did I. 'That's right, Chief,' I said.

He threw his chest a couple of inches farther. 'I look out of my northern windows and I see the busy bustle of Arguello Boulevard and the lovely California foothills, and in the near foreground one of the nicest little business sections a man could want to know. I look out of my southern windows, which I am looking out of right now, and I see the finest yacht harbour in the world, for a small yacht harbour. I don't have no eastern windows, but if I did have, I would see a residential section that would make your mouth water. No, sir, trouble is a thing we don't have a lot of on hand in our little town.'

'I guess I brought mine with me, Chief. Some of it at least. Do you have a man working for you named Galbraith, a plain-clothes sergeant?'

'Why yes, I believe I do,' he said, bringing his eyes around. 'What about him?'

'Do you have a man working for you that goes like this?' I described the other man, the one who said very little, was short, had a moustache and hit me with a blackjack. 'He goes around with Galbraith, very likely. Somebody called him Mister Blane, but that sounded like a phony.'

'Quite on the contrary,' the fat Chief said as stiffly as a fat man can say anything. 'He is my Chief of Detectives. Captain Blane.'

'Could I see these two guys in your office?'

He picked my card up and read it again. He laid it down. He waved a soft glistening hand.

'Not without a better reason than you have given me so far,' he said suavely.

'I didn't think I could, Chief. Do you happen to know of a man named Jules Amthor? He calls himself a psychic adviser. He lives at the top of a hill in Stillwood Heights.'

'No. And Stillwood Heights is not in my territory,' the Chief said. His eyes now were the eyes of a man who has other thoughts.

'That's what makes it funny,' I said. 'You see, I went to call on Mr Amthor in connection with a client of mine. Mr Amthor got the idea I was blackmailing him. Probably guys in his line of business get that idea rather easily. He had a tough Indian bodyguard I couldn't handle. So the Indian held me and Amthor beat me up with my own gun. Then he sent for a couple of cops. They happened to be Galbraith and Mister Blane. Could this interest you at all?'

Chief Wax flapped his hands on his desk top very gently. He folded his eyes almost shut, but not quite. The cool gleam of his eyes shone between the thick lids and it shone straight at me. He sat very still, as if listening. Then he opened his eyes and smiled.

'And what happened then?' he inquired, polite as a bouncer at the Stork Club.

'They went through me, took me away in their car, dumped me out on the side of a mountain and socked me with a sap as I got out.'

He nodded, as if what I had said was the most natural thing in the world. 'And this was in Stillwood Heights,' he said softly.

'Yeah.'

'You know what I think you are?' He leaned a little over the desk, but not far, on account of his stomach being in the way.

'A liar,' I said.

'The door is there,' he said, pointing to it with the little finger of his left hand.

I didn't move. I kept on looking at him. When he started to get mad enough to push his buzzer I said: 'Let's not both make the same mistake. You think I'm a small time private dick trying to push ten times his own weight, trying to make a charge against a police officer that, even if it was true, the officer would take damn good care couldn't be proved. Not at all. I'm not making any complaints. I think the mistake was natural. I want to square myself with Amthor and I want your man Galbraith to help me do it. Mister Blane needn't bother. Galbraith will be enough. And I'm not here without backing. I have important people behind me.'

'How far behind?' the Chief asked and chuckled wittily.

'How far is 862 Aster Drive, where Mr Merwin Lockridge Grayle lives?'

His face changed so completely that it was as if another man sat in his chair. 'Mrs Grayle happens to be my client,' I said.

'Lock the doors,' he said. 'You're a younger man than I am. Turn the bolt knobs. We'll make a friendly start on this thing. You have an honest face, Marlowe.'

I got up and locked the doors. When I got back to the desk along the blue carpet, the Chief had a nice looking bottle out and two glasses. He tossed a handful of cardamom seeds on his blotter and filled both glasses.

We drank. He cracked a few cardamom seeds and we chewed them silently, looking into each other's eyes.

'That tasted right,' he said. He refilled the glasses. It was my turn to crack the cardamom seeds. He swept the shells off his blotter to the floor and smiled and leaned back.

'Now let's have it,' he said. 'Has this job you are doing for Mrs Grayle anything to do with Amthor?'

'There's a connection. Better check that I'm telling you the truth, though.'

'There's that,' he said and reached for his phone. Then he took a small book out of his vest and looked up a number. 'Campaign contributors,' he said and winked. 'The Mayor is very insistent that all courtesies be extended. Yes, here it is.' He put the book away and dialled.

He had the same trouble with the butler that I had. It made his ears get red. Finally he got her. His ears stayed red. She must have been pretty sharp with him.

'She wants to talk to you,' he said and pushed the phone across his broad desk.

'This is Phil,' I said, winking naughtily at the Chief.

There was a cool provocative laugh. 'What are you doing with that fat slob?'

'There's a little drinking being done.'

'Do you have to do it with him?'

'At the moment, yes. Business. I said, is there anything new? I guess you know what I mean.'

'No. Are you aware, my good fellow, that you stood me up for an hour the other night? Did I strike you as the kind of girl that lets that sort of thing happen to her?'

'I ran into trouble. How about to-night?'

'Let me see – to-night is – what day of the week is it for heaven's sake?'

'I'd better call you,' I said. 'I may not be able to make it. This is Friday.'

'Liar.' The soft husky laugh came again. 'It's Monday. Same time, same place – and no fooling this time?'

'I'd better call you.'

'You'd better be there.'

'I can't be sure. Let me call you.'

'Hard to get? I see. Perhaps I'm a fool to bother.'

'As a matter of fact you are.'

'Why?'

'I'm a poor man, but I pay my own way. And it's not quite as soft a way as you would like.'

'Damn you, if you're not there——'

'I said I'd call you.'

She sighed. 'All men are the same.'

'So are all women – after the first nine.'

She damned me and hung up. The Chief's eyes popped so far out of his head they looked as if they were on stilts.

He filled both glasses with a shaking hand and pushed one at me.

'So it's like that,' he said very thoughtfully.

'Her husband doesn't care,' I said, 'so don't make a note of it.'

He looked hurt as he drank his drink. He cracked the cardamom seeds very slowly, very thoughtfully. We drank to each other's baby blue eyes. Regretfully the Chief put the bottle and glasses out of sight and snapped a switch on his call box.

'Have Galbraith come up, if he's in the building. If not, try and get in touch with him for me.'

I got up and unlocked the doors and sat down again. We didn't wait long. The side door was tapped on, the Chief called out, and Hemingway stepped into the room.

He walked solidly over to the desk and stopped at the end of it and looked at Chief Wax with the proper expression of tough humility.

'Meet Mr Philip Marlowe,' the Chief said genially. 'A private dick from L.A.'

Hemingway turned enough to look at me. If he had ever seen me before, nothing in his face showed it. He put a hand out and I put a hand out and he looked at the Chief again.

'Mr Marlowe has a rather curious story,' the Chief said, cunning, like Richelieu behind the arras. 'About a man named Amthor who has a place in Stillwood Heights. He's some sort of crystal-gazer. It seems Marlowe went to see him and you and Blane happened in about the same time and there was an argument of some kind. I forget the details.' He looked out of his windows with the expression of a man forgetting details.

'Some mistake,' Hemingway said. 'I never saw this man before.'

'There was a mistake, as a matter of fact,' the Chief said dreamily. 'Rather trifling, but still a mistake. Mr Marlowe thinks it of slight importance.'

Hemingway looked at me again. His face still looked like a stone face.

'In fact he's not even interested in the mistake,' the Chief dreamed on. 'But he is interested in going to call on this man Amthor who lives in Stillwood Heights. He would like someone with him. I thought of you. He would like someone who would see that he got a square deal. It seems that Mr Amthor has a very tough Indian bodyguard and Mr Marlowe is a little inclined to doubt his ability to handle the situation without help. Do you think you could find out where this Amthor lives?'

'Yeah,' Hemingway said. 'But Stillwood Heights is over the line, Chief. This just a personal favour to a friend of yours?'

'You might put it that way,' the Chief said, looking at his left thumb. 'We wouldn't want to do anything not strictly legal, of course.'

'Yeah,' Hemingway said. 'No.' He coughed. 'When do we go?'

The Chief looked at me benevolently. 'Now would be okey,' I said. 'If it suits Mr Galbraith.'

'I do what I'm told,' Hemingway said.

The Chief looked him over, feature by feature. He combed him and brushed him with his eyes. 'How is Captain Blane to-day?' he inquired, munching on a cardamom seed.

'Bad shape. Bust appendix,' Hemingway said. 'Pretty critical.'

The Chief shook his head sadly. Then he got hold of the arms of his chair and dragged himself to his feet. He pushed a pink paw across his desk.

'Galbraith will take good care of you, Marlowe. You can rely on that.'

'Well, you've certainly been obliging, Chief,' I said. 'I certainly don't know how to thank you.'

'Pshaw! No thanks necessary. Always glad to oblige a friend of a friend, so to speak.' He winked at me. Hemingway studied the wink but he didn't say what he added it up to.

We went out, with the Chief's polite murmurs almost carrying us down the office. The door closed. Hemingway looked up and down the hall and then he looked at me.

'You played that one smart, baby,' he said. 'You must got something we wasn't told about.'

33

The car drifted quietly along a quiet street of homes. Arching pepper trees almost met above it to form a green tunnel. The sun twinkled through their upper branches and their narrow light leaves. A sign at the corner said it was Eighteenth Street.

Hemingway was driving and I sat beside him. He drove very slowly, his face heavy with thought.

'How much you tell him?' he asked, making up his mind.

'I told him you and Blane went over there and took me away and tossed me out of the car and socked me on the back of the head. I didn't tell him the rest.'

'Not about Twenty-third and Descanso, huh?'

'No.'

'Why not?'

'I thought maybe I could get more co-operation from you if I didn't.'

'That's a thought. You really want to go over to Stillwood Heights, or was that just a stall?'

'Just a stall. What I really want is for you to tell me why you put me in that funny-house and why I was kept there?'

Hemingway thought. He thought so hard his cheek muscles made little knots under his greyish skin.

'That Blane,' he said. 'That sawed-off hunk of shin meat. I didn't mean for him to sap you. I didn't mean for you to walk home neither, not really. It was just an act, on account of we are friends with this swami guy and we kind of keep people from bothering him. You'd be surprised what a lot of people would try to bother him.'

'Amazed,' I said.

He turned his head. His grey eyes were lumps of ice. Then he looked ahead again through the dusty windshield and did some more thinking.

'Them old cops get sap-hungry once in a while,' he said. 'They just got to crack a head. Jesus, was I scared. You dropped like a sack of cement. I told Blane plenty. Then we run you over to Sonderborg's place on account of it was a little closer and he was a nice guy and would take care of you.'

'Does Amthor know you took me there?'

'Hell, no. It was our idea.'

'On account of Sonderborg is such a nice guy and he would take care of me. And no kickback. No chance for a doctor to back up a complaint if I made one. Not that a complaint would have much chance in this sweet little town, if I did make it.'

'You going to get tough?' Hemingway asked thoughtfully.

'Not me,' I said. 'And for once in your life neither are you. Because your job is hanging by a thread. You looked in the Chief's eyes and you saw that. I didn't go in there without credentials, not this trip.'

'Okey,' Hemingway said and spat out of the window. 'I didn't have any idea of getting tough in the first place except just the routine big mouth. What next?'

'Is Blane really sick?'

Hemingway nodded, but somehow failed to look sad. 'Sure is. Pain in the gut day before yesterday and it bust on him before they could get his appendix out. He's got a chance – but not too good.'

'We'd certainly hate to lose him,' I said. 'A fellow like that is an asset to any police force.'

Hemingway chewed that one over and spat it out of the car window.

'Okey, next question,' he sighed.

'You told me why you took me to Sonderborg's place. You didn't tell me why he kept me there over forty-eight hours, locked up and shot full of dope.'

Hemingway braked the car softly over beside the curb. He put his large hands on the lower part of the wheel side by side and gently rubbed the thumbs together.

'I wouldn't have an idea,' he said in a far-off voice.

'I had papers on me showing I had a private licence,' I said. 'Keys, some money, a couple of photographs. If he didn't know you boys pretty well, he might think the crack on the head was just a gag to get into his place and look around. But I figure he knows you boys too well for that. So I'm puzzled.'

'Stay puzzled, pally. It's a lot safer.'

'So it is,' I said. 'But there's no satisfaction in it.'

'You got the L.A. law behind you on this?'

'On this what?'

'On this thinking about Sonderborg.'

'Not exactly.'

'That don't mean yes or no.'

'I'm not that important,' I said. 'The L.A. law can come in here any time they feel like it – two-thirds of them anyway. The Sheriff's boys and the D.A.'s boys. I have a friend in the D.A.'s office. I worked there once. His name is Bernie Ohls. He's Chief Investigator.'

'You give it to him?'

'No. I haven't spoken to him in a month.'

'Thinking about giving it to him?'

'Not if it interferes with a job I'm doing.'

'Private job?'

'Yes.'

'Okey, what is it you want?'

'What's Sonderborg's real racket?'

Hemingway took his hands off the wheel and spat out of the window. 'We're on a nice street here, ain't we? Nice homes, nice gardens, nice climate. You hear a lot about crooked cops, or do you?'

'Once in a while,' I said.

'Okey, how many cops do you find living on a street even as good as this, with nice lawns and flowers? I'd know four or five, all vice squad boys. They get all the gravy. Cops like me live in itty-bitty frame houses on the wrong side of town. Want to see where I live?'

'What would it prove?'

'Listen, pally,' the big man said seriously. 'You got me on a string, but it could break. Cops don't go crooked for money. Not always, not even often. They got caught in the system. They get you where they have you do what is told them or else. And the guy that sits back there in the nice big corner office, with the nice suit and the nice liquor breath he thinks chewing on them seeds makes smell like violets, only it don't – he ain't giving the orders either. You get me?'

'What kind of man is the mayor?'

'What kind of guy is a mayor anywhere? A politician. You think he gives the orders? Nuts. You know what's the matter with this country, baby?'

'Too much frozen capital, I heard.'

'A guy can't stay honest if he wants to,' Hemingway said. 'That's what's the matter with this country. He gets chiselled out of his pants if he does. You gotta play the game dirty or you don't eat. A lot of bastards think all we need is ninety thousand F.B.I. men in clean collars and brief cases. Nuts. The percentage would get them just the way it does the rest of us. You know what I think? I think we gotta make this little world all over again. Now take Moral Rearmament. There you've got something. M.R.A. There you've got something, baby.'

'If Bay City is a sample of how it works, I'll take aspirin,' I said.

'You could get too smart,' Hemingway said softly. 'You might not think it, but it could be. You could get so smart you couldn't think about anything but bein' smart. Me, I'm just a dumb cop. I take orders. I got a wife and two kids and I do what the big shots say. Blane could tell you things. Me, I'm ignorant.'

'Sure Blane has appendicitis? Sure he didn't just shoot himself in the stomach for meanness?'

'Don't be that way,' Hemingway complained and slapped his hands up and down on the wheel. 'Try and think nice about people.'

'About Blane?'

'He's human – just like the rest of us,' Hemingway said. 'He's a sinner – but he's human.'

'What's Sonderborg's racket?'

'Okey, I was just telling you. Maybe I'm wrong. I had you figured for a guy that could be sold a nice idea.'

'You don't know what his racket is,' I said.

Hemingway took his handkerchief out and wiped his face with it. 'Buddy, I hate to admit it,' he said. 'But you ought to know damn well that if I knew or Blane knew Sonderborg had a racket, either we wouldn't of dumped you in there or you wouldn't ever have come out, not walking. I'm talking about a real bad racket, naturally. Not fluff stuff like telling old women's fortunes out of a crystal ball.'

'I don't think I was meant to come out walking,' I said. 'There's a drug called scopolamine, truth serum, that sometimes makes people talk without their knowing it. It's not sure fire, any more than hypnotism is. But it sometimes works. I think I was being milked in there to find out what I knew. But there are only three ways Sonderborg could have known that there was anything for me to know that might hurt him. Amthor might have told him, or Moose Malloy might have mentioned to him that I went to see Jessie Florian, or he might have thought putting me in there was a police gag.'

Hemingway stared at me sadly. 'I can't even see your dust,' he said. 'Who the hell is Moose Malloy?'

'A big hunk that killed a man over on Central Avenue a few days ago. He's on your teletype, if you ever read it. And you probably have a reader of him by now.'

'So what?'

'So Sonderborg was hiding him. I saw him there, on a bed reading newspapers, the night I snuck out.'

'How'd you get out? Wasn't you locked in?'

'I crocked the orderly with a bed spring. I was lucky.'

'This big guy see you?'

'No.'

Hemingway kicked the car away from the curb and a solid grin settled on his face. 'Let's go collect,' he said. 'It figures. It figures swell. Sonderborg was hiding hot boys. If they had dough, that is. His set-up was perfect for it. Good money, too.'

He kicked the car into motion and whirled around a corner.

'Hell, I thought he sold reefers,' he said disgustedly. 'With the right protection behind him. But hell, that's a small time racket. A peanut grift.'

'Ever hear of the numbers racket? That's a small time racket too – if you're just looking at one piece of it.'

Hemingway turned another corner sharply and shook his heavy head. 'Right. And pin ball games and bingo houses and horse parlours. But add them all up and give one guy control and it makes sense.'

'What guy?'

He went wooden on me again. His mouth shut hard and I could see his teeth were biting at each other inside it. We were on Descanso Street and going east. It was a quiet street even in late afternoon. As we got towards Twenty-third, it became in some vague manner less quiet. Two men were studying a palm tree as if figuring out how to move it. A car was parked near Dr Sonderborg's place, but nothing showed in it. Half-way down the block a man was reading water meters.

The house was a cheerful spot by daylight. Tea rose begonias made a solid pale mass under the front windows and pansies a blur of colour around the base of a white acacia in bloom. A scarlet climbing rose was just opening its buds on a fan-shaped trellis. There was a bed of winter sweet peas and a bronze-green humming bird prodding in them delicately. The house looked like the home of a well-to-do elderly couple who liked to garden. The late afternoon sun on it had a hushed and menacing stillness.

Hemingway slid slowly past the house and a tight little smile tugged at the corners of his mouth. His nose sniffed. He turned the next corner, and looked in his rear view mirror and stepped up the speed of the car.

After three blocks he braked at the side of the street again and turned to give me a hard level stare.

'L.A. law,' he said. 'One of the guys by the palm tree is called Donnelly. I know him. They got the house covered. So you didn't tell your pal uptown, huh?'

'I said I didn't.'

'The Chief'll love this,' Hemingway snarled. 'They come down here and raid a joint and don't even stop by to say hello.'

I said nothing.

'They catch this Moose Malloy?'

I shook my head. 'Not so far as I know.'

'How the hell far do you know, buddy?' he asked very softly.

'Not far enough. Is there any connection between Amthor and Sonderborg?'

'Not that I know of.'

'Who runs this town?'

Silence.

'I heard a gambler named Laird Brunette put up thirty grand to elect the mayor. I heard he owns the Belvedere Club and both the gambling ships out on the water.'

'Might be,' Hemingway said politely.

'Where can Brunette be found?'

'Why ask me, baby?'

'Where would you make for if you lost your hideout in this town?'

'Mexico.'

I laughed. 'Okey, will you do me a big favour?'

'Glad to.'

'Drive me back downtown.'

He started the car away from the curb and tooled it neatly along a shadowed street towards the ocean. The car reached the city hall and slid around into the police parking zone and I got out.

'Come round and see me some time,' Hemingway said. 'I'll likely be cleaning spittoons.'

He put his big hand out. 'No hard feelings?'

'M.R.A.' I said and shook the hand.

He grinned all over. He called me back when I started to walk away. He looked carefully in all directions and leaned his mouth close to my ear.

'Them gambling ships are supposed to be out beyond city and state jurisdiction,' he said. 'Panama registry. If it was me that was——' he stopped dead, and his bleak eyes began to worry.

'I get it,' I said. 'I had the same sort of idea. I don't know why I bothered so much to get you to have it with me. But it wouldn't work – not for just one man.'

He nodded, and then he smiled. 'M.R.A.' he said.

34

I lay on my back on a bed in a waterfront hotel and waited for it to get dark. It was a small front room with a hard bed and a mattress slightly thicker than the cotton blanket that covered it. A spring underneath me was broken and stuck into the left side of my back. I lay there and let it prod me.

The reflection of a red neon light glared on the ceiling. When it made the whole room red it would be dark enough to go out. Outside cars honked along the alley they called the Speedway. Feet slithered on the sidewalks below my window. There was a murmur and mutter of coming and going in the air. The air that seeped in through the rusted screens smelled of stale frying fat. Far off a voice of the kind that could be heard far off was shouting: 'Get hungry, folks. Get hungry. Nice hot doggies here. Get hungry.'

It got darker. I thought; and thought in my mind moved with a kind of sluggish stealthiness, as if it was being watched by bitter and sadistic eyes. I thought of dead eyes looking at a moonless sky, with black blood at the corners of the mouths beneath them. I thought of nasty old women beaten to death against the posts of their dirty beds. I thought of a man with bright blond hair who was afraid and didn't quite know what he was afraid of, who was sensitive enough to know that something was wrong, and too vain or too dull to guess what it was that was wrong. I thought of beautiful rich women who could be had. I thought of nice slim curious girls who lived alone and could be had too, in a different way. I thought of cops, tough cops that could be greased and yet were not by any means all bad, like Hemingway. Fat prosperous cops with Chamber of Commerce voices, like Chief Wax. Slim, smart and deadly cops like Randall, who for all their smartness and deadliness were not free to do a clean job in a clean way. I thought of sour old goats like Nulty who had given up trying. I thought of Indians and psychics and dope doctors.

I thought of lots of things. It got darker. The glare of the red neon sign spread farther and farther across the ceiling. I sat up on the bed and put my feet on the floor and rubbed the back of my neck.

I got up on my feet and went over to the bowl in the corner and threw cold water on my face. After a little while I felt a little better, but very little. I needed a drink, I needed a lot of life insurance, I needed a vacation, I needed a home in the country. What I had was a coat, a hat and a gun. I put them on and went out of the room.

There was no elevator. The hallways smelled and the stairs had grimed rails. I went down them, threw the key on the desk and said I was through. A clerk with a wart on his left eyelid nodded and a Mexican bellhop in a frayed uniform coat came forward from behind the dustiest rubber plant in California to take my bags. I didn't have any bags, so being a Mexican, he opened the door for me and smiled politely just the same.

Outside the narrow street fumed, the sidewalks swarmed with fat stomachs. Across the street a bingo parlour was going full blast and beside it a couple of sailors with girls were coming out of a photographer's shop where they had probably been having their photos taken riding on camels. The voice of the hot dog merchant split the dusk like an axe. A big blue bus blared down the street to the little circle where the street car used to turn on a turntable. I walked that way.

After a while there was a faint smell of ocean. Not very much, but as if they had kept this much just to remind people this had once been a clean open beach where the waves came in and creamed and the wind blew and you could smell something besides hot fat and cold sweat.

The little sidewalk car came trundling along the wide concrete walk. I got on it and rode to the end of the line and got off and sat on a bench where it was quiet and cold and there was a big brown heap of kelp almost at my feet. Out to sea they turned the lights on in the gambling boats. I got back on the sidewalk car the next time it came and rode back almost to where I had left the hotel. If anybody was tailing me, he was doing it without moving. I didn't think there was. In that clean little city there wouldn't be enough crime for the dicks to be very good shadows.

The black piers glittered their length and then disappeared into the dark background of night and water. You could still smell hot fat, but you could smell the ocean too. The hot dog man droned on:

'Get hungry, folks, get hungry. Nice hot doggies. Get hungry.'

I spotted him in a white barbecue stand tickling wienies with a long fork. He was doing a good business even that early in the year. I had to wait some time to get him alone.

'What's the name of the one farthest out?' I asked, pointing with my nose.

'*Montecito.*' He gave me the level steady look.

'Could a guy with reasonable dough have himself a time there?'

'What kind of a time?'

I laughed, sneeringly, very tough.

'Hot doggies,' he chanted. 'Nice hot doggies, folks.' He dropped his voice. 'Women?'

'Nix. I was figuring on a room with a nice sea breeze and good food and nobody to bother me. Kind of vacation.'

He moved away. 'I can't hear a word you say,' he said, and then went into his chant.

He did some more business. I didn't know why I bothered with him. He just had that kind of face. A young couple in shorts came up and bought hot dogs and strolled away with the boy's arm around the girl's brassiere and each eating the other's hot dog.

The man slid a yard towards me and eyed me over. 'Right now I should be whistling Roses of Picardy,' he said, and paused. 'That would cost you,' he said.

'How much?'

'Fifty. Not less. Unless they want you for something.'

'This used to be a good town,' I said. 'A cool-off town.'

'Thought it still was,' he drawled. 'But why ask me?'

'I haven't an idea,' I said. I threw a dollar bill on his counter. 'Put it in the baby's bank,' I said. 'Or whistle Roses of Picardy.'

He snapped the bill, folded it longways, folded it across and folded it again. He laid it on the counter and tucked his middle finger behind his thumb and snapped. The folded bill hit me lightly in the chest and fell noiselessly to the ground. I bent and picked it up and turned quickly. But nobody was behind me that looked like a dick.

I leaned against the counter and laid the dollar bill on it again. 'People don't throw money at me,' I said. 'They hand it to me. Do you mind?'

He took the bill, unfolded it, spread it out and wiped it off with his apron. He punched his cash-register and dropped the bill into the drawer.

'They say money don't stink,' he said. 'I sometimes wonder.'

I didn't say anything. Some more customers did business with him and went away. The night was cooling fast.

'I wouldn't try the *Royal Crown*,' the man said. 'That's for good little squirrels, that stick to their nuts. You look like dick to me, but that's your angle. I hope you swim good.'

I left him, wondering why I had gone to him in the first place. Play the hunch. Play the hunch and get stung. In a little while you wake up with your mouth full of hunches. You can't order a cup of coffee without shutting your eyes and stabbing the menu. Play the hunch.

I walked around and tried to see if anybody walked behind me in any particular way. Then I sought out a restaurant that didn't smell of frying grease and found one with a purple neon sign and a cocktail bar behind a reed curtain. A male cutie with henna'd hair drooped at a bungalow grand piano and tickled the keys lasciviously and sang Stairway to the Stars in a voice with half the steps missing.

I gobbled a dry martini and hurried back through the reed curtain to the dining-room.

The eighty-five cent dinner tasted like a discarded mail bag and was served to me by a waiter who looked as if he would slug me for a quarter, cut my throat for six bits, and bury me at sea in a barrel of concrete for a dollar and a half, plus sales tax.

35

It was a long ride for a quarter. The water taxi, an old launch painted up and glassed in for three-quarters of its length, slid through the anchored yachts and around the wide pile of stone which was the end of the breakwater. The swell hit us without warning and bounced the boat like a cork. But there was plenty of room to be sick that early in the evening. All the company I had was three couples and the man who drove the boat, a tough-looking citizen who sat a little on his left hip on account of having a black leather hip-holster inside his right hip pocket. The three couples began to chew each other's faces as soon as we left the shore.

I stared back at the lights of Bay City and tried not to bear down too hard on my dinner. Scattered points of light drew together and became a jewelled bracelet laid out in the show window of the night. Then the brightness faded and they were a soft orange glow appearing and disappearing over the edge of the swell. It was a long smooth even swell with no white caps, and just the right amount of heave to make me glad I hadn't pickled my dinner in bar whisky. The taxi slid up and down the swell now with a sinister smoothness, like a cobra dancing. There was cold in the air, the wet cold that sailors never get out of their joints. The red neon pencils that outlined the *Royal Crown* faded off to the left and dimmed in the gliding grey ghosts of the sea, then shone out again, as bright as new marbles.

We gave this one a wide berth. It looked nice from a long way off. A faint music came over the water and music over the water can never be anything but lovely. The *Royal Crown* seemed to ride as steady as a pier on its four hausers. Its landing stage was lit up like a theatre marquee. Then all this faded into remoteness and another, older, smaller boat began to sneak out of the night towards us. It was not much to look at. A converted seagoing freighter with scummed and rusted plates, the superstructure cut down to the boat deck level, and above that two stumpy masts just high enough for a radio antenna. There was light on the *Montecito* also and music floated across the wet dark sea. The spooning couples took their teeth out of each other's necks and stared at the ship and giggled.

The taxi swept around in a wide curve, careened just enough to give the passengers a thrill, and eased up to the hemp fenders along the stage. The taxi's motor idled and backfired in the fog. A lazy searchlight beam swept a circle about fifty yards out from the ship.

The taximan hooked to the stage and a sloe-eyed lad in a blue mess jacket with bright buttons, a bright smile and a gangster mouth, handed the girls up from the taxi. I was last. The casual neat way he looked me over told me something about him. The casual neat way he bumped my shoulder clip told me more.

'Nix,' he said softly. 'Nix.'

He had a smoothly husky voice, a hard Harry straining himself through a silk handkerchief. He jerked his chin at the taximan. The taximan dropped a short loop over a bitt, turned his wheel a little, and climbed out on the stage. He stepped behind me.

'No gats on the boat, laddy. Sorry and all that rot,' Mess-jacket purred.

'I could check it. It's just part of my clothes. I'm a fellow who wants to see Brunette, on business.'

He seemed mildly amused. 'Never heard of him,' he smiled. 'On your way, bo.'

The taximan hooked a wrist through my right arm.

'I want to see Brunette,' I said. My voice sounded weak and frail, like an old lady's voice.

'Let's not argue,' the sloe-eyed lad said. 'We're not in Bay City now, not even in California, and by some good opinions not even in the U.S.A. Beat it.'

'Back in the boat,' the taximan growled behind me. 'I owe you a quarter. Let's go.'

I got back into the boat. Mess-jacket looked at me with his silent sleek smile. I watched it until it was no longer a smile, no longer a face, no longer anything but a dark figure against the landing lights. I watched it and hungered.

The way back seemed longer. I didn't speak to the taximan and he didn't speak to me. As I got off at the wharf he handed me a quarter.

'Some other night,' he said wearily, 'when we got more room to bounce you.'

Half a dozen customers waiting to get in stared at me, hearing him. I went past them, past the door of the little waiting room on the float, towards the shallow steps at the landward end.

A big red-headed roughneck in dirty sneakers and tarry pants and what was left of a torn blue sailor's jersey and a streak of black down the side of his face straightened from the railing and bumped into me casually.

I stopped. He looked too big. He had three inches on me and thirty pounds. But it was getting to be time for me to put my fist into somebody's teeth even if all I got for it was a wooden arm.

The light was dim and mostly behind him. 'What's the matter, pardner?' he drawled. 'No soap on the hell ship?'

'Go darn your shirt,' I told him. 'Your belly is sticking out.'

'Could be worse,' he said. 'The gat's kind of bulgy under the light suit at that.'

'What pulls your nose into it?'

'Jesus, nothing at all. Just curiosity. No offence, pal.'

'Well, get the hell out of my way then.'

'Sure. I'm just resting here.'

He smiled a slow tired smile. His voice was soft, dreamy, so delicate for a big man that it was startling. It made me think of another soft-voiced big man I had strangely liked.

'You got the wrong approach,' he said sadly. 'Just call me Red.'

'Step aside, Red. The best people make mistakes. I feel one crawling up my back.'

He looked thoughtfully this way and that. He had me angled into a corner of the shelter on the float. We seemed to be more or less alone.

'You want on the *Monty*? Can be done. If you got a reason.'

People in gay clothes and gay faces went past us and got into the taxi. I waited for them to pass.

'How much is the reason?'

'Fifty bucks. Ten more if you bleed in my boat.'

I started around him.

'Twenty-five,' he said softly. 'Fifteen if you come back with friends.'

'I don't have any friends,' I said, and walked away. He didn't try to stop me.

I turned right along the cement walk down which the little electric cars come and go, trundling like baby carriages and blowing little horns that wouldn't startle an expectant mother. At the foot of the first pier there was a flaring bingo parlour, jummed full of people already. I went into it and stood against the wall behind the players, where a lot of other people stood and waited for a place to sit down.

I watched a few numbers go up on the electric indicator,

listened to the table men call them off, tried to spot the house players and couldn't, and turned to leave.

A large blueness that smelled of tar took shape beside me. 'No got the dough – or just tight with it?' the gentle voice asked in my ear.

I looked at him again. He had the eyes you never see, that you only read about. Violet eyes. Almost purple. Eyes like a girl, a lovely girl. His skin was as soft as silk. Lightly reddened, but it would never tan. It was too delicate. He was bigger than Hemingway and younger, by many years. He was not as big as Moose Malloy, but he looked very fast on his feet. His hair was that shade of red that glints with gold. But except for the eyes he had a plain farmer face, with no stagy kind of handsomeness.

'What's your racket?' he asked. 'Private eye?'

'Why do I have to tell you?' I snarled.

'I kind of thought that was it,' he said. 'Twenty-five too high? No expense account?'

'No.'

He sighed. 'It was a bum idea I had anyway,' he said. 'They'll tear you to pieces out there.'

'I wouldn't be surprised. What's *your* racket?'

' A dollar here, a dollar there. I was on the cops once. They broke me.'

'Why tell me?'

He looked surprised. 'It's true.'

'You must have been levelling.'

He smiled faintly.

'Know a man named Brunette?'

The faint smile stayed on his face. Three bingoes were made in a row. They worked fast in there. A tall beak-faced man with sallow sunken cheeks and a wrinkled suit stepped close to us and leaned against the wall and didn't look at us. Red leaned gently towards him and asked: 'Is there something we could tell you, pardner?'

The tall beak-faced man grinned and moved away. Red grinned and shook the building leaning against the wall again.

'I've met a man who could take you,' I said.

'I wish there was more,' he said gravely. 'A big guy costs money. Things ain't scaled for him. He costs to feed, to put clothes on, and he can't sleep with his feet in the bed. Here's how it works. You might not think this is a good place to talk, but it is. Any finks drift along I'll know them and the rest of the crowd is watching those numbers and nothing else. I got a boat with an under-water by-pass. That is, I can borrow one. There's a pier down the line without lights. I know a loading port on the *Monty* I can open. I take a load out there once in a while. There ain't many guys below decks.'

'They have a searchlight and lookouts,' I said.

'We can make it.'

I got my wallet out and slipped a twenty and a five against my stomach and folded them small. The purple eyes watched me without seeming to.

'One way?'

I nodded.

'Fifteen was the word.'

'The market took a spurt.'

A tarry hand swallowed the bills. He moved silently away. He faded into the hot darkness outside the doors. The beak-nosed man materialized at my left side and said quietly:

'I think I know that fellow in sailor clothes. Friend of yours? I think I seen him before.'

I straightened away from the wall and walked away from him without speaking, out of the doors, then left, watching a high head that moved along from electrolier to electrolier a hundred feet ahead of me. After a couple of minutes I turned into a space between two concession shacks. The beak-nosed man appeared, strolling with his eyes on the ground. I stepped out to his side.

'Good evening,' I said. 'May I guess your weight for a quarter?' I leaned against him. There was a gun under the wrinkled coat.

His eyes looked at me without emotion. 'Am I goin' to have to pinch you, son? I'm posted along this stretch to maintain law and order.'

'Who's dismaintaining it right now?'

'Your friend had a familiar look to me.'

'He ought to. He's a cop.'

'Aw hell,' the beak-nosed man said patiently. 'That's where I seen him. Good-night to you.'

He turned and strolled back the way he had come. The tall head was out of sight now. It didn't worry me. Nothing about that lad would ever worry me.

I walked on slowly.

36

Beyond the electroliers, beyond the beat and toot of the small sidewalk cars, beyond the smell of hot fat and popcorn and the shrill children and the barkers in the peep shows, beyond everything but the smell of the ocean and the suddenly clear line of the shore and the creaming fall of the waves into the pebbled spume. I walked almost alone now. The noises died behind me, the hot dishonest light became a fumbling glare. Then the lightless finger of a black pier jutted seaward into the dark. This would be the one. I turned to go out on it.

Red stood up from a box against the beginning of the piles and spoke upwards to me. 'Right,' he said. 'You go on out to the seasteps. I gotta go and get her and warm her up.'

'Waterfront cop followed me. That guy in the bingo parlour. I had to stop and speak to him.'

'Olson. Pickpocket detail. He's good too. Except once in a

while he will lift a leather and plant it, to keep up his arrest record. That's being a shade too good, or isn't it?'

'For Bay City I'd say just about right. Let's get going. I'm getting the wind up. I don't want to blow this fog away. It doesn't look much but it would help a lot.'

'It'll last enough to fool a searchlight,' Red said. 'They got Tommy-guns on that boat deck. You go on out the pier. I'll be along.'

He melted into the dark and I went out the dark boards, slipping on fish-slimed planking. There was a low dirty railing at the far end. A couple leaned in a corner. They when away, the man swearing.

For ten minutes I listened to the water slapping the piles. A night bird whirred in the dark, the faint greyness of a wing cut across my vision and disappeared. A plane droned high in the ceiling. Then far off a motor barked and roared and kept on roaring like half a dozen truck engines. After a while the sound eased and dropped, then suddenly there was no sound at all.

More minutes passed. I went back to the seasteps and moved down them as cautiously as a cat on a wet floor. A dark shape slid out of the night and something thudded. A voice said: 'All set. Get in.'

I got into the boat and sat beside him under the screen. The boat slid out over the water. There was no sound from its exhaust now but an angry bubbling along both sides of the shell. Once more the lights of Bay City became something distantly luminous beyond the rise and fall of alien waves. Once more the garish lights of the *Royal Crown* slid off to one side, the ship seeming to preen itself like a fashion model on a revolving platform. And once again the ports of the good ship *Montecito* grew out of the black Pacific and the slow steady sweep of the searchlight turned around it like the beam of a lighthouse.

'I'm scared,' I said suddenly. 'I'm scared stiff.'

Red throttled down the boat and let it slide up and down the swell as though the water moved underneath and the boat stayed in the same place. He turned his face and stared at me.

'I'm afraid of death and despair,' I said. 'Of dark water and drowned men's faces and skulls with empty eyesockets. I'm afraid of dying, of being nothing, of not finding a man named Brunette.'

He chuckled. 'You had me going for a minute. You sure give yourself a pep talk. Brunette might be any place. On either of the boats, at the club he owns, back east, Reno, in his slippers at home. That all you want?'

'I want a man named Malloy, a huge brute who got out of the Oregon State pen a while back after an eight-year stretch for bank robbery. He was hiding out in Bay City.' I told him about it. I told him a great deal more than I intended to. It must have been his eyes.

At the end he thought and then spoke slowly and what he said had wisps of fog clinging to it, like the beads on a moustache. Maybe that made it seem wiser than it was, maybe not.

'Some of it makes sense,' he said. 'Some not. Some I wouldn't know about, some I would. If this Sonderborg was running a hideout and peddling reefers and sending boys out to heist jewels off rich ladies with a wild look in their eyes, it stands to reason that he had an in with the city government, but that don't mean they knew everything he did or that every cop on the force knew he had an in. Could be Blane did and Hemingway, as you call him, didn't. Blane's bad, the other guy is just tough cop, neither bad nor good, neither crooked nor honest, full of guts and just dumb enough, like me, to think being on the cops is a sensible way to make a living. This psychic fellow doesn't figure either way. He bought himself a line of protection in the best market, Bay City, and he used it when he had to. You never know what a guy like that is up to and so you never know what he has on his conscience or is afraid of. Could be he's human and fell for a customer once in a while. Them rich dames are easier to make than paper dolls. So my hunch about your stay in Sonderborg's place is simply that Blane knew Sonderborg would be scared when he found out who you were – and the story they told Sonderborg is probably what he told you, that they found you wandering with your head dizzy – and Sonderborg wouldn't know what to do with you and he would be afraid either to let you go or to knock you off, and after long enough Blane would drop around and raise the ante on him. That's all there was to that. It just happened they could use you and they did it. Blane might know about Malloy too. I wouldn't put it past him.'

I listened and watched the slow sweep of the searchlight and the coming and going of the water taxi far over to the right.

'I know how these boys figure,' Red said. 'The trouble with cops is not that they're dumb or crooked or tough, but that they think just being a cop gives them a little something they didn't have before. Maybe it did once, but not any more. They're topped by too many smart minds. That brings us to Brunette. He don't run the town. He couldn't be bothered. He put up big money to elect a mayor so his water taxis wouldn't be bothered. If there was anything in particular he wanted, they would give it to him. Like a while ago one of his friends, a lawyer, was pinched for drunk driving felony and Brunette got the charge reduced to reckless driving. They changed the blotter to do it, and that's a felony too. Which gives you an idea. His racket is gambling and all rackets tie together these days. So he might handle reefers, or touch a percentage from some one of his workers he gave the business to. He might know Sonderborg and he might not. But the jewel heist is out. Figure the work these boys done for eight grand. It's a laugh to think Brunette would have anything to do with that.'

'Yeah,' I said. 'There was a man murdered too – remember?'

'He didn't do that either, nor have it done. If Brunette had that done, you wouldn't have found any body. You never know what might be stitched into a guy's clothes. Why chance it? Look what I'm doing for you for twenty-five bucks. What would Brunette get done with the money *he* has to spend?'

'Would he have a man killed?'

Red thought for a moment. 'He might. He probably has. But he's not a tough guy. These racketeers are a new type. We think about them the way we think about old time yeggs or needled-up punks. Big-mouthed police commissioners on the radio yell that they're all yellow rats, that they'll kill women and babies and howl for mercy if they see a police uniform. They ought to know better than to try to sell the public that stuff. There's yellow cops and there's yellow torpedoes – but damn few of either. And as for the top men, like Brunette – they didn't get there by murdering people. They got there by guts and brains – and they don't have the group courage the cops have either. But above all they're business men. What they do is for money. Just like other business men. Sometimes a guy gets badly in the way. Okey. Out. But they think plenty before they do it. What the hell am I giving a lecture for?'

'A man like Brunette wouldn't hide Malloy,' I said. 'After he had killed two people.'

'No. Not unless there was some other reason than money. Want to go back?'

'No.'

Red moved his hands on the wheel. The boat picked up speed. 'Don't think I *like* these bastards,' he said. 'I hate their guts.'

37

The revolving searchlight was a pale mist-ridden finger that barely skimmed the waves a hundred feet or so beyond the ship. It was probably more for show than anything else. Especially at this time in the evening. Anyone who had plans for hijacking the take on one of these gambling boats would need plenty of help and would pull the job about four in the morning, when the crowd was thinned down to a few bitter gamblers, and the crew were all dull with fatigue. Even then it would be a poor way to make money. It has been tried once.

A taxi curved to the landing stage, unloaded, went back shorewards. Red held his speedboat idling just beyond the sweep of the searchlight. If they lifted it a few feet, just for fun – but they didn't. It passed languidly and the dull water glowed with it and the speedboat slid across the line and closed in fast under the overhang, past the two huge scummy stern hausers. We sidled up to the greasy plates of the hull as coyly as a hotel dick getting set to ease a hustler out of his lobby.

Double iron doors loomed high above us, and they looked too high to reach and too heavy to open even if we could reach them. The speedboat scuffed the *Montecito's* ancient sides and the swell slapped loosely at the shell under our feet. A big shadow rose in the gloom at my side and a coiled rope slipped upwards through the air, slapped, caught, and the end ran down and splashed in water. Red fished it out with a boat-hook, pulled it tight and fastened the end to something on the engine cowling. There was just enough fog to make everything seem unreal. The wet air was as cold as the ashes of love.

Red leaned close to me and his breath tickled my ear. 'She rides too high. Come a good blow and she'd wave her screws in the air. We got to climb those plates just the same.'

'I can hardly wait,' I said, shivering.

He put my hands on the wheel, turned it just as he wanted it, set the throttle, and told me to hold the boat just as she was. There was an iron ladder bolted close to the plates, curving with the hull, its rungs probably as slippery as a greased pole.

Going up it looked as tempting as climbing over the cornice of an office building. Red reached for it, after wiping his hands hard on his pants to get some tar on them. He hauled himself up noiselessly, without even a grunt, and his sneakers caught the metal rungs, and he braced his body out almost at right angles to get more traction.

The searchlight beam swept far outside us now. Light bounced off the water and seemed to make my face as obvious as a flare, but nothing happened. Then there was a dull creak of heavy hinges over my head. A faint ghost of yellowish light trickled out into the fog and died. The outline of one half of the loading port showed. It couldn't have been bolted from inside. I wondered why.

The whisper was a mere sound, without meaning. I left the wheel and started up. It was the hardest journey I ever made. It landed me panting and wheezing in a sour hold littered with packing boxes and barrels and coils of rope and clumps of rusted chain. Rats screamed in dark corners. The yellow light came from a narrow door on the far side.

Red put his lips against my ear. 'From here we take a straight walk to the boiler room catwalk. They'll have steam in one auxiliary, because they don't have no Diesels on this piece of cheese. There will be probably one guy below. The crew doubles in brass up on the play decks, table men and spotters and waiters and so on. They all got to sign on as something that sounds like ship. From the boiler room I'll show you a ventilator with no grating in it. It goes to the boat deck and the boat deck is out of bounds. But it's all yours – while you live.'

'You must have relatives on board,' I said.

'Funnier things have happened. Will you come back fast?'

'I ought to make a good splash from the boat deck,' I said, and got my wallet out. 'I think this rates a little more money. Here. Handle the body as if it was your own.'

'You don't owe me nothing more, pardner.'

'I'm buying the trip back– even if I don't use it. Take the money before I bust out crying and wet your shirt.'

'Need a little help up there?'

'All I need is a silver tongue and the one I have is like a lizard's back.'

'Put your dough away,' Red said. 'You paid me for the trip back. I think you're scared.' He took hold of my hand. His was strong, hard, warm and slightly sticky. 'I *know* you're scared,' he whispered.

'I'll get over it,' I said. 'One way or another.'

He turned away from me with a curious look I couldn't read in that light. I followed him among the cases and barrels, over the raised iron sill of the door, into a long dim passage with the ship smell. We came out of this on to a grilled steel platform, slick with oil, and went down a steel ladder that was hard to hold on to. The slow hiss of the oil burners filled the air now and blanketed all other sound. We turned towards the hiss through mountains of silent iron.

Around a corner we looked at a short dirty wop in a purple silk shirt who sat in a wired-together office chair, under a naked hanging light, and read the evening paper with the aid of a black forefinger and steel-rimmed spectacles that had probably belonged to his grandfather.

Red stepped behind him noiselessly. He said gently:

'Hi, Shorty. How's all the bambinos?'

The Italian opened his mouth with a click and threw a

hand at the opening of his purple shirt. Red hit him on the angle of the jaw and caught him. He put him down on the floor gently and began to tear the purple shirt into strips.

'This is going to hurt him more than the poke on the button,' Red said softly. 'But the idea is a guy going up a ventilator ladder makes a lot of racket down below. Up above they won't hear a thing.'

He bound and gagged the Italian neatly and folded his glasses and put them in a safe place and we went along to the ventilator that had no grating in it. I looked up and saw nothing but blackness.

'Good-bye,' I said.

'Maybe you need a little help.'

I shook myself like a wet dog. 'I need a company of marines. But either I do it alone or I don't do it. So long.'

'How long will you be?' His voice still sounded worried.

'An hour or less.'

He stared at me and chewed his lip. Then he nodded. 'Sometimes a guy has to,' he said. 'Drop by that bingo parlour, if you get time.'

He walked away softly, took four steps, and came back. 'That open loading port,' he said. 'That might buy you something. Use it.' He went quickly.

38

Cold air rushed down the ventilator. It seemed a long way to the top. After three minutes that felt like an hour I poked my head out cautiously from the horn-like opening. Canvas-sheeted boats were grey blurs near by. Low voices muttered in the dark. The beam of the searchlight circled slowly. It came from a point still higher, probably a railed platform at the top of one of the stumpy masts. There would be a lad up there with a Tommy-gun too, perhaps even a light Browning. Cold job, cold comfort when somebody left the loading port unbolted so nicely.

Distant music throbbed like the phony bass of a cheap radio. Overhead a masthead light and through the higher layers of fog a few bitter stars stared down.

I climbed out of the ventilator, slipped my .38 from the shoulder clip and held it curled against my ribs, hiding it with my sleeve. I walked three silent steps and listened. Nothing happened. The muttering talk had stopped, but not on my account. I placed it now, between two lifeboats. And out of the night and the fog, as it mysteriously does, enough light gathered into one focus to shine on the dark hardness of a machine-gun mounted on a high tripod and swung down over the rail. Two men stood near it, motionless, not smoking, and their voices began to mutter again, a quiet whisper that never became words.

I listened to the muttering too long. Another voice spoke clearly behind me.

'Sorry, guests are not allowed on the boat deck.'

I turned, not too quickly, and looked at his hands. They were light blurs and empty.

I stepped sideways nodding and the end of a boat hid us. The man followed me gently, his shoes soundless on the damp deck.

'I guess I'm lost,' I said.

'I guess you are.' He had a youngish voice, not chewed out of marble. 'But there's a door at the bottom of the companion-way. It has a spring lock on it. It's a good lock. There used to be an open stairway with a chain and a brass sign. We found the livelier element would step over that.'

He was talking a long time, either to be nice, or to be waiting. I didn't know which. I said: 'Somebody must have left the door open.'

The shadowed head nodded. It was lower than mine.

'You can see the spot that puts us in, though. If somebody did leave it open, the boss won't like it a nickel. If somebody didn't, we'd like to know how you got up here. I'm sure you get the idea.'

'It seems a simple idea. Let's go down and talk to him about it.'

'You come with a party?'

'A very nice party.'

'You ought to have stayed with them.'

'You know how it is – you turn your head and some other guy is buying her a drink.'

He chuckled. Then he moved his chin slightly up and down.

I dropped and did a frogleap sideways and the swish of the blackjack was a long spent sigh in the quiet air. It was getting to be that every blackjack in the neighbourhood swung at me automatically. The tall one swore.

I said: 'Go ahead and be heroes.'

I clicked the safety catch loudly.

Sometimes even a bad scene will rock the house. The tall one stood rooted, and I could see the blackjack swinging at his wrist. The one I had been talking to thought it over without any hurry.

'This won't buy you a thing,' he said gravely. 'You'll never get off the boat.'

'I thought of that. Then I thought how little you'd care.'

It was still a bum scene.

'You want what?' he said quietly.

'I have a loud gun,' I said. 'But it doesn't have to go off. I want to talk to Brunette.'

'He went to San Diego on business.'

'I'll talk to his stand-in.'

'You're quite a lad,' the nice one said. 'We'll go down. You'll put the heater up before we go through the door.'

'I'll put the heater up when I'm sure I'm going through the door.'

He laughed lightly. 'Go back to your post, Slim. I'll look into this.'

He moved lazily in front of me and the tall one appeared to fade into the dark.

'Follow me, then.'

We moved Indian file across the deck. We went down brassbound slippery steps. At the bottom was a thick door. He opened it and looked at the lock. He smiled, nodded, held the door for me and I stepped through, pocketing the gun.

The door closed and clicked behind us. He said:

'Quiet evening, so far.'

There was a gilded arch in front of us and beyond it a gaming room, not very crowded. It looked much like any other gaming room. At the far end there was a short glass bar and some stools. In the middle a stairway going down and up this the music swelled and faded. I heard roulette wheels. A man was dealing faro to a single customer. There were not more than sixty people in the room. On the faro table there was a pile of yellowbacks that would start a bank. The player was an elderly white-haired man who looked politely attentive to the dealer, but no more.

Two quiet men in dinner jackets came through the archway sauntering, looking at nothing. That had to be expected. They strolled towards us and the short slender man with me waited for them. They were well beyond the arch before they let their hands find their side pockets, looking for cigarettes of course.

'From now on we have to have a little organization here,' the short man said. 'I don't think you'll mind?'

'You're Brunette,' I said suddenly.

He shrugged. 'Of course.'

'You don't look so tough,' I said.

'I hope not.'

The two men in dinner jackets edged me gently.

'In here,' Brunette said, 'We can talk at ease.'

He opened the door and they took me into dock.

The room was like a cabin and not like a cabin. Two brass lamps swung in gimbals hung above a dark desk that was not wood, possibly plastic. At the end were two bunks in grained wood. The lower of them was made up and on the top one were half a dozen stacks of phonograph record books. A big combination radio-phonograph stood in the corner. There was a red leather chesterfield, a red carpet, smoking stands, a tabouret with cigarettes and a decanter and glasses, a small bar sitting cattycorners at the opposite end from the bunks.

'Sit down,' Brunette said and went around the desk. There were a lot of business-like papers on the desk, with columns of figures, done on a book-keeping machine. He sat in a tall-backed director's chair and tilted it a little and looked me over. Then he stood up again and stripped off his overcoat and scarf and tossed them to one side. He sat down again. He picked a pen up and tickled the lobe of one ear with it. He had a cat smile, but I like cats.

He was neither young nor old, neither fat nor thin. Spending a lot of time on or near the ocean had given him a good healthy complexion. His hair was nut-brown and waved naturally and waved still more at sea. His forehead was narrow and brainy and his eyes held a delicate menace. They were yellowish in colour. He had nice hands, not babied to the point of insipidity, but well-kept. His dinner clothes were midnight blue, I judged, because they looked so black. I thought his pearl was a little too large, but that might have been jealousy.

He looked at me for quite a long time before he said: 'He has a gun.'

One of the velvety tough guys leaned against the middle of my spine with something that was probably not a fishing rod. Exploring hands removed the gun and looked for others.

'Anything else ?' a voice asked.

Brunette shook his head. 'Not now.'

One of the gunners slid my automatic across the desk.

Brunette put the pen down and picked up a letter opener and pushed the gun around gently on his blotter.

'Well,' he said quietly, looking past my shoulder. 'Do I have to explain what I want now?'

One of them went out quickly and shut the door. The other was so still he wasn't there. There was a long easy silence, broken by the distant hum of voices and the deep-toned music and somewhere down below a dull almost imperceptible throbbing.

'Drink?'

'Thanks.'

The gorilla mixed a couple at the little bar. He didn't try to hide the glasses while he did it. He placed one on each side of the desk, on black glass scooters.

'Cigarette?'

'Thanks.'

'Egyptian all right?'

'Sure.'

We lit up. We drank. It tasted like good Scotch. The gorilla didn't drink.

'What I want——' I began.

'Excuse me, but that's rather unimportant, isn't it?'

The soft catlike smile and the lazy half-closing of the yellow eyes.

The door opened and the other one came back and with him was Mess-jacket, gangster mouth and all. He took one look at me and his face went oyster-white.

'He didn't get past me,' he said swiftly, curling one end of his lips.

'He had a gun,' Brunette said, pushing it with the letter opener. 'This gun. He even pushed it into my back more or less, on the boat deck.'

'Not past me, boss,' Mess-jacket said just as swiftly.

Brunette raised his yellow eyes slightly and smiled at me. 'Well?'

'Sweep him out,' I said. 'Squash him somewhere else.'

'I can prove it by the taximan,' Mess-jacket snarled.

'You've been off the stage since five-thirty?'

'Not a minute, boss.'

'That's no answer. An empire can fall in a minute.'

'Not a second, boss.'

'But he can be had,' I said, and laughed.

Mess-jacket took the smooth gliding step of a boxer and his fist lashed like a whip. It almost reached my temple. There was a dull thud. His fist seemed to melt in mid-air. He slumped sideways and clawed at a corner of the desk, then rolled on his back. It was nice to see somebody else get sapped for a change.

Brunette went on smiling at me.

'I hope you're not doing him an injustice,' Brunette said. 'There's still the matter of the door to the companionway.'

'Accidentally open.'

'Could you think of any other idea?'

'Not in such a crowd.'

'I'll talk to you alone,' Brunette said, not looking at anyone but me.

The gorilla lifted Mess-jacket by the armpits and dragged him across the cabin and his partner opened an inner door. They went through. The door closed.

'All right,' Brunette said. 'Who are you and what do you want?'

'I'm a private detective and I want to talk to a man named Moose Malloy.'

'Show me you're a private dick.'

I showed him. He tossed the wallet back across the desk. His wind-tanned lips continued to smile and the smile was getting stagy.

'I'm investigating a murder,' I said. 'The murder of a man named Marriott on the bluff near your Belvedere Club last Thursday night. This murder happens to be connected with another murder, of a woman, done by Malloy, an ex-con and bank robber and all-round tough guy.'

He nodded. 'I'm not asking you yet what it has to do with me. I assume you'll come to that. Suppose you tell me how you got on my boat?'

'I told you.'

'It wasn't true,' he said gently. 'Marlowe is the name? It wasn't true, Marlowe. You know that. The kid down on the stage isn't lying. I pick my men carefully.'

'You own a piece of Bay City,' I said. 'I don't know how big a piece, but enough for what you want. A man named Sonderborg has been running a hideout there. He has been running reefers and stick-ups and hiding hot boys. Naturally, he couldn't do that without connections. I don't think he could do it without you. Malloy was staying with him. Malloy has left. Malloy is about seven feet tall and hard to hide. I think he could hide nicely on a gambling boat.'

'You're simple,' Brunette said softly. 'Supposing I wanted to hide him, why should I take the risk out here?' He sipped his drink. 'After all I'm in another business. It's hard enough to keep a good taxi service running without a lot of trouble. The world is full of places a crook can hide. If he has money. Could you think of a better idea?'

'I could, but to hell with it.'

'I can't do anything for you. So how did you get on the boat?'

'I don't care to say.'

'I'm afraid I'll have to have you made to say, Marlowe.' His teeth glinted in the light from the brass ship's lamps. 'After all, it can be done.'

'If I tell you, will you get word to Malloy?'

'What word?'

I reached for my wallet lying on the desk and drew a card from it and turned it over. I put the wallet away and got a pencil instead. I wrote five words on the back of the card and pushed it across the desk. Brunette took it and read what I had written on it. 'It means nothing to me,' he said.

'It will mean something to Malloy.'

He leaned back and stared at me. 'I don't make you out. You risk your hide to come out here and hand me a card to pass on to some thug I don't even know. There's no sense to it.'

'There isn't if you don't know him.'

'Why didn't you leave your gun ashore and come aboard the usual way?'

'I forgot the first time. Then I knew that toughie in the mess jacket would never let me on. Then I bumped into a fellow who knew another way.'

His yellow eyes lighted as with a new flame. He smiled and said nothing.

'This other fellow is no crook but he's been on the beach with his ears open. You have a loading port that has been unbarred on the inside and you have a ventilator shaft out of which the grating has been removed. There's one man to knock over to get to the boat deck. You'd better check your crew list, Brunette.'

He moved his lips softly, one over the other. He looked down at the card again. 'Nobody named Malloy is on board this boat,' he said. 'But if you're telling the truth about that loading port, I'll buy.'

'Go and look at it.'

He still looked down. 'If there's any way I can get word to Malloy, I will. I don't know why I bother.'

'Take a look at that loading port.'

He sat very still for a moment, then leaned forward and pushed the gun across the desk to me.

'The things I do,' he mused, as if he was alone. 'I run towns, I elect mayors, I corrupt police, I peddle dope, I hide out crooks, I heist old women strangled with pearls. What a lot of time I have.' He laughed shortly. 'What a lot of time.'

I reached for my gun and tucked it back under my arm.

Brunette stood up. 'I promise nothing,' he said, eyeing me steadily. 'But I believe you.'

'Of course not.'

'You took a long chance to hear so little.'

'Yes.'

'Well——' he made a meaningless gesture and then put his hand across the desk.

'Shake hands with a chump,' he said softly.

I shook hands with him. His hand was small and firm and a little hot.

'You wouldn't tell me how you found out about this loading port?'

'I can't. But the man who told me is no crook.'

'I could make you tell,' he said, and immediately shook his head. 'No. I believed you once. I'll believe you again. Sit still and have another drink.'

He pushed a buzzer. The door at the back opened and one of the nice-tough guys came in.

'Stay here. Give him a drink, if he wants it. No rough stuff.'

The torpedo sat down and smiled at me calmly. Brunette went quickly out of the office. I smoked. I finished my drink. The torpedo made me another. I finished that, and another cigarette.

Brunette came back and washed his hands over in the corner, then sat down at his desk again. He jerked his head at the torpedo. The torpedo went out silently.

The yellow eyes studied me. 'You win, Marlowe. And I have one hundred and sixty-four men on my crew list. Well——' he shrugged. 'You can go back by the taxi. Nobody will bother you. As to your message, I have a few contacts. I'll use them. Good-night. I probably should say thanks. For the demonstration.'

'Good-night,' I said, and stood up and went out.

There was a new man on the landing stage. I rode to shore

233

on a different taxi. I went along to the bingo parlour and leaned against the wall in the crowd.

Red came along in a few minutes and leaned beside me against the wall.

'Easy, huh?' Red said softly, against the heavy clear voices of the table men calling the numbers.

'Thanks to you. He bought. He's worried.'

Red looked this way and that and turned his lips a little more close to my ear. 'Get your man?'

'No. But I'm hoping Brunette will find a way to get him a message.'

Red turned his head and looked at the tables again. He yawned and straightened away from the wall. The beak-nosed man was in again. Red stepped over to him and said: 'Hiya, Olson,' and almost knocked the man off his feet pushing past him.

Olson looked after him sourly and straightened his hat. Then he spat viciously on the floor.

As soon as he had gone, I left the place and went along to the parking lot back towards the tracks where I had left my car.

I drove back to Hollywood and put the car away and went up to the apartment.

I took my shoes off and walked around in my socks feeling the floor with my toes. They would still get numb again once in a while.

Then I sat down on the side of the pulled-down bed and tried to figure time. It couldn't be done. It might take hours or days to find Malloy. He might never be found until the police got him. If they ever did – alive.

39

It was about ten o'clock when I called the Grayle number in Bay City. I thought it would probably be too late to catch her, but it wasn't. I fought my way through a maid and the butler and finally heard her voice on the line. She sounded breezy and well-primed for the evening.

'I promised to call you,' I said. 'It's a little late, but I've had a lot to do.'

'Another stand-up?' Her voice got cool.

'Perhaps not. Does your chauffeur work this late?'

'He works as late as I tell him to.'

'How about dropping by to pick me up? I'll be getting squeezed into my commencement suit.'

'Nice of you,' she drawled. 'Should I really bother?' Amthor had certainly done a wonderful job with her centres of speech – if anything had ever been wrong with them.

'I'd show you my etching.'

'Just one etching?'

'It's just a single apartment.'

'I heard they had such things,' she drawled again, then changed her tone. 'Don't act so hard to get. You have a lovely build, mister. And don't ever let anyone tell you different. Give me the address again.'

I gave it to her and the apartment number. 'The lobby door is locked,' I said. 'But I'll go down and slip the catch.'

'That's fine,' she said. 'I won't have to bring my jimmy.'

She hung up, leaving me with a curious feeling of having talked to somebody that didn't exist.

I went down to the lobby and slipped the catch and then

took a shower and put my pyjamas on and lay down on the bed. I could have slept for a week. I dragged myself up off the bed again and set the catch on the door, which I had forgotten to do, and walked through a deep hard snowdrift out to the kitchenette and laid out glasses and a bottle of liqueur Scotch I had been saving for a really high-class seduction.

I lay down on the bed again. 'Pray,' I said out loud. 'There's nothing left but prayer.'

I closed my eyes. The four walls of the room seemed to hold the throb of a boat, the still air seemed to drip with fog and rustle with sea wind. I smelled the rank sour smell of a disused hold. I smelled engine oil and saw a wop in a purple shirt reading under a naked light bulb with his grandfather's spectacles. I climbed and climbed up a ventilator shaft. I climbed the Himalayas and stepped out on top and guys with machine-guns were all around me. I talked with a small and somehow very human yellow-eyed man who was a racketeer and probably worse. I thought of the giant with the red hair and the violet eyes, who was probably the nicest man I had ever met.

I stopped thinking. Lights moved behind my closed lids. I was lost in space. I was a gilt-edged sap come back from a vain adventure. I was a hundred dollar package of dynamite that went off with a noise like a pawnbroker looking at a dollar watch. I was a pink-headed bug crawling up the side of the City Hall.

I was asleep.

I woke slowly, unwillingly, and my eyes stared at reflected light on the ceiling from the lamp. Something moved gently in the room.

The movement was furtive and quiet and heavy. I listened to it. Then I turned my head slowly and looked at Moose Malloy. There were shadows and he moved in the shadows, as noiselessly as I had seen him once before. A gun in his hand had a dark oily business-like sheen. His hat was pushed back on his black curly hair and his nose sniffed, like the nose of a hunting dog.

He saw me open my eyes. He came softly over to the side of the bed and stood looking down at me.

'I got your note,' he said. 'I make the joint clean. I don't make no cops outside. If this is a plant, two guys goes out in baskets.'

I rolled a little on the bed and he felt swiftly under the pillows. His face was still wide and pale and his deep-set eyes were still somehow gentle. He was wearing an overcoat tonight. It fitted him where it touched. It was burst out in one shoulder seam, probably just getting it on. It would be the largest size they had, but not large enough for Moose Malloy.

'I hoped you'd drop by,' I said. 'No copper knows anything about this. I just wanted to see you.'

'Go on,' he said.

He moved sideways to a table and put the gun down and dragged his overcoat off and sat down in my best easy chair. It creaked, but it held. He leaned back slowly and arranged the gun so that it was close to his right hand. He dug a pack of cigarettes out of his pocket and shook one loose and put it into his mouth without touching it with his fingers. A match flared on a thumbnail. The sharp smell of the smoke drifted across the room.

'You ain't sick or anything?' he said.

'Just resting. I had a hard day.'

'Door was open. Expecting someone?'

' A dame.'

He stared at me thoughtfully

'Maybe she won't come,' I said. 'If she does, I'll stall her.'

'What dame?'

'Oh, just a dame. If she comes, I'll get rid of her. I'd rather talk to you.'

His very faint smile hardly moved his mouth. He puffed

his cigarette awkwardly, as if it was too small for his fingers to hold with comfort.

'What made you think I was on the *Monty*?' he asked.

'A Bay City cop. It's a long story and too full of guessing.'

'Bay City cops after me?'

'Would that bother you?'

He smiled the faint smile again. He shook his head slightly.

'You killed a woman,' I said. 'Jessie Florian. That was a mistake.'

He thought. Then he nodded. 'I'd drop that one,' he said quietly.

'But that queered it,' I said. 'I'm not afraid of you. You're no killer. You didn't mean to kill her. The other one – over on Central – you could have squeezed out of. But not out of beating a woman's head on a bedpost until her brains were on her face.'

'You take some awful chances, brother,' he said softly.

'The way I've been handled,' I said, 'I don't know the difference any more. You didn't mean to kill her – did you?'

His eyes were restless. His head was cocked in a listening attitude.

'It's about time you learned your own strength,' I said.

'It's too late,' he said.

'You wanted her to tell you something,' I said. 'You took hold of her neck and shook her. She was already dead when you were banging her head against the bed-post.'

He stared at me.

'I know what you wanted her to tell you,' I said.

'Go ahead.'

'There was a cop with me when she was found. I had to break clean.'

'How clean?'

'Fairly clean,' I said. 'But not about to-night.'

He stared at me. 'Okey, how did you know I was on the

Monty?' He had asked me that before. He seemed to have forgotten.

'I didn't. But the easiest way to get away would be by water. With the set-up they have in Bay City you could get out to one of the gambling boats. From there you could get clean away. With the right help.'

'Laird Brunette is a nice guy,' he said emptily. 'So I've heard. I never even spoke to him.'

'He got the message to you.'

'Hell, there's a dozen grapevines that might help him to do that, pal. When do we do what you said on the card? I had a hunch you were levelling. I wouldn't take the chance to come here otherwise. Where do we go?'

He killed his cigarette and watched me. His shadow loomed against the wall, the shadow of a giant. He was so big he seemed unreal.

'What made you think I bumped Jessie Florian?' he asked suddenly.

'The spacing of the finger marks on her neck. The fact that you had something to get out of her, and that you are strong enough to kill people without meaning to.'

'The johns tied me to it?'

'I don't know.'

'What did I want out of her?'

'You thought she might know where Velma was.'

He nodded silently and went on staring at me.

'But she didn't,' I said. 'Velma was too smart for her.'

There was a light knocking at the door.

Malloy leaned forward a little and smiled and picked up his gun. Somebody tried the doorknob. Malloy stood up slowly and leaned forward in a crouch and listened. Then he looked back at me from looking at the door.

I sat up on the bed and put my feet on the floor and stood up. Malloy watched me silently, without a motion. I went over to the door.

'Who is it?' I asked with my lips to the panel.

It was her voice all right. 'Open up, silly. It's the Duchess of Windsor.'

'Just a second.'

I looked back at Malloy. He was frowning. I went over close to him and said in a very low voice: 'There's no other way out. Go in the dressing-room behind the bed and wait. I'll get rid of her.'

He listened and thought. His expression was unreadable. He was a man who had now very little to lose. He was a man who would never know fear. It was not built into even that giant frame. He nodded at last and picked up his hat and coat and moved silently around the bed and into the dressing-room. The door closed, but did not shut tight.

I looked around for signs of him. Nothing but a cigarette butt that anybody might have smoked. I went to the room door and opened it. Malloy had set the catch again when he came in.

She stood there half smiling, in the high-necked white fox evening cloak she had told me about. Emerald pendants hung from her ears and almost buried themselves in the soft white fur. Her fingers were curled and soft on the small evening bag she carried.

The smile died off her face when she saw me. She looked me up and down. Her eyes were cold now.

'So it's like that,' she said grimly. 'Pyjamas and dressing gown. To show me his lovely little etching. What a fool I am.'

I stood aside and held the door. 'It's not like that at all. I was getting dressed and a cop dropped in on me. He just left.'

'Randall?'

I nodded. A lie with a nod is still a lie, but it's an easy lie. She hesitated a moment, then moved past me with a swirl of scented fur.

I shut the door. She walked slowly across the room, stared blankly at the wall, then turned quickly.

'Let's understand each other,' she said. 'I'm not this much of a pushover. I don't go for hall bedroom romance. There was a time in my life when I had too much of it. I like things done with an air.'

'Will you have a drink before you go?' I was still leaning against the door, across the room from her.

'Am I going?'

'You gave me the impression you didn't like it here.'

'I wanted to make a point. I have to be a little vulgar to make it. I'm not one of these promiscuous bitches. I can be had – but not just by reaching. Yes, I'll take a drink.'

I went out into the kitchenette and mixed a couple of drinks with hands that were not too steady. I carried them in and handed her one.

There was no sound from the dressing-room, not even a sound of breathing.

She took the glass and tasted it and looked across it at the far wall. 'I don't like men to receive me in their pyjamas,' she said. 'It's a funny thing. I liked you. I liked you a lot. But I could get over it. I have often got over such things.'

I nodded and drank.

'Most men are just lousy animals,' she said. 'In fact it's a pretty lousy world, if you ask me.'

'Money must help.'

'You think it's going to when you haven't always had money. As a matter of fact it just makes new problems.' She smiled curiously. 'And you forget how hard the old problems were.'

She got out a gold cigarette case from her bag and I went over and held a match for her. She blew a vague plume of smoke and watched it with half-shut eyes.

'Sit close to me,' she said suddenly.

'Let's talk a little first.'

'About what? Oh – my jade?'

'About murder.'

Nothing changed in her face. She blew another plume of smoke, this time more carefully, more slowly. 'It's a nasty subject. Do we have to?'

I shrugged.

'Lin Marriott was no saint,' she said. 'But I still don't want to talk about it.'

She stared at me coolly for a long moment and then dipped her hand into her open bag for a handkerchief.

'Personally, I don't think he was a finger man for a jewel mob, either,' I said. 'The police pretend that they think that, but they do a lot of pretending. I don't even think he was a blackmailer, in any real sense. Funny, isn't it?'

'Is it?' The voice was very, very cold now.

'Well, not really,' I agreed and drank the rest of my drink. 'It was awfully nice of you to come here, Mrs Grayle. But we seem to have hit the wrong mood. I don't even, for example, think Marriott was killed by a gang. I don't think he was going to that canyon to buy a jade necklace. I don't even think a jade necklace was ever stolen. I think he went to that canyon to be murdered, although he thought he went there to help commit a murder. But Marriott was a very bad murderer.'

She leaned forward a little and her smile became just a little glassy. Suddenly, without any real change in her, she ceased to be beautiful. She looked merely like a woman who would have been dangerous a hundred years ago, and twenty years ago daring, but who to-day was just Grade B Hollywood.

She said nothing, but her right hand was tapping the clasp of her bag.

'A very bad murderer,' I said. 'Like Shakespeare's Second Murderer in that scene in *King Richard III*. The fellow that had certain dregs of conscience, but still wanted the money, and in the end didn't do the job at all because he couldn't make up his mind. Such murderers are very dangerous. They have to be removed – sometimes with blackjacks.'

She smiled. 'And who was he about to murder, do you suppose?'

'Me.'

'That must be very difficult to believe – that anyone would hate you that much. And you said my jade necklace was never stolen at all. Have you any proof of all this?'

'I didn't say I had. I said I thought these things.'

'Then why be such a fool as to talk about them?'

'Proof,' I said, 'is always a relative thing. It's an overwhelming balance of probabilities. And that's a matter of how they strike you. There was a rather weak motive for murdering me – merely that I was trying to trace a former Central Avenue dive singer at the same time that a convict named Moose Malloy got out of jail and started to look for her too. Perhaps I was helping him find her. Obviously, it was possible to find her, or it wouldn't have been worth while to pretend to Marriott that I had to be killed and killed quickly. And obviously he wouldn't have believed it, if it wasn't so. But there was a much stronger motive for murdering Marriott, which he, out of vanity or love or greed or a mixture of all three, didn't evaluate. He was afraid, but not for himself. He was afraid of violence to which he was a part and for which he could be convicted. But on the other hand he was fighting for his meal ticket. So he took the chance.'

I stopped. She nodded and said: 'Very interesting. If one knows what you are talking about.'

'And one does,' I said.

We stared at each other. She had her right hand in her bag again now. I had a good idea what it held. But it hadn't started to come out yet. Every event takes time.

'Let's quit kidding,' I said. 'We're all alone here. Nothing either of us says has the slightest standing against what the other says. We cancel each other out. A girl who started in the gutter became the wife of a multi-millionaire. On the way up a shabby old woman recognized her – probably heard her singing at the radio station and recognized the voice and went to see — and this old woman had to be kept quiet. But she was cheap, therefore she only knew a little. But the man who dealt with her and made her monthly payments and owned a trust deed on her home and could throw her into the gutter any time she got funny — that man knew it all. He was expensive. But that didn't matter either, as long as nobody else knew. But some day a tough guy named Moose Malloy was going to get out of jail and start finding things out about his former sweetie. Because the big sap loved her — and still does. That's what makes it funny, tragic-funny. And about that time a private dick starts nosing in also. So the weak link in the chain, Marriott, is no longer a luxury. He has become a menace. They'll get to him and they'll take him apart. He's that kind of lad. He melts under heat. So he was murdered before he could melt. With a blackjack. By you.'

All she did was take her hand out of her bag, with a gun in it. All she did was point it at me and smile. All I did was nothing.

But that wasn't all that was done. Moose Malloy stepped out of the dressing-room with the Colt .45 still looking like a toy in his big hairy paw.

He didn't look at me at all. He looked at Mrs Lewin Lockridge Grayle. He leaned forward and his mouth smiled at her and he spoke to her softly.

'I thought I knew the voice,' he said. 'I listened to that voice for eight years — all I could remember of it. I kind of liked your hair red, though. Hiya, babe. Long time no see.'

She turned the gun.

'Get away from me, you son of a bitch,' she said.

He stopped dead and dropped the gun to his side. He was still a couple of feet from her. His breath laboured.

'I never thought,' he said quietly. 'It just came to me out of the blue. *You* turned me in to the cops. *You*. Little Velma.'

I threw a pillow, but it was too slow. She shot him five

times in the stomach. The bullets made no more sound than fingers going into a glove.

Then she turned the gun and shot at me but it was empty. She dived for Malloy's gun on the floor. I didn't miss with the second pillow. I was around the bed and knocked her away before she got the pillow off her face. I picked the Colt up and went away around the bed again with it.

He was still standing, but he was swaying. His mouth was slack and his hands were fumbling at his body. He went slack at the knees and fell sideways on the bed, with his face down. His gasping breath filled the room.

I had the phone in my hand before she moved. Her eyes were a dead grey, like half-frozen water. She rushed for the door and I didn't try to stop her. She left the door wide, so when I had done phoning I went over and shut it. I turned his head a little on the bed, so he wouldn't smother. He was still alive, but after five in the stomach even a Moose Malloy doesn't live very long.

I went back to the phone and called Randall at his home. 'Malloy,' I said. 'In my apartment. Shot five times in the stomach by Mrs Grayle. I called the Receiving Hospital. She got away.'

'So you had to play clever,' was all he said and hung up quickly.

I went back to the bed. Malloy was on his knees beside the bed now, trying to get up, a great wad of bedclothes in one hand. His face poured sweat. His eyelids flickered slowly and the lobes of his ears were dark.

He was still on his knees and still trying to get up when the fast wagon got there. It took four men to get him on the stretcher.

'He has a slight chance – if they're .25's,' the fast wagon doctor said just before he went out. 'All depends what they hit inside. But he has a chance.'

'He wouldn't want it,' I said.

He didn't. He died in the night.

40

'You ought to have given a dinner party,' Anne Riordan said looking at me across her tan figured rug. 'Gleaming silver and crystal, bright crisp linen – if they're still using linen in the places where they give dinner parties – candlelight, the women in their best jewels and the men in white ties, the servants hovering discreetly with the wrapped bottles of wine, the cops looking a little uncomfortable in their hired evening clothes, as who the hell wouldn't, the suspects with their brittle smiles and restless hands, and you at the head of the long table telling all about it, little by little, with your charming light smile and a phony English accent like Philo Vance.'

'Yeah,' I said. 'How about a little something to be holding in my hand while you go on being clever?'

She went out to her kitchen and rattled ice and came back with a couple of tall ones and sat down again.

'The liquor bills of your lady friends must be something fierce,' she said and sipped.

'And suddenly the butler fainted,' I said. 'Only it wasn't the butler who did the murder. He just fainted to be cute.'

I inhaled some of my drink. 'It's not that kind of story,' I said. 'It's not lithe and clever. It's just dark and full of blood.'

'So she got away?'

I nodded. 'So far. She never went home. She must have had a little hideout where she could change her clothes and appearance. After all she lived in peril, like the sailors. She was alone when she came to see me. No chauffeur. She came in a small car and she left it a few dozen blocks away.'

'They'll catch her – if they really try.'

'Don't be like that. Wilde, the D.A. is on the level. I

worked for him once. But if they catch her, what then? They're up against twenty million dollars and a lovely face and either Lee Farrell or Rennenkamp. It's going to be awfully hard to prove she killed Marriott. All they have is what looks like a heavy motive and her past life, if they can trace it. She probably has no record, or she wouldn't have played it this way.'

'What about Malloy? If you had told me about him before, I'd have known who she was right away. By the way, how did *you* know? Those two photos are not of the same woman.'

'No. I doubt if even old lady Florian knew they had been switched on her. She looked kind of surprised when I shoved the photo of Velma – the one that had Velma Valento written on it – in front of her nose. But she may have known. She may have just hid it with the idea of selling it to me later on. Knowing it was harmless, a photo of some other girl Marriott substituted.'

'That's just guessing.'

'It had to be that way. Just as when Marriott called me up and gave me a song and dance about a jewel ransom pay-off it had to be because I had been to see Mrs Florian asking about Velma. And when Marriott was killed, it had to be because he was the weak link in the chain. Mrs Florian didn't even know Velma had become Mrs Lewin Lockridge Grayle. She couldn't have. They bought her too cheap. Grayle says they went to Europe to be married and she was married under her real name. He won't tell where or when. He won't tell what her real name was. He won't tell where she is. I don't think he knows, but the cops don't believe that.'

'Why won't he tell?' Anne Riordan cupped her chin on the backs of her laced fingers and stared at me with shadowed eyes.

'He's so crazy about her he doesn't care whose lap she sat in.'

'I hope she enjoyed sitting in yours,' Anne Riordan said acidly.

'She was playing me. She was a little afraid of me. She didn't want to kill me because it's bad business killing a man who is a sort of cop. But she probably would have tried in the end, just as she would have killed Jessie Florian, if Malloy hadn't saved her the trouble.'

'I bet it's fun to be played by handsome blondes,' Anne Riordan said. 'Even if there is a little risk. As, I suppose, there usually is.'

I didn't say anything.

'I suppose they can't do anything to her for killing Malloy, because he had a gun.'

'No. Not with her pull.'

The gold-flecked eyes studied me solemnly. 'Do you think she meant to kill Malloy?'

'She was afraid of him,' I said. 'She had turned him in eight years ago. He seemed to know that. But he wouldn't have hurt her. He was in love with her too. Yes, I think she meant to kill anybody she had to kill. She had a lot to fight for. But you can't keep that sort of thing up indefinitely. She took a shot at me in my apartment – but the gun was empty then. She ought to have killed me out on the bluff when she killed Marriott.'

'He was in love with her,' Anne said softly. 'I mean Malloy. It didn't matter to him she hadn't written to him in six years or ever gone to see him while he was in jail. It didn't matter to him that she had turned him in for a reward. He just bought some fine clothes and started to look for her the first thing when he got out. So she pumped five bullets into him, by way of saying hello. He had killed two people himself, but he was in love with her. What a world.'

I finished my drink and got the thirsty look on my face again. She ignored it. She said:

'And she had to tell Grayle where she came from and he didn't care. He went away to marry her under another name and sold his radio station to break contact with anybody who might know her and he gave her everything that money can buy and she gave him – what?'

'That's hard to say.' I shook the ice cubes at the bottom of my glass. That didn't get me anything either. 'I suppose she gave him a sort of pride that he, a rather old man, could have a young and beautiful and dashing wife. He loved her. What the hell are we talking about it for? These things happen all the time. It didn't make any difference what she did or who she played around with or what she had once been. He loved her.'

'Like Moose Malloy,' Anne said quietly.

'Let's go riding along the water.'

'You didn't tell me about Brunette or the cards that were in those reefers or Amthor or Dr Sonderborg or that little clue that set you on the path of the great solution.'

'I gave Mrs Florian one of my cards. She put a wet glass on it. Such a card was in Marriott's pockets, wet glass mark and all. Marriott was not a messy man. That was a clue, of sorts. Once you suspected anything it was easy to find out other connections, such as that Marriott owned a trust deed on Mrs Florian's home, just to keep her in line. As for Amthor, he's a bad hat. They picked him up in a New York hotel and they say he's an international con man. Scotland Yard has his prints, also Paris. How the hell they got all that since yesterday or the day before I don't know. These boys work fast when they feel like it. I think Randall has had this thing taped for days and was afraid I'd step on the tapes. But Amthor had nothing to do with killing anybody. Or with Sonderborg. They haven't found Sonderborg yet. They think he has a record too, but they're not sure until they get him. As for Brunette, you can't get anything on a guy like Brunette. They'll have him before the Grand Jury and he'll refuse to say anything; on his constitutional rights. He doesn't have to bother about his reputation. But there's a nice shakeup here in Bay City. The Chief has been canned and half the detectives have been reduced to acting patrolmen, and a very nice guy named Red Norgaard, who helped me get on the *Montecito*, has got his job back. The mayor is doing all this, changing his pants hourly while the crisis lasts.'

'Do you have to say things like that?'

'The Shakespearean touch. Let's go riding. After we've had another drink.'

'You can have mine,' Anne Riordan said, and got up and brought her untouched drink over to me. She stood in front of me holding it, her eyes wide and a little frightened.

'You're so marvellous,' she said. 'So brave, so determined, and you work for so little money. Everybody bats you over the head and chokes you and smacks your jaw and fills you with morphine, but you just keep right on hitting between tackle and end until they're all worn out. What makes you so wonderful?'

'Go on,' I growled. 'Spill it.'

Anne Riordan said thoughtfully: 'I'd like to be kissed, damn you!'

41

It took over three months to find Velma. They wouldn't believe Grayle didn't know where she was and hadn't helped her get away. So every cop and newshawk in the country looked in all the places where money might be hiding her. And money wasn't hiding her at all. Although the way she hid was pretty obvious once it was found out.

One night a Baltimore detective with a camera eye as rare as a pink zebra wandered into a night club and listened to the band and looked at a handsome black-haired, black-browed torcher who could sing as if she meant it. Something in her face struck a chord and the chord went on vibrating.

He went back to Headquarters and got out the Wanted file and started through the pile of readers. When he came to the one he wanted he looked at it a long time. Then he straightened his straw hat on his head and went back to the night club and got hold of the manager. They went back to the dressing-rooms behind the shell and the manager knocked on one of the doors. It wasn't locked. The dick pushed the manager aside and went in and locked it.

He must have smelled marijuana because she was smoking it, but he didn't pay any attention then. She was sitting in front of a triple mirror, studying the roots of her hair and eyebrows. They were her own eyebrows. The dick stepped across the room smiling and handed her the reader.

She must have looked at the face on the reader almost as long as the dick had down at Headquarters. There was a lot to think about while she was looking at it. The dick sat down and crossed his legs and lit a cigarette. He had a good eye, but he had over-specialized. He didn't know enough about women.

Finally she laughed a little and said: 'You're a smart lad, copper. I thought I had a voice that would be remembered. A friend recognized me by it once, just hearing it on the radio. But I've been singing with this band for a month – twice a week on a network – and nobody gave it a thought.'

'I never heard the voice,' the dick said and went on smiling.

She said: 'I suppose we can't make a deal on this. You know, there's a lot in it, if it's handled right.'

'Not with me,' the dick said. 'Sorry.'

'Let's go then,' she said and stood up and grabbed up her bag and got her coat from a hanger. She went over to him holding the coat out so he could help her into it. He stood up and held it for her like a gentleman.

She turned and slipped a gun out of her bag and shot him three times through the coat he was holding.

She had two bullets left in the gun when they crashed the

door. They got half-way across the room before she used them. She used them both, but the second shot must have been pure reflex. They caught her before she hit the floor, but her head was already hanging by a rag.

'The dick lived until the next day,' Randall said, telling me about it. 'He talked when he could. That's how we have the dope. I can't understand him being so careless, unless he really was thinking of letting her talk him into a deal of some kind. That would clutter up his mind. But I don't like to think that, of course.'

I said I supposed that was so.

'Shot herself clean through the heart – twice,' Randall said. 'And I've heard experts on the stand say that's impossible, knowing all the time myself that it was. And you know something else?'

'What?'

'She was stupid to shoot that dick. We'd never have convicted her, not with her looks and money and the persecution story these high-priced guys would build up. Poor little girl from a dive climbs to be wife of rich man and the vultures that used to know her won't let her alone. That sort of thing. Hell, Rennenkamp would have half a dozen crummy old burlesque dames in court to sob that they'd blackmailed her for years, and in a way that you couldn't pin anything on them but the jury would go for it. She did a smart thing to run off on her own and leave Grayle out of it, but it would have been smarter to have come home when she was caught.'

'Oh you believe now that she left Grayle out of it?' I said.

He nodded. I said: 'Do you think she had any particular reason for that?'

He stared at me. 'I'll go for it, whatever it is.'

'She was a killer,' I said. 'But so was Malloy. And *he* was a long way from being all rat. Maybe that Baltimore dick wasn't so pure as the record shows. Maybe she saw a chance – not to get away – she was tired of dodging by that time – but to give a break to the only man who had ever really given her one.'

Randall stared at me with his mouth open and his eyes unconvinced.

'Hell, she didn't have to shoot a cop to do that ' he said.

'I'm not saying she was a saint or even a half-way nice girl. Not ever. She wouldn't kill herself until she was cornered. But what she did and the way she did it, kept her from coming back here for trial. Think that over. And who would that trial hurt most? Who would be least able to bear it? And win, lose or draw, who would pay the biggest price for the show? An old man who had loved not wisely, but too well.'

Randall said sharply: 'That's just sentimental.'

'Sure. It sounded like that when I said it. Probably all a mistake anyway. So long. Did my pink bug ever get back up here?'

He didn't know what I was talking about.

I rode down to the street floor and went out on the steps of the City Hall. It was a cool day and very clear. You could see a long way – but not as far as Velma had gone.

MORE ABOUT PENGUINS
AND PELICANS

Penguinews, which appears every month, contains details of all the new books issued by Penguins as they are published. From time to time it is supplemented by *Penguins in Print*, which is a complete list of all titles available. (There are some five thousand of these.)

A specimen copy of *Penguinews* will be sent to you free on request. For a year's issues (including the complete lists) please send 50p if you live in the British Isles, or 75p if you live elsewhere. Just write to Dept EP, Penguin Books Ltd, Harmondsworth, Middlesex, enclosing a cheque or postal order, and your name will be added to the mailing list.

In the U.S.A.: For a complete list of books available from Penguin in the United States write to Dept CS, Penguin Books Inc., 7110 Ambassador Road, Baltimore, Maryland 21207.

In Canada: For a complete list of books available from Penguin in Canada write to Penguin Books Canada Ltd, 41 Steelcase Road West, Markham, Ontario

PLAYBACK

Raymond Chandler

'There was nothing to it ... the subject was as easy to spot as a kangaroo in a dinner jacket.'

And with that Philip Marlowe is off on the tail of a girl who makes all the rest look like pick-ups.

Once aboard the train to San Diego you travel fast with Philip Marlowe, into situations your senses half expected, up against characters you'd rather not encounter, wise-cracking in the face of piano-wire tension. There's the parrot that sneers and the body that disappears ... and all the time you're piecing the evidence together.

Playback, as the *Guardian* said, 'carries the genuine Chandler label'. It does things to your subconscious. And it was the last and not the least publication of a great crime writer.

Also available

The Big Sleep
Killer in the Rain
The Little Sister
The High Window
The Lady in the Lake
The Long Good-Bye
Smart-Aleck Kill
Pearls are a Nuisance